#GIRL FIGHT

A NOVEL BY
SUZANNE MCKENNA LINK

#GIRLFIGHT

Copyright © 2024 by Suzanne McKenna Link

First Edition 2024

ISBN 978-1-7347215-2-2 (print-pbk)

ISBN 978-1-7347215-3-9 (epub)

Library of Congress Control Number: 2024903554

Cover design by Sonia Freitas / chloebellearts.com

Editing by Veronica Jorden, Kelley Riegert

Proofreading by Erin McClary

Also By Suzanne McKenna Link

Saving Toby (Save Me Series Book 1)

Keeping Claudia (Save Me Series Book 2)

Finding Edward (Save Me Series Book 3)

For Bruce ~

Who lives forever in our hearts

"You always become the thing you fight the most."
~Carl Jung

ONE

I stand to the side of my professor's office doorway, fingers touching my left cheek. The swelling is gone, but the shiner was still noticeable in this morning's mirror. Bruises on the body are easier to hide. Out of necessity, my skill in makeup application has vastly improved.

Students usually wait to be called in, but I ball my fists, take a steadying breath, and step into her office. Despite the light being on and the computer screen flickering with a colorful, animated screen saver, my academic advisor is nowhere to be seen. The smell, a blend of a library and well-worn leather, evokes a strong sense of familiarity. Dad's small office at the courthouse was much like this one, but less tidy than my advisor's.

Itching to touch one of the thick-spined tomes on her shelves, same as when I visited my father at work, I tug out a book on legal treatises and crack it open. The thin, onionskin-like pages remind me of years ago, when I passed time sprawled across the office's natty, coffee-stained rug, a law book before me, pretending to read legal cases while Dad worked. Sometimes, he'd let me sit in the swivel chair and play on his phone.

"Jones and Daughter," I'd answer, the old-fashioned phone receiver pressed to my ear.

"Jones and Daughter. I like the sound of that." He'd tugged on a piece of my dark hair.

As I grew, so did my interest in the law, and instead of playing with the books, I started reading them. I believed one day when I earned my law degree, we'd be associates. And here I am, working towards that degree, even though the possibility of teaming up with my father is no longer possible.

"Jayden Jones." Professor Dumfries strolls briskly into her office and motions to the chair in front of her desk. "Please, have a seat."

I slide the book back into place as the older woman sits behind her desk, slips on her reading glasses, and flips through several sheets of printouts. No doubt copies of the warning notes I'd received from this semester's professors. Stupidly and irresponsibly disregarded.

I sit and cross my legs, wincing at sore muscles.

She removes her glasses, holding them poised in the air. "Are you okay?"

"Yes. Fine, thanks."

"Jayden, if there's something you'd like to talk about—"

Heat collars my neck. "There's nothing to talk about. I'm fine, really."

"I have reports that say otherwise." Her gaze briefly challenges mine, but when she speaks again, her voice softens. "Professor Beardsley reported you came to class in physical distress, more than once. I have statements of bruises and a blackened eye. No one has to put up with being treated poorly—"

"Professor Dumfries." I tip forward, interrupting again. "I appreciate your concern, but it isn't what you think."

"What is it then?" The older woman scrutinizes me.

I self-consciously touch my face, wondering if she's noticed the bruise. "They were... incidents," I say. "At work." Not a lie, exactly.

Dumfries drops her reading glasses on the desk and sits back. "You need to be more convincing if you plan to have a successful career in litigation."

I twist in my seat, searching for words to explain, but how can I explain my situation to the professor, a woman whose livelihood and passion is to teach law and dispense justice?

Talk about a bad look for a future law career.

When I offer nothing more, my professor places her hands on the desk and exhales, showing impressive control by holding back what she really wants to say.

"As your first semester proves, you're a capable student, Jayden. But frankly, your grades have noticeably slipped this semester." She hands me a sheet of paper. "As your academic advisor, it pains me to have to inform you that your GPA dropped below the 3.5 needed to maintain your scholarship."

I cannot meet her eyes.

"I've lost the scholarship?"

"Unfortunately, yes."

A numbness creeps into my limbs as I stare at the printout before me, my grades listed with the accumulated second-term GPA circled in red ink: 3.2.

"Would it help to write the board? Do extra credit? Promise I'll over-perform in the fall?" I'm already struggling to stay afloat. Without the scholarship, I have no way to pay for law school.

She taps a pen on the desk, her eyes trained on me.

"Please, I'll do anything."

She taps the pen again and shifts forward. "Okay. How about writing a mission statement? Law school is hard. It's not for everyone. Spend the summer thinking about why you're here and what you plan to do with a law degree. Email it to me before fall term." She scribbles a note and raises her eyes. "If I'm convinced that you belong here, perhaps the board will reconsider your scholarship."

"I can do that." I clasp my hands between my knees and nod, the heel of my left foot involuntarily bumping up and down on the carpeted floor. "Thank you."

"Don't thank me," her firm tone returns. "You need to do this for yourself as much as the board."

With my agreement, she stands, snaps a business card from her desk, and holds it out to me. "Take this phone number. Please consider calling."

I take the card and thank her.

Outside, past the stonework at the entrance of the law school, several students are sitting at benches and tables in the courtyard, but this close to the end of the term, many more are empty. I stride down the sidewalk, catching the pedestrian walk light, and cross the busy street to the subway entrance in a shaft of sunlight. The early May sun works its way through my thick hair, heating my already warm scalp.

Despite the pervading taint of soured food, sewage, and track dust, the coolness of the subterranean station is a welcome relief. I swipe my credit card, push through the turnstile, and shuffle foot to foot on the platform waiting for my train.

Dumfries is right; law school isn't a cakewalk. It's challenging but shying away from challenges is not in my DNA. I lost focus. It began last year when Troy jetted off to Vegas to be part of *Sin City Fight Club*, a new MMA reality show, two days after college commencement services. My boyfriend is living the life of a competitive fighter with a serious paycheck as I watch from a distance, scraping the barrel.

My face warms uncomfortably. After my last 1L final, I anticipated the freedom and lack of stress that comes with summer—but now I'll spend the break worrying about financing law school.

The air shifts, followed by a reverberating shutter as the subway car rounds the tracks and screeches to a stop before me. I grab the first spot on the molded communal bench, phone out, and find Rick in my contacts. My fingers hover over the keypad. I'm still a little sore. Is it too soon?

Rent is due, and with plans to visit Troy in Vegas, I need travel money. Money wins, and I send the text.

Me: *Any action tonight?*

Rick: *Brooklyn.*

Without hesitating, I send my reply. *I want in.*

Rick: *Deets to come. Stay tuned.*

I sit back to take a deep breath and realize I still have the business card Dumfries gave me in my hand. I glance at it, expecting the name and number of a tutor to help me raise my grades or a financial aid counselor. But no, it's a domestic violence hotline.

On the back of the card is a handwritten message:

If I can be of help, please call 231-783-9990–Glenda Dumfries.

I don't peg Dumfries as an MMA fan, but it's possible that she, or any of my professors, has gotten wind of my boyfriend's occupation. Troy's becoming a household name. And as his significant other, I'm caught in the periphery of his growing prominence. The professor, a perceptive woman, might be clued into my situation. Then, her assumption of domestic abuse makes more sense. Troy Murphy is a big, powerful guy. He beats people up for a living.

I appreciate the professor's concern, but it's misplaced. Troy is no Raging Bull. He's rather soft-spoken and non-confrontational. Anyone who knows Troy knows he would never hurt me.

I save Dumfries's number to my cell and scribble over it, then tuck the hotline card in the window frame of the nearest seat, hoping someone who truly needs help will find the number.

As promised, Rick texts me with a time and place: *The Uppercut, Brooklyn, 9 pm.*

The Rocky theme plays in my head as I sprint the last few blocks, throwing punches left and right, visualizing Sylvester Stallone trekking through the streets of Philadelphia in the famous training montage.

But I'm not in Philly, and definitely not in training to fight the reigning world heavyweight champion. I'm just an unknown ready to throw down at a backstreet MMA gym.

I stop just outside the gym, sucking air, my workout clothes damp with sweat, and watch people flow inside. Nerves bounce around my stomach, the same as on other fight nights.

I didn't win the previous fight nights I'd entered, but incrementally, with each fight, I got better. Less blood, less time on the mat. Fewer injuries overall, though my professors didn't seem to appreciate that.

Each fight I enter is a chance to do better, even if it's only to prove to myself that I can. Despite any drawbacks, in less than an hour, I walk away with a pocketful of cash. With the cost of rent and upcoming fall tuition looming, it's the money, despite any fear, that propels me to follow the crowd inside, into a recipe of air conditioning, sweat, and disinfectant.

A few hundred people—mostly men—bump around in the spaces between two identical octagonal-shaped fight stages. Bets are being placed and money changes hands as excited voices echo and bounce off the gym's high ceiling.

There's little formality to these events. Fighters weigh in, put on gloves, and get to it. The prospect of cops showing up enlivens the crowd and impels an urgency for organizers and fighters to start and finish without getting busted.

At a makeshift folding table registration area, I sign in as The Bruiser, a nickname given to me by my high school wrestling teammates. In my shorts and sports bra and holding my sneakers, I wait behind several men for my turn to step on the scale.

"Hey, I'm up." I elbow a guy who tries to cut the line.

"Sorry. Thought you were here to watch," he says.

I roll my eyes. Being a female athlete in a male-dominated sport is something I've learned to get comfortable with, but my patience with ignorant lunkheads is still a work in progress.

Rick stands nearby, his baggy jeans and beer gut out of place amid the muscled hard bodies. The odds and money guy is my only connection to this underground world. He fist bumps me and records my name and weight class, which is on the lighter side of MMA bantamweight.

"You're in cage two with Diva." Rick points to a muscled woman skipping rope, and my confidence takes a detour.

I've seen Diva at Fight Night before. In her early thirties and almost ten years older than me, she's a regular here and a local favorite. Once again, I'm a wrestler competing against a boxer. Years of training taught me effective maneuvers to put my opponent off balance and pin her, but academic wrestling never taught me how to avoid flying fists or legs. In academia, striking an opponent is a violation. If you hit or kick your opponent, you'll get penalized or ejected, a major difference in this arena. Here, everything goes.

I move off to the side to stretch and warm up and remind myself that I've been coached by the best, from high school to college, and have notable wrestling career wins. Fear is a useless, defeatist attitude.

Through tinny overhead speakers, over the persistent excited shouts and general clamor of the crowd, my match is called.

"In cage two, female bantamweights, Diva of Death versus The Bruiser."

Compared to Diva of Death, Bruiser sounds toothless. I collect my things and head toward the second platform, kicking myself for not being more creative when, twenty feet back, overhead lights form an angelic halo above a head of wavy golden-brown hair and a familiar face.

Cooper.

Watching the fight in cage one. I stop to stare as my hand snakes up my right bicep.

"You ready?" Rick asks, pulling me back.

"Yeah." I drop my hand and mentally zip myself up. I can't think about Cooper or anything else but this fight. If you're not ready when your bout is called, you lose your place. This crowd doesn't take kindly to competitors who balk. They're here to watch combat, even better if there's blood. I've seen them shake their fists at and boo hesitant fighters right out of the venue.

Diva of Death cuts me an over-the-shoulder sneer and steps ahead of me to be the first in the ring. A rush of adrenaline gluts my body, awakening every nerve. I dump my stuff next to the three steps that lead up to the cage, its perimeter encircled in a black plastic-coated chain-link fence to keep the fighters from tumbling out. I climb the steps, pop in my rubber mouthguard to protect my teeth, and swing my arms back and forth, my bare feet leaving short-lived imprints on the dense foam-covered black canvas flooring.

Across from me, Diva drops into a combat stance, fists raised, legs slightly bent, ready to drive forward, and trying to intimidate me with furious scowls and flexing muscle. I steel myself, adopt my own battle-ready stance, and when the brawny ref barks, "Fight!" we explode toward each other.

I swing my fists, right then left, but Diva deflects the punches and returns the attack, pummeling me with so many body shots that I lose count. Despite the pain, I edge forward, hands up to protect my face. Wrestling is the only way I can control the outcome of this fight, and to do that, I need to get closer.

Although I twist, dip, and use my elbows to block her, Diva throttles me with a series of punches to the gut.

Oomph. Her punches burn like a branding iron, and I drop my left arm to guard my stomach. Diva takes full advantage of my lowered fist and wallops me with a solid cross to the left side of my face. My head snaps right. The crowd roars, chanting, "Diva, Diva!" as the metallic taste of blood floods my mouth.

Anger blurs my vision. In my head, I hear my high school coach command, "Shoot low." I crouch and leap forward, rushing Diva and knocking her fists aside to seize her. In one fluid motion, I twist and haul her over my hip, a classic underhook throw.

Diva's breath whooshes out noisily as her body slams to the floor. Before she recovers, I'm on top of her, slamming her with my full weight, and then springing backward to grapple for control of her right arm.

Within seconds, I have the arm extended, clamped between my legs in an arm bar, one of the most painful and dangerous holds in wrestling. There's little hope of escaping without breaking bones. This fight is all mine now, and the crowd knows it too. They're screaming, feasting on this unexpected twist.

Diva bucks against my hold, thrashing about on the blood-stained mat of the ring, but the ref jumps in and taps out for her, giving me the win.

I release my hold on Diva and jump to my feet, amped by the endorphins of my victory. I offer a hand to help my opponent to her feet, a habit ingrained by Coach McCaffrey in high school, but the other woman snubs me.

Fighters endure a lot—injuries, sore muscles, love, and hate from the crowd. It all comes with the territory, but poor sportsmanship shouldn't be one of them.

Despite the bite, when the ref lifts my arm and announces me as the winner, I nod at Diva and say, "Good fight," before strutting from the enclosure.

"That win just made you a nice bit of pocket change." Rick finds me, a huge grin on his face and hands me a wad of cash. "Next time you fight, it'll be even more."

He gives me a gruff thump on the back and moves off to watch another fight. I shove the cash into my sports bra, slick with sweat. I estimate it's nearly a grand, much more than I'd made last time. After I catch up on bills and put some cash aside for Vegas, I hope there's money left over for a rare steak at Delmonico's.

Swiping my hand across my mouth sends a ripple of pain shooting up the side of my face and a trail of blood across my knuckles—another injury to conceal.

The next match is called, and the fighters pass me to climb into the cage, as the night swiftly moves on. I make it a habit not to stick around past my bout. No need to push my luck. Limbs pulsing and growing heavier and achier by the moment, I move through the crowd on my way to the women's locker room to clean up before heading home. It takes two trains and a bus to get back to my apartment. I pat the cash in my bra. Maybe I'll treat myself to an Uber.

Pushing through the crowd, my feet grow roots, and my celebratory mood vanishes. Cooper stands between me and the locker room. This time, he sees me. For a long, heavy moment, we stare at one another. I grapple for an appropriate greeting, but when he takes a step my way, I turn and bolt in the opposite direction.

I circle around the gym, hugging the outer wall, and enter the locker room. In a bathroom stall, I press the side of my face to the cool metal door and slide my sweaty palm over the upper part of my right arm. After high school graduation, Cooper, Troy, and I got identical tattoos—three crossed swords with our initials: TM, JJ, and CM.

Troy recently had his lasered off. Has Cooper? I will once I can afford to. The three of us were tight and had vowed our friendship would last forever. After that night in his car, though, I cut him out, and then Troy cut him out, too. We haven't talked to him in years.

Two

I spend the next day icing sore muscles, holed up in my apartment in Williamsburg, a third-floor walkup I share with two roommates. It's an added expense I probably could've avoided, but after finishing my undergrad, going home to live with Mom wasn't an option.

Sprawled across my bed, with a small notebook propped on my knees, I jot down numbers, guestimating how many fight nights I'll need to enter to cover the next several month's living expenses and fall tuition. After buying a roundtrip airline ticket to Vegas to visit Troy for the summer, as we'd planned, there isn't much money left over.

Dad set up a college savings account for me, which, combined with my scholarship, is scarcely enough to last the duration of law school. Without the scholarship, I'll need a backup plan. As I consider whether to apply for a loan or seek a waitressing or entry-level legal job, my cell lights up with a call from Kara. I answer, feeling a surge of homesickness for my sister.

"Thought you'd want to know Mr. McCaffrey is in the hospital."

Icy fingers of alarm race down my back. "What happened?"

"Heart trouble," she says.

It's been too long between visits with my high school wrestling coach. The possibility of running into Cooper has kept me away. But with this terrible news, I want to see Coach. I *need* to see him.

I take the train out to Long Island and Uber to the hospital where Coach is laid up. With makeup camouflaging leftover facial marks from the fight, I ride the elevator to the cardiac care floor, a visitor pass, candy, and a small bouquet of yellow tulips in hand.

Past the nurse's station, numbered placards next to each doorway lead me to Coach's room. I hesitate outside the open door, punched by a sudden sense of trepidation. If Cooper is here, this visit will be awkward.

I draw in a steadying breath and step into the doorway. Midday sunshine pours in from a double-wide window and brightens the room, its ledge jam-packed with a cheerful array of flowers and an assortment of greeting cards tucked in among them. A white curtain obscures the bed from the doorway.

I rap the knuckles of my free hand on the open door and call out, "Hello."

Cooper appears from behind the curtain, pocketing his cell phone. My forward motion stalls, the sight of him a gut punch. The worst place for a reunion is not at an unsanctioned fight. It's at the hospital.

"Jayden?" An unmistakable surprise colors his voice as he eats up the several feet between us.

"Cooper, hey!" I lift my voice and smile to cover my disappointment.

He returns the smile, his more authentic, and pulls me in for a hug. "It's good to see you."

The warm greeting throws me off, and I'm stiff in his embrace.

We step apart, and I give him a quick once-over. He's still stupid handsome. His broadened shoulders and thickened build make him appear older, more mature, and somehow even better-looking than in high school.

I never liked pretty boys. They attract too much undeserved adulation. But Cooper, even as a teen, had a rare kindness about him. For this reason, I'd never held his beauty against him.

"How have you been?" I ask.

"The car accident put me off my game a bit." He gives me a careless shrug. It's a casual indifference unnatural to the Cooper I once knew so well. "Totaled my Mustang. I miss that car."

"It was a nice car," I say, though the memory of the classic honey gold car makes my hands clammy. I'd sent Cooper a few texts when I'd heard about the accident last spring. After the niceties and well wishes, our communication once again died off. I study his face, looking for evidence: scars or blemishes. But he looks completely intact. "Glad you didn't get hurt too badly."

"Yeah, the guy blew a point one-five on the breathalyzer. Could have been much, much worse."

The thought turns my stomach, but the sensation somersaults into something different when his green eyes, fringed with incredibly long, thick eyelashes, sweep lazily over me.

"But you, Jayden, you look great."

I glance away. I'd forgotten how disarming those peepers of his can be. The intensity of his gaze makes me feel like I'm standing in Times Square with a guitar, in nothing but tighty-whities.

"Oh, no. I'm a mess." I pass the flowers and candy to him and run a hand over my ponytail, hoping I don't look half as disheveled as I feel. "Those are for your dad. Think he's up for a quick visit?"

"He sleeps on and off, but we'll wake him. He'll be excited to see you." Cooper's easygoing smile slips into place as he acknowledges my gifts. "Caramels are his favorite."

"I remember." Relieved he doesn't mention seeing me at the fight, I edge forward as he wedges the tulips onto the windowsill where several larger bouquets dwarf my small offering.

"How did you know to come?"

"Kara. She heard at school."

A few feet farther into the room, past the curtain, a hospital bed dominates the space. Under a white cotton blanket, Coach Kellan McCaffrey sleeps. I haven't seen him in a couple of years. My stout and hearty mentor has never been a giant in the physical sense. Like his son, he stands less than six feet tall, but striding the length of a classroom chalkboard, energetically retelling a period in history, or shouting encouragement from the sidelines at sports competitions, he'd never had a problem commanding attention.

But here, in front of me, he appears to have shrunk, and his usually ruddy complexion is grayish. He looks sickly. Old.

Anguish wiggles in the back of my throat. I should have been better about staying in touch.

Cooper crosses to the far side of the bed and gives his father's arm a gentle nudge. "Pop, you have a visitor."

Coach's eyes draw open, his tired blue gaze fixed on his son. Their physical resemblance is undeniable. The same defined chin; straight, celestial nose; and a shock of thick, wavy hair. Cooper's hair, though mostly grown out of his regular crew cut style, is chestnut, burnished with natural golden highlights, and his face is clean-shaven, while his father has a salt-and-pepper mop that matches the woolly mustache concealing his upper lip.

"You must be special. Look who came to see you," Cooper says, motioning to me.

Coach's gaze clicks left until he finds me. As tears threaten my eyes, I step forward and smile, like I've been called onto the stage.

"Hey, Coach." I take his warm, thick hand in mine.

"Jayden 'Courageous Cat' Jones, as I live and breathe. How about that? This is a good day." Coach's voice is wispy and gruff, but he smiles. "Is Troy with you?"

Cooper tips his head, giving my answer his full attention.

"No. He'd be here if he could, but he's in Nevada," I say.

"Right, right. This soggy old noodle loses track of things." He taps the side of his head, making fun of the memory failure. "He's out in Las Vegas filming the television show. All that attention going to his head?"

I laugh. "You think that enormous ego has room to grow?"

"I'm teasing. You know Troy is one of three of my all-time favorite students. You can guess the other two." Coach looks from Cooper to me, a smile deep in his eyes. "Those were good years. You, Troy, and Coop, the Three Musketeers."

Across the bed, Cooper and I look at each other. His expression reflects a loss I feel, too. Guilt warms my face, and I break eye contact.

"I followed your wrestling stats at North Central." Unaware of the angst between Cooper and me, Coach rambles on. "Impressive record, Cat."

"Thanks, Coach. It was an amazing way to end my wrestling career. Moving on from it, losing the routine of that level of competitive fighting, has been a hard adjustment, like leaving a piece of my heart behind. I've been reduced to living vicariously through Troy's MMA journey."

"Hogwash. You could easily get yourself on Troy's show."

"Me on *Sin City Fight Club?*" I chuckle. "Thanks for the vote of confidence."

Cooper raises his hands. "Why not? You're one of the best wrestlers I've ever seen. And you know jiu-jitsu—"

"I took a few classes," I push back. Enough to hold my own in unsanctioned fights, and he knows it.

"Still, with the right training..." Cooper leaves the sentence unfinished.

"Nice thought, but I'm in law school."

"The next Notorious RBG," Coach says, proving much of his memory is still intact. He'd gifted me a Ruth Bader Ginsburg pin when I graduated high school. "How's that going?"

I swallow, fighting a blister of frustration the subject creates. "Harder than I expected."

"I believe in you." Coach pats my hand. "You'll achieve whatever you set your mind to, Cat."

A bloom of warmth fills my chest. I didn't realize how much I needed to hear those words, and more so from him, someone I've always respected.

With labored breath, Coach squeezes my hand; his tired grin stirs my deep affection. "Winners don't sit back on their heels. They lean into the fight."

His words prompt a memory of myself in a blue wrestling singlet, the only girl on the high school wrestling team, facing off with my male opponent, Coach urging me to make a move. Tears prick the back of my eyes as I'm slammed with the reminder of why this man held an important place in my life. He always knew how to motivate me to do better, and to be my best.

I sandwich his large hand in mine and recite from memory: "'You already have all you need to succeed.'"

"You remember."

I nod. "You taught me much more than just wrestling."

He smiles as his eyes grow glossy. "Your eagerness to learn made my job easy. I'd have taken a hundred students like you."

"And I'd have taken a hundred teachers like you," I say.

"Courageous Cat, you've made my day. Thank you for coming to see me." His fingers curl around my hand, then go slack. "I wish I were better company, but this old man can't keep his eyes open."

"Don't worry about it, Pop. I'm sure Jayden understands." Cooper brushes a hand through his father's hair. The simple, loving gesture chokes me up. "You want anything?"

"No, I'm good, son," he says.

"You rest and get better," I whisper, and press a kiss to the side of Coach's stubbled face. Heavy eyelids flutter closed over those earnest sky-blue eyes.

I catch Cooper's attention and motion to the door. The two of us shuffle out to the main corridor, where I check the time. I'll have to leave soon if I want to catch my train.

"When did all this happen?" I ask.

"He started having chest pains about eight months ago. I don't suppose you knew that."

I wince. "No, I hadn't heard."

"His cardiologist recommended retirement. He resisted, but after graduation last June, he did. Letting teaching go was tough for him, but continuing to work wasn't an option."

I cross my arms over my chest, hugging myself. "Where does that leave him now?"

"It's a wait-and-see and pray-for-the-best kind of situation," he says. "Top order of business, though, is to keep him comfortable."

The note of acceptance in his tone makes my heart heavy.

"If there's anything I can do for him, for you, or your family, please let me know."

"Thanks," he says with a smile that doesn't reach his eyes. From behind him, the ringing of the hospital room's phone disrupts the silence. "Let me get that. Don't go anywhere." He shakes a warning finger at me before he goes back into his father's room as if I might scurry away before he returns.

Our conversation is all too familiar. *If there's anything I can do…* I'm saying the same words to him that people had said to me when my father was dying. Unpleasant memories stuffed away in the recesses of my mind creep back in—how I'd sought comfort from Cooper the night we buried my father.

With guests at the house after the funeral services, all the well-wishers and well-meaning, it'd been an unending, heavy day. Cooper offered a reprieve. A ride to the beach in his Mustang, to get away from my mother and the guests who'd remained at my house.

I sat in the passenger seat and told him I planned to give up my scholarship and leave North Central to come home. My younger sister needed me. In a calm, reassuring voice, Cooper reminded me of my dreams and told me to trust my mother, that Kara would be fine.

I was frightened and overwhelmed, and once the tears started, they wouldn't stop. I'd never experienced such a loss of control. I had to stop the spinout and put a bullet in that day. When Cooper pulled me into his arms, it was like he was there in answer to my prayers.

And I kissed him.

Something I'd wanted to do since the first time I met him. He kissed me back with an intensity I'd only dreamed of.

I craved more touch, more heat—to feel instead of think. I pushed the straps of my dress and bra off my shoulders and put his hands on me.

He flinched and pulled away like he'd touched a hot stove.

I quickly turned away to cover myself and ordered him to take me home. He tried to explain, to make me feel better during the drive, but I understood. I'd crossed a line he hadn't wanted to cross.

My face burns with the memory all over again. Here we are today, basically strangers, because, in my grief, I'd done something stupid and reckless and closed the door on our friendship.

I'd further sealed that door closed by then sleeping with Troy.

"More well-wishers." Cooper returns, and with a sigh, leans against the doorjamb.

His gaze slips away from me, down the wide hospital corridor, and I can't help thinking that every time he sees me, he remembers that night too.

He watches a nurse walk by before he looks at me again.

"What you said back there, about leaving a piece of your heart behind. I get that. I miss our wrestling days, too. But after seeing you at Uppercut last week, obviously you haven't stopped competing." I cringe, waiting for him to ask why I took off, but he simply asks, "Underground fights, are they a regular thing for you?"

"No. Only done it a few times. Just a way to let off steam and make a few bucks."

"The ankle holding up?"

His father followed my college stats, but I'm surprised Cooper knows about my ankle, which I had injured during a college wrestling tournament my senior year.

It's my turn to shrug. "It's fine. Hasn't given me any trouble."

"Heard *Sin City Fight Club* has rolling auditions. Why not give it a try? MMA is intense but you might enjoy the challenge."

"Yeah, maybe. I'm actually headed to Vegas next week."

Frown lines bracket his mouth. "To join Troy Murphy's entourage?"

"I'm his girlfriend, not a fangirl." A rise of defiance sharpens my response.

"No, fangirling isn't your style." He slides his hands into the front pockets of his jeans. "What about law school?"

"It's summer break. I'll be back in a few weeks." I shift my weight, glancing toward the exit sign. I don't want to think about the fall, the persuasive mission statement I need to write, or the hoops I'll need to jump through to pay tuition and pull my grades up.

"You and Troy, finally in the same city. That's convenient."

I brace myself for a lecture, remembering the heated argument that ensued after he found me in Troy's bed. Before today, I could count on one hand the number of words we've exchanged since then.

But all he says is, "That'll be good for you guys." His gaze dips before it returns to me. "I never thought you'd stay together this long."

I bristle at the comment, but to be fair, I don't think any of us could have foreseen that after a thoughtless night of drunken sex, Troy and I, hampered by the distance between our colleges, would still be together four years later.

"You should try out for Sin City." He wants to say more, I can tell, but when I arch my brow, he just smiles and adds, "Good luck, Jayden, whatever you decide."

"Thanks," I say, realizing that though we aren't close anymore, his opinion still holds weight with me. "So, how about you? You start grad school?"

"Not yet. I took some time off after the accident and to be home with Dad, so I had some classes to catch up on. Just finished my undergrad a few weeks ago at Stony Brook."

"But that school doesn't have a wrestling program," I say.

"No, they don't. I let it go, switched things up." He holds my gaze. "That we know so little about each other's lives shows how cut off we've been from each other, doesn't it?"

The bitterness in his tone stuns me. I don't know how to respond, so I don't.

"Jess and my mom will be upset that they missed you." He breaks the unnerving silence. "I insisted they go home and relax for a few hours."

Despite wanting to leave, I'm anchored in place by the brave face he puts on. When my father was in the hospital, the exhaustion and worry wore me down.

"Please let them know I'm thinking of them, and that I'll try to come back before I leave," I say.

"I hope you will."

I graze his forearm with my fingertips, surprised when the touch sends tingles up my arm, shocked that he still affects me like this.

"It's going to be okay." We both know I'm lying. It's what people say in this situation, to be kind. A false, brief whisper of hope.

It's what they said to me before Dad died. Of course, nothing was okay. And it still isn't.

As I'm waiting on the train platform, Coach and Cooper's words about *Sin City Fight Club* reverberate in my head. I won my last underground fight, but am I good enough to be on the show? My cell pulses with an incoming text, interrupting my internal debate.

Cooper: *Thanks for coming.*

Me: *Of course. I love your dad.*

I pause and add: *Please keep me updated on his condition.*

Cooper: *I will. It was great to see you.*

I smile and type back: *You, too.*

Cooper: *We should get together before you leave for Vegas. Dinner or something?*

Me: *Let me check my calendar.*

It's pure lip service. Even if I have time, we both know I won't meet up with him. The hospital visit is enough to know the unease between us continues.

Cooper: *Sounds like an it's-not-gonna-happen if ever I heard one.*

Busted.

Me: *The next time Troy and I are home, all three of us can go out together.*

A lengthy pause follows before he replies.

Cooper: *You'll only agree if we include Troy?*

Me: *Of course not. My train just pulled up. Talk soon.*

I drop into a row of empty seats and stare out the window. Cooper is extending an olive branch to me, not Troy. After all this time, and all the water under our collective bridges, to agree to meet for a social outing without Troy feels disloyal.

When Troy and I became a couple, Cooper made it clear he didn't agree with our choice. I'd never seen Cooper lose his cool as he did when he'd barged into Troy's room unannounced and found us in bed together that day.

Cooper had dragged Troy bare-assed into the hallway to chew him out. The guys had argued bitterly, and things got heated.

The memory of Cooper's expression that morning still makes the hair on the back of my neck stand up. I think we both understood that if things had gone differently between us, I wouldn't have slept with Troy.

But I was protective of Troy and our relationship. He had saved me—saved me from a freefall into sadness after my father died.

The railroad car vibrates as it rolls along the tracks. I scroll through my cell phone images to one of Troy and I mugging for a selfie. Though the times we see each other are infrequent, we talk often. He always has my back, and that means everything.

Being the ones who changed the dynamics of the friendship, it became difficult for Troy and me to hang out with Cooper without an ever-present elephant in the room. Every month that ticked by expanded the divide. I missed Cooper. Missed his steadying presence in my life. But there didn't seem to be a way back to the camaraderie of our high school days.

Our connection had dwindled. None of us tried to save it.

Uninterested in dwelling on the unfortunate history, I return to the idea of trying out for *Sin City Fight Club*. If I got on the show, my financial problems would vanish, but it's the prospect of training and fighting alongside Troy that excites me. Like a strike of lightning, I know I want to do this. I need to.

Crossing my left leg over my right, I pull up my pant leg to look at my ankle. I'd been honest when I'd told Cooper the ankle was fine. It hasn't bothered me in some time, likely because I haven't consistently tested it.

Would my ankle hold up for the full season of Fight Club? I reposition the pant leg over my ankle and put my foot back on the floor.

There's only one way to find out.

THREE

I catch the subway back to my apartment and message Troy about Coach, adding that I need his opinion on an idea I have. We agree to talk later, and then I make an impulsive decision to get off before my regular stop. I exit the train and move past the slower foot traffic with Cooper McCaffrey lingering in the back of my thoughts.

At street level, the rush of traffic greets my ears: car horns and radios blend with the constant sound of tires rattling over the scarred and repaired blacktop. Across Joralemon Street, long, colorful banners hang between the tall stone columns of the entrance of Brooklyn Law. The flags declare OPPORTUNITY, EXCELLENCE, LEADERSHIP.

Brooklyn Law was both Grandpa Jones's and Dad's alma mater. Grandpa had been a respected circuit court judge, and Dad, a public defender. That I planned to continue in their footsteps pleased my father.

Becoming a lawyer is all I ever wanted to do; all I ever saw myself doing. Maybe if Troy had gotten a regular job, a gym teacher or sports trainer, I'd be happily looking forward to the upcoming fall semester. But now, standing before the law school I'd attended for the past year, I feel as though I've been struck by lightning, and everything is upside down. This small fleeting opportunity to jump back into competitive fighting may amount to nothing, but something tells me I must grab onto it.

My breath catches until my lungs ache.

"Daddy, I know I promised, but I just can't do it right now," I whisper and turn away from Brooklyn Law to walk a few blocks before catching another subway to my apartment.

I unlock the door and immediately spot the kitchen sink filled with Miguel's dirty dishes. Down the hall, I slip into my bedroom, flip on the light, and fall onto my bed. Staring up at the water-stained ceiling, I hear Miguel and his girlfriend laughing through the thin wall that separates us.

My room is small and windowless. A three-drawer dresser and a double bed take up most of the space. It's cramped, but that's not what bothers me about it. Since I moved back to New York for law school, I've been alone. Troy is supposed to be here, sharing this rental with me, but our plans went out the window once he was selected for the show.

An internet search for the *Sin City Fight Club* yields the production company's website, and within seconds, I find the casting application. Tentatively, I begin filling it in until my cell erupts with a series of beeps, and with a swipe, the new and improved version of the face I know and love fills the screen.

To me, Troy is Troy, the often-stupid boy I grew up with, who, on colt-like legs, used to trip over his own enormous feet. The early inelegance is all but gone, morphed into unshakeable confidence. He has a bit of cauliflower ear, a telltale sign of many years of wrestling, but Troy's been professionally manscaped for the show. His dirty blond hair is shaved close to his skull but a long curly tuft in the front softens the cut and makes him look a touch boyish and sweet. He's been waxed and tweezed, and the stubble on the lower half of his face has been stylishly groomed. He's a grownup Hollywood-ized version of the lovable oaf I used to wrestle with in the mud.

Standing at six-four and ripped with muscle, he's always been popular with the girls, but it's a mistake to think of Troy Murphy as just another pretty face. His looks bring him attention, but his prowess in the octagon, his new stage, eclipses all of that. Troy dazzles.

"Hey, Hollywood," I tease.

He grimaces, clearly not in the mood for light banter. "How's Coach?"

"It's his heart. He doesn't look good." I think of Coach lying in that hospital bed. "Cooper said his doctor forced him to retire last year."

Troy curses under his breath and sweeps the top of his head with a heavy hand.

For several minutes, we reminisce about our time with Coach.

"Can you come home to visit him?" I ask.

"The show schedule is intense."

"Don't sweat it." I quickly give him a pass. "Cooper has my number. He promised to keep me updated."

"Cooper... how is he?"

"Um, he seems good. Older, but the same. Still questioning my choices."

"He never liked us together. Probably hasn't gotten over you." He grins. "He was going to ask you to senior prom."

"I'm sure he was just being kind." Troy didn't know what happened between Cooper and me that night at the beach. I never told him. A few moments, a blip in time years ago. Certainly nothing Cooper wouldn't have gotten over.

"*I* didn't think to ask you," he says.

"Cooper was always nicer than you."

"Burn." Troy shakes his hand like it's on fire.

"He was nicer than both of us. Anyway, you had a date. And a string of backup options." I make a raspberry sound with my lips. "Doesn't matter. I didn't want to go."

Just before prom, my father's health plummeted. Glitzy socials were at the bottom of my to-do list.

"Yeah, I know, Jay. I remember," he says in a somber tone.

We're the same, him and me. Every wrestling season, we challenged each other to work out and perform at our best. Through high school and college, and even somewhat now, we eat, breathe, and sleep competitive fighting. We both want to live in a big city, and we dream about traveling the world. We like the same foods and drink the same beer. Our likenesses calm me. Being with him helped me survive the year after I lost my father. I wouldn't have finished my freshman year of college if it weren't for Troy. I'm jazzed that I'll soon be in Vegas, sleeping beside him.

"Hey, I had an idea. Thought I'd audition for Sin City." In my excitement, the words shoot off my tongue like a bullet. "If I make it, we'll be coworkers."

"You want to be on the show? What about law school?"

"I need a break. I can always go back later and pick up where I left off." I lay it out for him as well as myself. "Even if I don't make the show, I think I might stay. We'll get a place together. I mean, that's always been our plan."

His eyes stray from the screen, and he absently scratches his chin. "Yeah. All right, cool."

It's not exactly the enthusiastic response I anticipated, but I sprung this on him. I've known Troy for a long time. He'll come around.

"I'll work out the details when I arrive. I'm nearly done packing." I angle the cell camera to show him my giant suitcase stowed against the wall, most of my possessions packed inside. When he doesn't comment, I study his face. A fat lip and a blaze of scarlet across his right cheek are the only lingering signs of his last MMA bout. Despite appearing physically fit, Troy seems tired and preoccupied.

"Hey, you okay?" I ask.

"Huh? Oh, yeah. I'm fine." He pauses. "Like I said, the show schedule is intense. We won't have much time to hang out."

"Still better than working around our college training schedules." We used to spend our college breaks together, but the rest of the year, time together consisted of video calls, same as now. I sense he misses me despite the lack of words. Troy and I don't do emo. We don't need to. We know how we feel about one another. "Cheer up, your best pal will soon be in Vegas with you!"

"Can't wait." He gives me a thumbs up.

We end the call, and the telltale thump against the wall and faint moans tell me Miguel and his girlfriend are at it again. The noisy sex highlights my solitude. Troy and I haven't been in the same bed in a while. A *long* while.

The wall vibrates with each slap of the bed. I lie down and hitch a ride, slipping a hand under the waistband of my lace panties to touch myself, imagining green eyes on me, a soft voice. My hand is his. Minutes after me, the lovebirds finish up, and the apartment finally goes quiet.

I fold a pillow over my face, embarrassed I'd fantasized about Cooper instead of Troy. I haven't thought about him in a long time. Seeing him brought it all back.

Damn him for looking so good.

That night, I locate a video of my college wrestling highlights, a gift from my coach at North Central, and email the file to *Sin City Fight Club*. A few days later, while cleaning out the last of my things from the apartment, a show assistant calls me, enthusiastic. We schedule an in-person interview for the day I arrive in Vegas.

The morning of my flight, I surrender my key to the building's super. As he hands me a check for my security deposit, he informs me he's already found someone to rent my room. I bid him goodbye, and then, flushed with adrenaline, I grab my timeworn suitcase, the zipper straining under the pressure of my belongings, and head to the airport.

The flight from JFK to Las Vegas gets in a little early. I call Troy and send him a text, but he doesn't answer or reply. Annoyed, but also too wired to sit around and wait, I order an Uber. I have the address of Troy's condo, where I plan to hang out until my interview. I sweep out of the terminal with my suitcase, and just in the few steps from the arrival terminal to my ride, I experience the temperature. The heat in the basin of the Mojave Desert is shockingly brutal, and it's only May.

The air-conditioned car traverses the Vegas strip toward the condo development where Troy lives with his castmates. I've seen the stretch of hotels and casinos before, but I'm still amazed by the glitter and glam that make up Las Vegas Boulevard, the 4.2 miles that everyone thinks of as Las Vegas. The stately hotels, one after the other: The Venetian, Caesars Palace, and the Bellagio with its fountains. Unlike New York where you'll get a touch of vertigo to go with the crick in your neck from looking up at the skyscrapers, there's a lot more space in Vegas, and though hotels are everywhere, they have room to breathe.

The Uber driver stops at a light, and a large electronic billboard in front of the MGM Grand flashes with images of *Sin City Fight Club*, advertising the show. Displayed 50 feet tall over the strip, the two teams—ten men and six women, half of them dressed in red, the other in blue—face each other. As I'm watching, the image changes, and Troy's face, along with his name, appears on the giant screen. That magnetic smile lights up the display. The image changes again, to a torso shot of Troy flexing. It hits me: He's made the Big Time. It's hardly a surprise, though. I knew he would, as did many in our small Long Island town. He has that charm, that personality that small towns like ours can't keep to ourselves. Troy Murphy was meant to be a star.

Now is my chance to show the world what Jayden Jones is capable of.

The car pulls up to the front of the manicured condo development, and a surge of exhilaration rises within me. I'm steps away from living and breathing the world of competitive fighting, working out in a state-of-the-art gym with the best professional coaching money can buy. I can taste it.

Outside, the brick wall of heat has me dash for the door of the men's unit and the A/C. Milo, one of the three male teammates Troy shares the condo with, currently the dead weight on the team, is leaving the unit. Though I'm not sure he remembers my name, he grins broadly and holds the door open for me.

"*Superstar* is in the shower." Milo follows the cynical dub with a wink.

I thank Milo and pass by, lugging my suitcase behind me. From the start, Troy had pulled ahead of the pack, becoming the main event. Some of his teammates aren't happy falling in line behind him. It's a dog-eat-dog world.

Part of the fighters' contract requires them to live together during the show's filming. The producers claim they want to depict the men and women fighters beyond the octagon, to give the audience a sense of who they are before they step into the cage and pummel each other black and blue. Totally a ploy to create drama and drive ratings up. As a former wrestler, I know the highs and lows of competitive fighting, the tension, the euphoria, the frustration. All the right ingredients for good entertainment. People are tuning in. Ratings are good—*really good*. Apparently, the producers know what they're doing.

Thankfully, Troy hasn't gotten pulled into any off-color drama. I'm not into that. I wheel my suitcase down the hallway to his bedroom. As

Milo informed me, the room is vacant—the blinds drawn and, à propos to Troy's nature, starkly unadorned. His phone is on the night table, blinking with my missed calls and texts. I kick off my sneakers and eye the rumpled, slept-in bed. No surprise there. Dude's never made a bed in his life.

The faint hum of the shower vibrates through the bedroom wall. Anticipation trumps my fatigue as I strip down to my birthday suit. A long, steamy shower with Troy will drive thoughts of Cooper from my head. I grab the door handle, remembering that, though not in the bedrooms, the production company wired the condo with cameras. I pick up Troy's crumpled T-shirt from the floor and put it on.

The bathroom door is unlocked, and when I push it open, wafting steam hangs in the air. Troy's silhouette moves beyond the frosted glass shower door. He is grunting repeatedly, and for a moment, this confuses me. But only until a higher-pitched feminine moan responds.

My breath catches as the forms beyond the steamed-up shower doors take the shape of two bodies moving together.

I leave the bathroom soundlessly, but the loud and formidable thump–thump–thump of my heart deafens and disorients me. Fine motor skills leave me as I struggle to put my clothes back on. Somehow, dressed again, I am in the kitchen pacing like a caged tiger. The morning sun glints off an impressive collection of liquor bottles on the counter—greens, blues, and clear glass—and draws my attention. I seize the nearest bottle, tequila, my hands shaking, and pour myself a generous shot. Drawing it to my lips, I drain the glass. Aged and pricey, the stuff goes down smoothly. I wish it would burn my throat or make me gag. Pushing the glass aside, I lay my hands on the counter. My head throbs like a ticking time bomb, counting down seconds, *tick, tick, tick,* before it explodes.

Part of me wants to leave, to sneak away and never speak of this. Pretend it never happened. The other, more willful part of me wants to stay, to see Troy's face when he realizes I'm here. And that I know what he's done.

The shower stops, and the sound of their muffled voices grow louder. I imagine them drying each other off. In my heart, anger and grief wage war. I *cannot* believe he's done this to me.

When the bathroom door opens, it's Troy's voice I hear first. I take a deep breath and raise my eyes as he boldly strides into the kitchen naked. He rubs his head with a white terrycloth towel, the rest of his body glistening with the traces of his shower.

It takes two full steps for him to realize he's not alone.

"Whoa," he says, raising a hand to his chest.

My presence startles him. Even now, amid his betrayal, I almost laugh at his reaction. Odd for a tough, professional fighter. But I'm too angry. I curl my lips in and glare at him.

"Jay, how'd you get here?" He recovers and hurriedly wraps the towel around his waist. "How'd you get in?"

"Who were you in the shower with?" I ask, relatively composed despite the tightness in my throat.

He freezes, eyes darting toward the hallway. We both hear the pitter-patter of bare feet coming our way. My heart hammers in my chest.

"Troy, baby, do you have a blow dryer?" She's wrapped in white fluffy towels, one around her torso, the other around her hair, the thick cotton curled high like the headdress of Nefertiti, queen of the Nile.

She's darker skinned than him, pretty, with a build similar to mine. My gaze falls to her arms—defined and dense with muscle. She's a fighter.

I've never met her, but I recognize her. A Canadian bantamweight, and a member of the Fight Club. She's on Team Diego—the same as Troy.

Zoe Bocek.

The towel is low, exposing the rounded top of her breasts. Breasts that Troy, moments ago, pawed.

A blackness shutters my thoughts, and before I consciously plan to act, I'm hurtling toward Troy. I go for his legs, shouldering his left and hooking the right. Unsuspecting, he's an easy target, and though he outweighs me by over seventy pounds, he topples backward from the force. The two of us crash to the cool, hard tile floor, Troy taking the brunt of the impact. I round on him, head into his armpit, and snake my arm around his neck, grasping him in a headlock.

He quickly overpowers my grip and loosens my hold on him when a loud, hissing shriek pierces the room. I look up and see Zoe cock her leg before she delivers a punishing boot to the right side of my face.

The force of the blow sends me reeling backward, off Troy. I raise my arms and shield myself. A series of punches punish my shoulders and arms and then stop altogether. I roll away and scurry to my feet, fists raised. Zoe is still swinging, but Troy has her restrained, her towel in a heap at her feet.

The uproar shakes Troy's teammates out of bed. Two muscular fighters stand in the kitchen bare-chested, offsetting Zoe's nakedness. The bitch glowers at me, hair and eyes wild. The look of loathing and insanity in her expression outstrips my rage.

"Enough, Zoe! Go wait in the bedroom, please?" Troy returns her lost towel to her and avoids meeting anyone's eyes.

"No," I blurt out. "Don't bother. I'm leaving."

I push past Troy and the rest of them and make for the door.

"Jay, wait." Troy follows, hand extended. "Let me explain."

"No need. I have eyes, Troy." I shove his hand aside and yank the door shut behind me.

My hands shake as I park myself on a bench next to the walkway in front of the condo unit to wait for the Uber I previously ordered to take me to the audition. I'd rather melt in the heat than spend another minute with Troy.

The blistering air causes the sky and trees to shimmer and waver before my eyes. My stomach churns. I lean my elbows on my knees and cradle my head in my hands, hoping I don't throw up. There are footsteps and my suitcase is set down beside me. The wooden bench bows slightly with Troy's added weight. Peeking out from my hands, I see he's still barefoot but dressed now in shorts and a T-shirt.

"Jay, I'm sorry. So, so sorry," he whispers, a tentative hand on my back. "This thing with Zoe, it just happened. I wish you hadn't found out like this."

I glare at him, a slow-burning sob inching its way up my throat. "You're only sorry because I found out? How about being sorry you cheated on me, Troy?"

The Uber rolls up in front of us.

"Go to the audition." He motions to the car. "We'll talk afterward—"

"Fuck you." I shoot to my feet and grab the handle of my suitcase. "You're dead to me."

He stands looking like he wants to stop me, but reading the look on my face, he knows better. I march to the Uber. The driver pops the trunk so I can load my luggage. I get in the car and slam the door. As the driver pulls away, I chance a look back. Troy's face is in his hands. I feel nothing but the burn of anger.

The show's production offices are housed in the business district. I make for the nearest restroom to catch my breath and refresh my makeup, doing my best to hide the damage Zoe did to my face. More composed, I sign in and take a seat. I sit, waiting nearly forty minutes, eyeing the exit, and talking myself out of leaving, until a suited assistant leads me to a glass-enclosed meeting room.

Seconds after I take a seat at a large modern conference table, a lean blonde strides in, an employee nametag clipped to her jacket lapel.

I stand, and she reaches across the table to shake my hand. "Pleasure to meet you, Ms. Jones. My name is Kathleen Contreras. I'm the casting director," she says but doesn't sit down. "We loved your audition video, but it doesn't appear you'll be a good fit for *Sin City Fight Club* after all."

"Why?"

"We received a call from Ms. Bocek. I understand there's been an unfortunate turn of events in the men's condo. She refuses to work with you."

"That bitch is screwing *my* boyfriend and I'm being punished?"

"Ms. Bocek is popular with our viewers. Our hands are tied," she says with a shrug.

And just like that, it's over. Contreras says I should stop by the receptionist to pick up comp tickets for dinner and a show. This way, my trip to Vegas isn't a complete waste of time.

I exit the office, mind spinning. Troy, the show, and this move to Vegas had been the holy grail. I gave up my apartment and put my law degree on indefinite hold to move across the country and do the thing I loved with the person I loved most—my best friend.

Only my best friend is a lying cheater.

He screwed her, and I screwed myself. I'm in an unknown place, without Troy, and without a backup plan. There's no Hail Mary.

Life off the rails, I Uber back to the airport, but once inside the terminal, my stomach twists violently. I book it to the nearest women's restroom where I retch and empty my stomach, but it does little to make me feel better.

"Asshole!" I stomp the flush button with my foot. Something snaps inside me, and I stomp it again, more forcefully.

"Stupid fucking asshole!" I continue to hammer the button over and over. By the time I get out of the stall, I've gained several onlookers.

"What?" I lower my chin, daring them to say something. They turn and scatter. No one wants to challenge the mad chick beating up the toilet bowl. Seeing my reflection in the mirror, I don't blame them. Tears have made my mascara run and given me a set of angry raccoon eyes. With my knotted and messy hair and red, puffy face, I look like I've crawled out of the gutter.

Back in the check-in area, I claim a bank of seats to myself and scroll my cell for flight schedules, thinking I'll call my Brooklyn landlord next, and see if he has another place I can afford to rent.

My phone rings mid-scroll and my stomach drops when I see Cooper's name.

I answer with surprisingly still hands.

"Jayden." The soft, broken way he says my name makes the skin on my arms pimple. "My father passed away last night."

The sounds and sights of the airport fade.

"Oh, God, no." I drop my forehead to my hand, tears filling my eyes. "Cooper, I'm so sorry. Are you... okay?"

It's a stupid question, and I reach for something else to say, something that will make him feel better, but I know all too well no words will make this hurt any less.

"I'm hanging in there," he says. "The four of us were all together. They sedated him for the pain. He passed quietly. Peacefully."

I press my lips together, afraid I'll burst out crying and wreck the composure he's working hard to maintain.

"We're planning the services," he adds. "I'll let you know the details when we have them."

"Please do. I'll be there."

"Good. I was worried you'd left for Las Vegas. Where are you?"

Gripping my phone, I stare at the industrial carpet of the airport check-in area. "Nowhere special. I'll see you in a couple of days."

"Okay, see you." Cooper ends the call without waiting for me to say goodbye.

The stabbing sensation in my heart makes it difficult to think straight. It's not fair. Coach was too young. He had more living to do, many more lives to have a positive impact on. As he did mine.

All the opportunities over the years I had to visit or call him, gone forever.

The question of where to go next is answered. Home. I have to go home for Coach's funeral services.

Onboard a flight back to New York, I take a window seat and wait for the plane to take off. My cell pings with an incoming text. I look, hoping it's Cooper, but it's Troy.

I've known Troy Murphy most of my life. We became best friends in elementary school, chasing frogs and turtles down at the pond at the end of the street where we grew up. We've never been apart since. A duo—like a pair of shoes or salt and pepper shakers—you don't find one without the other. I can't remember life before him.

It's hard to imagine moving on without him, but I don't see any other option. A string of texts follows. Apologies, all of them. I know he'll continue. You don't throw away a relationship of over fifteen years without some remorse. The plane prepares for takeoff, and I switch the phone to airplane mode.

I have forgiven Troy for many things, but this, this kind of betrayal is unforgivable.

Four

It's edging into the afternoon rush hour when I arrive in New York. The trains are packed with daily commuters. People grunt and roll their eyes as I bustle through the busy terminal with my old cumbersome suitcase in tow and hop on the next available eastbound train.

The only logical place to go is to my mother's house, where I can lie low and figure out my next step. I call my mother.

"Mom, it's me. I'm coming home."

"Now?"

"About an hour. I just got on the train."

"Is something wrong?"

"I'll explain when I see you," I say.

"I'm at work until five, and Kara is babysitting after school until seven."

"Okay. I'll wait outside until you get home."

"Why? Did you lose your key?"

"No." I bite my tongue. She requested I hand over my copy when I last saw her. "I gave it back to you."

"Oh, well, I'll see you a few minutes after five," she says.

The Long Island Railroad car sways, clickety-clacking on the rails as it passes first through the boroughs and then through the counties, from Nassau into Suffolk, making brief stops at stations along the way. The landscape outside the train window grows noticeably different. The buildings are shorter, from residential high-rises to two- and three-storied structures, and more spaced out until it's populated by single-family homes with paved driveways and green lawns. The Long Island suburbs.

There's a light drizzle of rain when I exit the train at the Ronkonkoma station and approach the row of taxis waiting for passengers. I pick one since they're already there and mutely watch as we coast through the familiar tree-lined streets.

Bayport is a small hamlet bordering Long Island's southern coastline, so small it's rarely noted on maps of the area. It doesn't even have a true main street. Located on the Great South Bay, the town consists mostly of residential homes with schools and a smattering of small businesses. Years ago, the town was known for its abundance of oysters, mussels, and clams, but that was long before my time. For anything worth doing, we cross over into other towns, like Sayville or Patchogue. This town was surely what the first writer had envisioned when they coined the phrase "sleepy town" and is why the show picked *Country* as a nickname for Troy.

When the taxi pulls up in front of the house, I settle the fare and glance at Troy's childhood home across the street, but I can't spare any mental energy for him.

The rain is steady, the kind that often comes in spring—big heavy drops that the earth, bursting with new life, sucks up unapologetically. Trees come to life, fattening with shiny leaves. Cherry trees, overburdened with soft pastel flowers, line the side of the house, and the grass is plump and full like a plush carpet. The perfumed scent of flowering lilacs fill the air and reminds me of how much I always loved Long Island this time of year.

It also makes me think of Coach and how he won't be here this spring or summer. He'll never pass another season with us. I still can't believe he's gone.

Tears fill my eyes as I pull my suitcase up the driveway.

I wait for Mom on the covered porch. The rain has picked up and slants sideways, and no matter where I try to hide, it finds me. At twenty minutes past the hour, I check my messages, but Mom hasn't texted. I shoot her another message, then leave my suitcase to check the garage. It's locked. So is the back door. I'm not thrilled about being stuck outside, but locked doors are good. Locked doors keep my family safe. Resigned to wait, I return to the porch.

I moved to Brooklyn after graduating college and haven't been home in a while. The last few Christmases, Mom, Kara, and I met in the city because we couldn't bear to be in the house during the holidays without Dad. We had nice dinners and took pictures in front of the Rockefeller tree, fabricating smiles so we could tell ourselves we were okay, that we were making this new reality work.

I notice things while waiting, like the faded white clapboard and peeling black trim on the house, the lawn needs mowing, and the bushes that edge the driveway are out of control. Before Dad got sick, he took pride in our home's upkeep. The current scruffy state illuminates his absence.

My teeth chatter, and I do jumping jacks and run in place, which makes my swollen jaw ache. Mom's car pulls into the driveway just before six.

"I got a phone call just as I was leaving work, and I totally forgot about you," she says and unlocks the door.

I say nothing as I follow her inside, dragging my suitcase behind me.

My mother kicks off her shoes in the foyer. "Alejandro called. That man makes me forget everything."

I do not know who that is. Watching Mom embrace her widowhood, being single and dating other men, is more than I can tolerate. I don't ask about Alejandro.

Coming back home feels like falling into a warp-speed vortex and teleporting back in time. No matter the years I've been out from under this roof, being here brings out my mulish side.

The kitchen looks like it has exploded. A teetering tower of dirty dishes fills the sink, and open boxes of cereal and granola bars litter the counter. The tabletop is covered with food crumbs and coffee.

Beneath the mess is a beautiful room with top-of-the-line appliances. When Dad's life insurance paid out, my mother had gone on a tear, a full-on spending spree, and renovated the house. Neither the money nor all the shiny new objects have made up for my father's absence. As far as I could tell, they haven't made my mother any happier.

The state of the house is only slightly better than my Brooklyn apartment. The mess irritates me, and I feel a powerful urge to clean it.

No, Jayden. It's not your mess. You will *not* clean it.

Mom walks straight to the sink and begins tackling the dishes, loading them into the dishwasher. The place is unkempt, and she knows I see it.

I dig out an ice pack from the freezer and, pressing it to my face, lean against the counter and check her out from behind. She put on some weight since the last time I saw her. But extra weight be damned. It hasn't held her back. At forty-six, Naomi Jones's beauty is still appreciated by the opposite sex, as her dating life attests to. Our differences are striking. From her dressy work clothes—well-cut slacks and bright, feminine blouse—to my athletic, slept-in clothes, her light skin to my deep-toned skin, her wavy blonde hair brushed to a gleaming shine to my messy dark hair that hasn't seen a brush in two days, and her pretty wedge sandals to my well-worn sneakers.

"So, you decided to come for a visit, eh?" she says over her shoulder.

Visit.

Yep, with Dad gone, they have demoted me to the rank of visitor.

Mom and I fought about my father's wish to die at home. She won. He died in the hospital, surrounded by us, but also the medical staff and beeping machines, instead of the familiar, comforting things of home. And since then, our relationship has become somewhat business-like. Dad's death illuminated our genetic-free relationship. Before Naomi was in the picture, Dad had me. I have no memory of my biological mother. She died when I was a newborn. They weren't married and had no plans for a future together. Dad said I was a happy accident. But Naomi and I never talk about *Before*. Before Dad married her.

Because we shared the same blood, Dad and me, he was mine in a way Naomi isn't. Still, I was too little to remember anything before her. Naomi is the only mother I know. I've always thought of myself as her daughter, but Dad's death left us in a weird place, stepping around each other.

"Aren't you supposed to be in Las Vegas or something?" Mom draws me back into conversation, continuing to load the dishwasher haphazardly.

"There and back. I'm home for Coach McCaffrey's funeral services."

"I heard he passed." She closes the dishwasher, wipes her hands on a dish towel, and for the first time, she looks at me. "What on earth happened to your face?"

"Intense workout." I'm not up for her judgment.

"I am sorry about Coach. Such a shame. He was a kind man," she says and tries to hug me. I stay still, let her hold me. I can't remember the last time she hugged me. Or me her. "I'll put a sympathy card in the mail." She pushes a lock of my dark brown hair behind my right ear. "Your hair got long since the last time I saw you. I like it much better this way. So much more feminine."

My shoulders stiffen, but I resist the bait.

"Haven't gotten around to getting a haircut." I pull away and finger-comb my hair. It is much longer than usual.

"How's Troy?" she asks, a spark of interest in her eyes. Troy's the son she never had. Over the years, he carried in her bags of groceries, ate her meatloaf dinners with gusto, flattered her new outfit or hairstyle, and watched over both of her daughters with a big brother's eye. How could any mother resist? In her eyes, the only thing I've ever done right was hook up with Troy. "Will he be home for Mr. McCaffrey's services?"

I grunt under my breath. I didn't tell him about Coach.

"He'll be home," I say.

He *has* to come. Which means we'll have to face each other. I'm not ready for that, but with Coach's funeral, do I have a choice?

Holding the ice pack to my face, I carry my suitcase up the carpeted staircase to the second floor, not stopping to look at anything. My only mission is to get to my bedroom, lie down, close my eyes, and silence the world.

The hinges on my bedroom door creak when I push the door open, but the thick off-white carpet absorbs the sound of my footsteps. The room smells stale and unused, and stepping past the door sends a visual whorl of dust motes into flight.

It feels familiar, though, like reuniting with an old childhood friend. One that's nice to see, but after many years of separation, I have little in common with anymore.

The most prevalent objects in the room are several large cardboard shipping boxes that obscure the view of the bed, Amazon's arched arrow logo on most of them. I squeeze past them and find the same old blue plaid comforter on my bed, buried beneath piles of clothes stacked impossibly high. A cat, a gray tabby I've never seen before, is asleep amongst the mounds. She lifts her head; her green luminous eyes watch me with curiosity.

"Get." I shake my hands in its direction and the cat scampers.

I push aside the piles of clothes, dumping some on the floor, until I have a space big enough to lie down. I climb onto the mattress and curl my knees into my chest. The cardboard shipping cartons form an uneven border around the bed, like a safety shield. The rain taps against the windowpane and lulls me to sleep.

Mom is gone when I wake up the next morning. My jaw is tight and sports an angry red welt. From the bedroom window, I spy my sister's newer model car in the driveway. My cell pings with an incoming text. It's from Cooper. The details of his father's services.

I text back: *Thinking of you.*

He responds with a broken heart emoji, which makes my heart ache.

I discard yesterday's rumpled, slept-in clothes, put on clean shorts and a T-shirt from my luggage, and head downstairs, where Gordon Ramsay berates someone's kitchen skills, his snarling face filling the family room's large screen TV.

My little sister is prone on the couch, focused on her cell phone. A blur of vivid orange manicured fingernails flutter over the screen. Kara is way more girly than I ever was. Even now, I prefer my nails short and unembellished. The Favored One is the polished and primped mini-me my mother always wanted.

"Hey," I say.

Her head jerks upward and a yelp of surprise leaps from her lips.

"Jayden!" she snaps, hand pressed to her chest. "You scared me!"

I laugh. "Sorry."

"Yeah, right." Kara sits up and stretches her arms over her head, yawning.

At seventeen, I still think of Kara as a kid. I was six when she was born, and I thought of her as more of a toy doll than a live baby. We are half-sisters, but with her pale skin and blonde hair, she strongly favors our mother. Her freckled but smooth, unblemished skin implies youth, but the well-rounded boobs and hips make it clear she's not a little girl.

"What are you doing here?"

"Good to see you, too."

Kara, cell in hand, stands to give me a brief hug. "It's good to see you, but where did you come from?"

"I came in yesterday and slept in my room. Mom didn't tell you?"

"No, I got in late. She was already sleeping," she says. "What's up with your face?"

"Disagreed with some chick." I laugh it off. "No school today?"

"Teacher conferences. Gives me time to study for a trig test tomorrow." She tips a notebook full of scribbled equations toward me. "Right angles and hypotenuses. Nothing but good times."

I frown in understanding. "Who's this Alejandro our mother keeps talking about?"

"I can't believe she didn't tell you *all* about him. She met him on a dating site and literally never stops talking about him." My sister rolls her eyes. "Morning, noon, and night, it's *Alejandro said this. Alejandro did that.*"

I cringe, thinking back to our mother's flirtations, crying on the shoulders of other men, and the high, lilting pitch of her voice as she spoke with them in the weeks following my father's passing. Her pitch was different with the husbands than with their wives and blatantly disrespectful of my father. Her behavior pushed my buttons, and with Dad no longer there to mediate and run interference, a sharp fallout began between us. It's easier to limit my time under the same roof as her.

"What happened to Jerry?"

"You mean Gary?" Kara quirks a groomed eyebrow. "He was two boo-thangs ago, before Artie."

"She dated a guy named *Artie*?"

"Gross, I know." She scrunches her face. "He used to sleep over on weekends."

"I never heard that."

"Mom made me swear to keep my mouth shut. She thought you'd judge her." She shrugs. "I thought he might move in at one point, but then Delia intervened."

Bedelia Rooney has been my mother's best friend for as long as I can remember.

"Intervened how?"

"She hooked up with Artie. Heard they're living together. Mom hasn't talked to Delia in almost a year."

"Wow. That's terrible." Delia is the closest thing Mom has to a sister. Before yesterday, I wouldn't have been able to imagine such betrayal. "How's Mom been handling it?"

"She seems okay. Though more determined to find a man. But seriously, the woman has about a three-month shelf life. I gotta give the chick credit where it's due. She doesn't sit around crying. She gets right out there and finds another man."

I shake my head.

"How long has she been seeing this latest guy?"

"I don't know. Two months? He's some kind of bigwig banker with an investment thing side hustle. Mom says he's dreamy—calls him her Latin lover." She adds the last bit with a wide grin.

"Nope." I hold out a hand. "Don't want to hear it."

Kara laughs and drops back on the dove gray sectional. "So, what are you doing home? Thought you were moving to Vegas."

She twirls long, bleached blonde strands around an index finger.

"I royally bombed my audition, and I had to come home for Mr. McCaffrey's funeral services. You talk to Jess since he passed away?"

"Just through texts," she says. I wish it were more, but it's nice that Cooper's sister and Kara keep in touch. "People are talking about it at school. Everyone's so sad. Kids were crying. He was everyone's favorite teacher."

My throat thickens, imagining the classrooms and school hallways full of grieving students and faculty. "I have the service times. We'll go together?"

"Yeah, sure."

Something is off about the den. I take a few seconds to pinpoint it, then it hits me.

"Where is Daddy's chair?"

Kara rolls her lips into a flat line. "Mommy wanted to give it to Goodwill."

"Oh, hell no." Anger constricts my breath.

The old recliner was his favorite. The brown leather smelled like him, and the seat dimpled in the shape of his butt. I'd found Kara asleep in that chair several times after he died.

"She didn't. Only because I convinced her to let me put it in my bedroom," my sister says.

"Good." I exhale. "So, I might stay for a while. I gave up my apartment and I'm in-between places. Hopefully that's okay with you and Mom."

"Fine with me." Kara shrugs.

"Do you know if Dad's car still starts?"

"Dunno." This time, Kara's eyes drop to her cell, and I know I've lost her. Asking if she knows where the keys are is pointless.

Leaving her to study, I head toward the garage. The wide door rolls up with a hum after I press the door opener. Yesterday's rain clouds are gone, replaced by cottony wisps.

Dad's old maroon Chevy Impala, the one I learned how to drive in, is sleeping under the canvas cover we put over it when Dad could no longer drive. I strip the heavy cloth off the car. It's old, funky, and ugly, or *fungly* as I called it back then to tease my father, but I begged my mother not to get rid of it. I'd boasted, that someday, when I have a place to park it, I'm taking it.

Looks like she took me seriously on that.

I put a hand on the faded roof and think of the many hours spent driving to wrestling practices, to the movies, and out for burgers and ice cream. In Brooklyn, it had been easier to compartmentalize, to put aside memories that made me both happy and sad. But here at home, I can't escape thinking about my father and the bundle of emotions that comes with those thoughts. Mom has moved things around and taken down many of our family photos. It's like she's trying to erase him. Even his car has stayed hidden under a tarp. Though Dad's physical items are out of sight, it's impossible to remove him from this house. It's been over four years, but he's still here. I feel him.

The car doors are locked, and I debate asking Mom for the keys or just searching all the usual hiding places myself. I pass by the car and stand in the open garage doorway, looking out over the neighborhood. An older couple, perhaps young retirees, holds hands as they stride by, in perfect step with each other. They move at a brisk pace, arms swinging, exercising, so the handholding looks uncomfortable—and silly. An excessive way to say we're together—we can't bear to not be always touching each other.

I roll my eyes as they pass, but my attention once again turns to the overgrown lawn. My nostrils fill with the sweet, sharp scent of mowed grass—from every house on the block, except my own. Mom must have forgotten to start up the lawn service for the season.

Irritation creeps up my back, but then, I remind myself, she's only one person. I make a mental note to make the call myself. I'll be helpful. I will keep the peace. A mowed lawn and harmony between my mother and me. I imagine my father smiling down from the heavens.

Inside again, I sit at the kitchen table and hold my cell out in front of me. I've resisted calling Troy about Coach for a day and a half. My father always said, no matter how hard, it's best to do the right thing. Telling Troy about Coach is the right thing. I pull up Troy's number, my finger hovering over the call button when "Renegades" from X Ambassadors bursts out, and I nearly drop my phone. The song from our high school wrestling days is Troy's ringtone.

"Jay, I heard about Coach," he rushes out when I answer.

His words suck the air from my lungs.

"Who told you?"

"Lee Kaminski. I still can't believe it."

Even though I'm angry with him, I feel guilty that a former classmate from our wrestling team told him before I did.

"I don't care what the producers say, I'm coming home for the funeral," he says. At least we both agree this isn't something he can miss. "And maybe, while I'm home, we can talk?"

I cover my eyes with a hand and take a deep breath. "There is nothing to talk about. You cheated on me. It's over. We're done."

It sounds final. It *is* final. Silence ensues over the line.

"We need to talk, but not over the phone. We'll do it when I come home," he says. "How do you want to handle the wake?"

"What do you mean?"

"You and me. If we don't show up together, people will talk."

"You afraid everyone will find out you cheated on me?" My voice rises.

"Do you want people to find out about us at Coach's funeral?"

Though I hate to admit it, the cheater has a valid point. We'll be there for Coach, and out of respect, neither of us wants to draw attention to ourselves.

"Fine. We'll walk in together and give our condolences. That's it."

I hang up without asking how long he'll stay or what his plans are. I don't care what he does.

The Chevy keys are in the top drawer of Dad's old antique desk in his office. I run a finger over the #1 DAD key ring, the one Kara and I gave him ten years ago. The name Alejandro pops into my mind. I know nothing about this new guy in my mother's life. From Mom's behavior and what Kara said, Mom seems hung up on him. Sight unseen, already I don't like him.

I pocket the keys and go online to the DMV to start the registration process so I can legally drive the car. Life in suburbia without a car is stifling. I bark out a harsh laugh at the absurdity of it all. A month ago, I was a law student and in a committed relationship. A day ago, I was a potential MMA fighter. Today, I'm back at my childhood home, single, and trying to secure a set of wheels.

Oh, how the mighty fall.

After I submit the application, I dig through piles of mail on the desk until I locate an old statement from O'Brien's lawn service. Katie, Mr. O'Brien's daughter, and I went to high school together. I dial the office number on the statement, and when a woman answers, I say, "Mrs. O'Brien? It's Jayden Jones. I need to start up the lawn service."

Mrs. O'Brien and I exchange a few pleasantries, and I find out Katie is working and living in Manhattan. "That's great," I say, keeping the envy out of my tone. She agrees to add our house to the team's maintenance schedule and tells me to say hello to my mother for her.

I wander upstairs to find a dress to wear to Coach's wake. I have a few appropriate options, but I'd rather not wear anything I own. The clothes I wear to Mr. McCaffrey's wake will forever hold a memory of losing him. I will never wear those clothes again. The dress from Dad's funeral got tossed out as soon as I returned home from Troy's house. That one dress had a surplus of unsettling memories.

Even though she's downstairs and could come talk to me, Kara texts me that she's going to a friend's house to study.

"Okay, bye!" I yell down to her, hoping while I'm home the two of us can bridge whatever gap between us my negligence the past couple of years has created.

With the sound of her car growing distant, I decide to poke around in her closet for a dress to wear to Coach's funeral. Dad's recliner sits in the corner of her bedroom, angled toward the window. I settle down into its soft leather and hold the armrests, an unsteady smile on my lips. My sister has this one special item of his, and I'm glad. I got his law books—which are special to me, and which I plan to find while I'm home. I suspect they're buried somewhere under the mess in my room.

Pushing out of the chair, I stand before Kara's closet, running my fingers along the fabrics hanging inside. Tags dangle from outfits bought and yet to be worn. I notice a few of my things, borrowed and not returned. *Little sisters.*

There are several dresses, but trying a couple on, I find they are too tight on my arms and chest. Kara has a slender, graceful figure. Many years of weightlifting have broadened the upper half of my body.

My mother's closet is next. As I step into her walk-in, I am hit with un-expected memories of playing dress-up, Kara and I wearing our mother's clothes and fancy shoes, too big on our feet. Of my teenage years, poking around for something vintage that had become fashionable again.

Unlike my sister's closet, my mother's is filled *beyond* capacity. I step over shopping bags and piles of shoes and move several boxes to look at her dresses. In Brooklyn, space comes at a premium price, but on the Island, lots of space is the norm. The house is large for two people. So much space, and yet my sister and mother have filled it up and used my bedroom to accommodate the overflow.

A few men's Oxford shirts hang in the back, and I run my fingers over the sleeve of a blueish-purple one. I remember teasing my father about the color. Said only a few men could pull off wearing periwinkle. And he had.

My mother is in the bedroom with her laptop as I exit the closet. I stop short, unsure if she's going to be annoyed that I'm rooting around in her closet.

"You don't mind if I borrow a dress for the wake service, do you?" I ask.

"Sure." She sits on the bed to slip off her heels, her pale hair swept back off her face and held in place by a clip. She opens her laptop, barely registering my presence. "You find something?"

Relieved, I hold up the black dress. "This, but it looks new."

"Take it. Probably doesn't fit me right now, anyway." Mom doesn't look up. Her attention is on the screen in front of her.

"Laptop, huh?" I motion to the computer.

"The girls at work got me into online chats a few months ago. It's so fun," she says, eyes never leaving the screen. Mom using a laptop. Sure, she bought into cell phone culture, texting and using Siri, but it's weird to see her using a computer. Even weirder that she's talking to strangers online.

"Hey, so, I might stay home awhile. I mean, if that's okay with you. I gave up my apartment in Brooklyn, and I haven't figured out where to go next."

Brown eyes pop up over the top of the computer. "How long?"

She wants an end date, to know when I'll be out of her hair.

I shrug. "Maybe for the summer?"

"What about Troy? You could take a job in Las Vegas for the summer."

"I don't want to stay out there." I shake my head. "It's too hot."

"Won't Troy miss you?"

"He'll be fine." Pushing aside a mental image of Troy and Zoe in the shower, I glance out the window. "What's up with the yard? Everything is overgrown."

"Oh, that. So busy. I forgot, is all."

"Well, I called O'Brien's and requested service."

Again, her eyes pop up to meet mine, followed by a moment of silence. "Worrying about the yard. Just like your father. If you're staying, then you can take care of the outdoor stuff. It'll cover your rent."

"*Okkaay*," I say, on a long breath. This is how we're doing this.

A series of musical beeps erupt from the computer. Mom's attention drops to the screen, and she laughs.

"Oh, Alejandro, you are too, too much!" She looks up with a megawatt smile. "I found myself a *wonderful* man."

"I heard." My enthusiasm falls short. "You should be careful. People aren't always what they seem."

Hell, Troy wasn't who I thought he was, and I'd known him for most of my life.

She waves off my concerns. "I've got nothing to worry about with Alejandro."

FIVE

That evening, Troy sends me a text that he's home, which is confirmed by the sight of a new sleek, black Mercedes in his driveway. It's a first that I don't rush across the street to see him. I feel sick to my stomach thinking about all the firsts that will follow. The summer, the holidays—all done separately. I can't remember a summer or any significant amount of time, other than college, not spent with Troy. And telling people we are no longer together and being asked why? The mere thought makes me want to avoid people for the next century.

Troy texts me in the morning with the time he plans to leave for the wake. My sister and I dress and prep with care. I wear makeup, something I don't do often, but it helps camouflage the bruise from Zoe's kick. Troy backs the Mercedes out of his driveway and zips up to the curb in front of our house. Walking a few steps ahead of Kara, I reach the car before her and take the back seat. Kara shrugs and launches into the front seat.

"Nice ride," she says to Troy.

"Perks of being a star, baby." He winks at her. His suit is new, a better cut and fit than anything I've ever seen him wear. "Dang, little sister, you grew up. I so want to mess your hair up like I used to, but you're too old for that, aren't you?"

"You touch my hair, and I'll punch you in the balls." She laughs and flips down the visor to check her appearance.

Troy grins at me in the back seat, but I give him a tight-lipped frown. His smile disappears.

"How're you doing?"

"Fine. Can we just go?" I say a little too sharply.

In the light-up visor mirror, my sister catches my eye. Questions flash across her expression. I turn and stare out the window.

My sister has always looked up to Troy. To her, he's the brother we never had. The day is already too heavy with grief for me to pop that balloon.

It's a short drive through town, and Troy pulls into the funeral home parking lot minutes later.

"Wow, it's really crowded," Kara says as Troy rounds the over-burdened lot a second time before he finds a spot to park.

The McCaffrey family is well-known and connected in our community, and it seems the entire town has come to pay their respects. As we step through the entrance, Kara gives me a sideways glance. I imagine she's feeling an uncomfortable sense of trepidation, the same as me. The last time we were in this funeral home together was for our father's services.

I take her hand.

"Don't," she says through clenched teeth and tugs her hand free.

Her reaction stings. She held onto my hand like a lifeline during our father's funeral. I'm completely at a loss when, without a backward glance, she marches ahead, merging into the fold of sympathizers.

Kara is connected to these people in a way I no longer am. Having been away for the last few years, Troy and I have become out-of-towners. For this one occasion, I'm glad he's with me, that I'm not alone, but as we move further into the main room, I feel armor-less and exposed. The humorless sights and sounds and the reality of why I'm here cause me to break out in a cold sweat.

My earlier hope to get in and out without too much attention becomes wishful thinking because as soon as Troy takes his sunglasses off, it's like he's stepped into the spotlight. Everyone turns to gawk. Faces light up with recognition.

He tries to put an arm around me, but I slip away from him using the excuse that I'll hold a place for us in the long line of people waiting to see the family. I don't want him to forget that we're here together for appearances only, nothing more. I scan the room to get the layout, avoiding eye contact with everyone around me. My chest is tight, and I focus on breathing in and out, in and out.

White display boards atop easels have been placed between tabletops laden with the photographic history of Kellan McCaffrey's life. I keep my gaze low, surfing from one photo to the next until the guy in front of me points to the photograph I'm staring at.

"Great shot," he says.

It's a younger version of Coach in front of a black classroom chalk-board wearing a big green Mexican sombrero and holding maracas. The photo eggs a smile out of me.

"It was never boring in his history class," I say, finally looking at the owner of the voice. He's a bit older. Easy on the eyes, as Mom often says.

"Everyone says he was an outstanding teacher," the guy says. One arm hangs casually across the back of a woman I assume is his wife.

"He was a legend. The teacher everyone wanted and a great coach, too. I was on the wrestling team. They took this the year before I joined." I point to a framed photo of the high school wrestling team, where Coach and I are off to the side. Troy and Cooper, two popular freshmen boys, are next to us. They are, like the other boys on the team, in their wrestling gear, their youthful bodies sinewy and muscled. I, the only girl in the photo and wearing jeans and a school hoodie, clipboard in hand, was relegated to the scorekeeper. That was the last season of a boys-only team.

"Ah, you're Jayden Jones—the first female wrestler in the district." The woman gives me a warm smile.

They make the connection surprisingly fast. "Guilty as charged."

"Claudia and Toby Faye," she says and holds out a hand. "We're neighbors and good friends of the family. I work with his wife."

I shake both of their hands.

"Kellan told us how you campaigned to join the wrestling team," Toby says. "He was so proud of your accomplishments. You could see it in his face whenever he spoke of you."

I drop my chin as a rush of emotion makes me unable to speak. There's no disguising my response.

"They are the nicest, friendliest family I've ever met." Claudia kindly continues talking to give me time to compose myself. "Kel's death is a terrible blow... to us all."

The McCaffrey's neighbors and I carry on a polite conversation as the line painstakingly inches forward. When we reach the front of the room, Toby and Claudia peel away from me to kneel in front of the casket. My gaze strays to Cooper standing beside his father's coffin. I watch my former friend and classmate greet each guest warmly, hugging most, shaking hands with others, and graciously accepting their sympathies. Even in the face of this momentous loss, he is level-headed, controlled, and respectable, reminding me why every year we wrestled, he was unanimously voted team captain. I admire his composure until Troy cuts the line and steps next to me, his large stature obstructing my view of Cooper.

I glue my eyes to Coach's lifeless body. Troy fills the silence between us with ramblings that float over me. Large pale hands, one positioned over the other. It's the only part of him I will allow myself to look at. I begin a chant of *You're okay, you're okay, you're okay* inside my head. If I start to cry, I may never stop.

When it's our turn, I kneel before the body, and out of habit, cross myself. Inside the coffin, along the pearlescent fabric-lined back, are three more photos of Coach and his immediate family—Mrs. McCaffrey, Jess, and Cooper. I glance at the images, then quickly avert my eyes. My last memories of Coach won't be this cold, lifeless body lying in the coffin. I won't look at him.

I can't.

In my periphery, Troy openly stares at Coach's body. He even dares to reach into the casket to touch something inside. I'm tempted to elbow him, to make him stop. Behind us, someone cries. *Sobs.* The sound cuts through me and rips a hole in my heart. A glance over my shoulder confirms the audible grief is coming from Jess sitting on the loveseat across from the coffin. Mrs. McCaffrey holds her daughter and whispers in her ear, murmuring something sweet, I'm sure, as she runs a hand over the teenager's hair, comforting her. God, I know what she's feeling. I understand this family's pain.

Their lives are forever changed. It isn't fair. *It just isn't fair.*

I look up to catch my breath, knowing I'll lose it if I don't get away from the coffin.

"Your family still needs you, Coach. Watch over them. And if you see my dad..." Heat swarms my eyes. "Tell him I miss him—so very much." I cross myself again before pushing onto my feet. Troy points at something inside the casket, and before I can stop myself, my gaze lands on Mr. McCaffrey's inert face. Now that I've looked, I cannot look away.

His face appears restful as if he's fallen asleep—like I could reach in and nudge him, and he'd open his eyes. My heart expands as I imagine him sitting up, greeting me with that big, contagious, mustached smile of his.

Coach was the one adult in my life who made me feel worthy simply by sharing his valuable time and wisdom with me. He'd helped me work through my difficulties, and without hesitation, had thrown his weight, time, and effort into helping me achieve my dreams. Teacher, mentor, father figure. He was all that and more.

He will never smile at me again.

He'll never playfully ruffle my hair.

I'll never again hear him say "Good job, Courageous Cat," with unmistakable pride in his voice.

The unfathomable loss rocks me to my core. I sink to my knees and lower my head.

"Jay?" Troy's fingers curl around my forearm. He attempts to pull me back to my feet, but I am a statue, locked in place, unable to move.

I should have made a point of staying in touch. Come home and see him. I've been so stupid to have stayed away. And now he's gone.

A long sorrowful howl pierces the quiet. A room full of sympathetic eyes turns to *me*.

The pitiful cry is mine. I slap a hand over my mouth as it fills with saliva, and hot tears flood my eyes. The room becomes a flurry of fuss in slow motion. A well-meaning funeral home staffer in his impeccable dark suit and shiny black shoes lunges at me—tissue box and water in hand.

"It's okay." Troy puts an arm around my shoulders and tries to coax me to my feet.

"Let go!" I jerk out of his grasp and, jumping to my feet, I bolt through the nearest door. The restroom door blows open as I charge it, shoulder first, and burst inside, my heart thumping against my ribcage. The bathroom is cold and quiet. And thankfully unoccupied. With my back pressed against the door, I mash my lips together as a wave of grief capsizes me. Tears stream unchecked down my face.

My relationship with Coach was a casualty of my need to put space between me, my mother, Cooper, and a home where Dad no longer existed. I never imagined Coach's final act would come so soon. There's a fallacy in believing we have more time. We never can be sure.

I choke out a few straggled breaths and rest my head back on the door. I'm not fragile like this, damn it. My face burns afresh with the realization of the scene I created. I consider an Irish Exit so I don't have to face anyone, but then I think of Mr. McCaffrey's family—of Cooper and his mother and sister—and I know I can't.

There's a knock, and a soft whisper comes from the other side of the door.

"Can I come in?"

"Oh, yeah. Sure." I zip up my emotional corset and step free of the door.

Jess McCaffrey emerges from the other side of the door.

"You okay, Jayden?" Wavy auburn hair surrounds her pale freckled face, and her cheeks are stained red, as are the whites of her large brown eyes, all from crying.

"Jess, oh my God. I'm so sorry." I pull her into a tight hug. "I'm so, so sorry."

She stays in my embrace until I release her.

"Thank you. I lost it out there myself." Her voice wavers and tears slide down her cheeks. She swallows and tries to rouse a smile for me. "Mom says we've got to hold each other up. I think she's right. Dad would want it that way."

"Yes, definitely. He would." I seize a box of tissues from nearby and hold it out to her. She grabs a few. I grab some, too. Simultaneously, we both move to the mirrors over the row of sinks to blot our eyes and wipe away smeared mascara.

She meets my eyes in the mirror. "Cooper was about to charge into the ladies' room after you. I blocked him, but maybe come out and let him see you're all right?"

Cooper still worries about me. I shouldn't be flattered, though. I'm nothing special. That's just how he is—with everyone.

"Yes, of course." I turn away from the mirror and wrangle my bottom lip under my teeth. Talking to Cooper is the least I can do.

Jess dabs her eyes a final time, pulls the door open, and steps back. "Ready?"

With a nod, I go.

"Oh!" pops from my lips as I collide with Cooper. He catches me like a football pass, his hands curling around my upper arms. I feel every one of his fingertips on my skin.

"I was worried. Are you okay?" he asks.

It's his kindness, the sincerity in his eyes, that strips away the thin veneer I'd shellacked in place moments ago.

"Yes, I'm fine." I squeeze my lids shut as tears fill my eyes, knowing I'm the one who should be consoling him. Instead of letting me go, he wraps his arms around me. My cheek finds his collarbone. It's been years, but I remember the feel of his arms around me, the warm, solid strength of his embrace. The pressure against my face makes me wince. I pull back and cover the injury Zoe inflicted with a protective hand.

He tugs my hand away, and those keen eyes laser in on the swollen tissue under a layer of tinted makeup.

"What happened?"

"It's nothing." I shake my head. "I'm sorry for making a scene. I'm so embarrassed."

"Don't sweat it." A phrase he often said in high school. "This is tough. We're all emotional."

I'm glad he doesn't press for an answer about my face. On the other side of the room, Troy stands in the parlor doorway, watching us, his hands shoved in his pockets. He wants to do something, but he doesn't know what. A seed of empathy rises within me, but before it can take hold, I pull my gaze away from him.

I step back from Cooper and wipe my eyes with the back of my hand. "I'm okay. Let's go back in."

Jess and Cooper exchange glances.

"You don't have to." He shakes his head. "It's mobbed."

"Your mom," I say. "I didn't get to talk to her."

"I'm sure she'd like it better if you came to see her at the house after this is all over. I'll tell her you'll come by, okay?"

He waits patiently for me to respond and relieved, I gesture my agreement.

"Now, get out of here, Courageous Cat." The smile he gives me doesn't reach his eyes.

I feel anything but courageous, but I squeeze his hand. "Cooper..."

His name hangs on my lips with nothing to follow it.

I remember the day I said goodbye to my father, and how it made me feel like a rag doll, dull and empty. It's a horrible feeling I'd wish on no one, especially not on people as kind as the McCaffrey family.

He lays a hand over mine. "I know, Jayden. I know."

When he walks away, I notice Troy has garnered another crowd around him, probably entertaining them with his stories.

I catch up with Kara and message Troy that we're ready to go and to meet us outside. Head low, I buzz through the crowded foyer, unable to breathe until my sister and I get to the parking lot. Troy emerges a few minutes later and gets behind the wheel without a word.

On the ride home, my sister stays engaged with her cell and acts as if we don't exist. Her behavior embarrasses me, but Troy turns up the volume on the radio and sings along. The music averts a need to fill any awkward silences. He drops Kara and me off in our driveway, and instead of pulling into his driveway, he guns the engine and zips away down the street.

"What's up with you and Troy? How come he didn't come in?" my sister asks, letting us into the house.

"He has people he wants to catch up with."

"That's it?" She stops in the foyer and turns to look at me. "You guys seemed off."

"We're fine." I walk past her toward the kitchen. "You want something to eat?"

"Nope. Going out." She kicks off her heels in favor of flip-flops left near the front door and leaves without another word.

I don't know why I didn't tell her about Troy. I'm afraid, I suppose. Kara loves Troy. Everyone loves Troy. And until a few days ago, I'd loved him, too, and imagined my future with him. Now, I feel nothing but resentment. He pushed my life off its axis, and the seismic shift has left the ground beneath my feet unstable. I don't have a clue where to stand or what to hold on to.

The following day is the funeral. It's just Troy and me this time. Kara is at school. The weather is cool and unusually blustery. At the gravesite, the mourners huddle together, bracing against forceful gusts that lift the hemlines of dresses and blow hair into reddened eyes. Troy agrees to stay in the back and draw less attention as we pay silent tribute to the man who helped shape our teenage years. Troy puts his arm around me, and I move closer at first, thankful we've got each other to lean on for this. As the funeral liturgy proceeds several rows of people ahead of us, I'm distracted by Troy's warm hand resting on my shoulder. The large, strong hand that used to touch me, used to bring me pleasure. My stomach tightens as I think of that hand on Zoe's skin, touching her the way he used to touch me. I shrug his arm off and shift away. He glances my way but lowers his arm to his side and says nothing because he knows.

The family invites everyone to a restaurant afterward. We make a brief appearance to be respectful, and then Troy drives us home. In front of my house, I'm about to hop out, but Troy's hand on my forearm stops me.

"Jay, we need to talk."

"Not now. Not today." I fist a tissue and shake my head vehemently.

"I know saying I'm sorry isn't enough." He continues as if I haven't spoken.

"It isn't, not by a long shot." I look out the car window.

"The show is a lot more pressure than I let on," he says. Though I'm not looking at him, I know he's lowering his eyes, giving me that humble-pie, little-boy sorry look that he's mastered over the years.

"Stop. Just stop." The smooth grain leather seat squeaks as I spin to face him. "We just buried Coach. Are you that self-consumed that you can't see I'm wrecked, completely and utterly wrecked, Troy? You think you've had it hard? Think about Jess and Cooper and Mrs. McCaffrey."

He maintains a stretch of silence to show he's apologetic. But who cares? It changes nothing. Coach is still dead. Troy still cheated. I throw open the door and push out of the car.

"C'mon on, Jay." He drops a hand on the passenger seat and stares at me, unblinking. "I know I messed up, but does this have to end our friendship? You're still my best friend."

I pucker my lips and lean down to look at him. "If you wanted to remain friends, you should have thought about that *before* you slept with Zoe Bocek."

He grips the steering wheel with both hands. "I just want to go back to the way it used to be."

"That's rich coming from you, Troy. I packed up my life to move across the country to be *with* you, so we could be together, like we used to be." With a grunt, I slam the Mercedes's door.

In a flash, he's out of the car, shouting across the top of it. "Ever since I left to do the show, you've been in a funk." He shakes his head and blows out a breath. "You were stoked at the idea of coming to Vegas, doing the show together. I couldn't take that away from you."

My vision goes red, blood red as a rush of air bursts through my lips. "You are the biggest asshole I've ever known! If you didn't want me there, you should have told me."

I do an about-face and charge across the front lawn, blinded by anger. Inside the house, I lean against the closed front door to catch my breath and swipe an arm across my face. The wetness on my cheeks enrages me. He doesn't deserve my tears. I wrench the borrowed heels from my feet and heft each one across the room. They bang violently, one after the other, against the wall.

I race up the stairs and tear the dress from my body. Unzipping my suitcase, I upend the contents on the carpet and toss the clothes around until I find my shoddiest, most comfortable sweatpants and T-shirt. I leave the mess on the floor.

My mother's pantry is packed with carbs, sugar, and empty calories — all I need to eat through the onslaught of heavy emotions I'm drowning in. I nuke a box of neon-colored mac and cheese and eat through a bag of sour cream and onion chips and half a batch of microwave brownies.

Somewhere along the way, Troy disconnected from me. Our relationship ended, and I didn't see it coming.

Loss and sadness merge with shame and humiliation. Coach, Troy, Mom, Cooper, my tanked audition—a week of hell. I'm spinning without direction. I cry nonstop, gasping at times to catch my breath in between mouthfuls of processed food, chewing without tasting any of it.

Six

Troy stays only for Coach's services. I watch him leave from my bedroom window. The same window he and I, as kids, used flashlights to signal to each other. We fought the first time we met. We were seven years old, and he'd said girls weren't as strong as boys. I'd called him a liar and challenged him to arm wrestle. Our match turned into a full-on, rolling-on-the-floor brawl that required our fathers to pull us apart. Troy never again disparaged me for being a girl, and we became inseparable. The summer following fifth grade, Mr. Murphy signed Troy up for wrestling camp. My mother had wanted me to go to cheerleading camp, but I refused. Instead, I waited for Troy to get home and teach me everything he learned. So many childhood memories. The loss hits me hard, and I alternate jaggedly between crying and cursing him out.

I emerge from my room every so often to slam cabinet doors or swear at uncooperative appliances. Mom and Kara exchange wary looks.

"Troy and I had a fight," I finally admit. "But I don't want to talk about it."

The cat, my sister's—whose name I learn is Adele—follows me around, watching me with her big moon eyes as I mope around the house. My days become an endless cycle of sameness. I sleep late, wake up, and send Cooper a text. A short quick message, like *Thinking of you. Hope you're doing okay. Sending prayers*. Then I crawl out of bed to make pots of strong coffee from the expensive bags of coffee beans my mother has accumulated. Sipping the bold brews, I scroll through the endless feeds on Instagram and TikTok for hours at a time.

A week after the funeral, I manage to rise before ten o'clock. Ramped up on caffeine, open, unplanned hours make me antsy with the need to do something, yet not having anything to do. In all my life, I've never been this idle for this long. I'm ready to crawl up the walls, but the caffeine spike is all bluster, a mirage of oomph. I don't really have the energy for anything until I step onto my mother's fancy digital bathroom scale, and it shows my body fat up and muscle mass down.

I drop my head into my hands and groan. I need to do something other than sit around, eat, and feel sorry for myself. Join a gym. Go to the beach. Anything to get out of this house.

The wide door of the faded maroon Impala protests with a groan as I pull it open. I slide into the warm oversized velour driver's seat and grip the steering wheel as I look around the car's interior: the beaded cross that hangs from the review mirror, the silly pink fuzzy foot sticker Kara gave him years ago still stuck to the dashboard, the worn armrest between the seats where my father perched his right forearm while he drove. I close my eyes and inhale. It could be a trick of my mind, but I swear I can still smell Dad's cologne in the car.

The car has been sitting idle for years, and I have no idea if it'll even start. I slide the key into the ignition slot and twist. The engine wheezes, coughs, and tries to catch but doesn't. The battery is dead. I search the garage until I find an electric battery charger and hook up the cables to the car's battery—black to negative, red to positive—just as Dad taught me, and plug it in. The charge will take several hours. Then, fingers crossed, she'll start.

Back in the house, jonesing for a project, I set my sights on my disaster zone of a room. Looks as if I'm going to be here for the summer. In that case, I need orderliness or risk going insane.

I focus on Mom's and Kara's overflow items that have been taking up residence in my bedroom. I open each box, one after the other, and lay out the prizes inside, make piles, and put clothes on hangers. I break down the boxes and carry them out to the recycling bin in the garage. It's late afternoon by the time I finish, but the space feels less like a place to disappear and more like the room I remember. I head to the kitchen, ready for another cup of coffee and to lay claim to the chocolate chip cookies calling my name, when I notice a text from Cooper: *Since you're home, how about we get together for that dinner?*

It's only been a week since his father's funeral, but that he's ready to go out and socialize is good.

Sure. I respond, because I have zippo plans, and really, how can I refuse?

Cooper: *I tried to include Troy but seems he flew back to Las Vegas?*

Yeah, he did, I reply stroking my neck to soothe my nerves.

Cooper: *What time should I pick you up?*

I'm not ready to sit alone with him in a car. *Tell me when and where. I'll meet you.*

Cooper: *Tonight, Dockside Café, seven o'clock.*

A local place I haven't been to in ages.

I pull jeans and a blouse from my suitcase dump that I've yet to tackle and still lies in a heap in the middle of my bedroom floor. Even though I hate Troy, his presence at dinner would be welcome. Other than the few minutes in the hospital, I haven't been alone, really alone, with Cooper since my father's funeral, and the thought of what might come up leaves me anxious. What if he talks about what happened between us? What if he asks me about Troy? I can still hear the condescension in his voice the morning he found me, naked, in Troy's bed.

"What did you do?" His expression hardened.

I tucked the bed sheet under my arms and raised my chin. "Isn't it obvious?"

"I didn't give you what you wanted, so you went to him?" He pointed to Troy in bed next to me.

He'd called what we'd done "a stupid, stupid move that would destroy our friendship." In all our years of friendship, the dressing down was the meanest Cooper McCaffrey had ever been. The rebuff needles me to this day. I suppose, after he rejected me earlier that day, my sleeping with Troy might have appeared to be revenge on my part. But truthfully, it wasn't. I'd had a thing for Cooper back then, even imagined I loved him. That he didn't want me was simply another deposit to the worst day of my life, and going to Troy, my best friend and refuge, was a natural response to a bad day.

You could say if Cooper hadn't refused me, I wouldn't be in this mess with Troy, how different everything would be right now. It feels good to blame Cooper, though it's not his fault. I can only imagine how superior he'll feel when he finds out Troy and I are done—our lifelong friendship destroyed. It'll mean he'd been right—something I'm not ready to concede.

I need something or *someone* as a go-between to help keep the conversation light and bearable. Downstairs, Kara is on the couch with her phone, another cooking show unwatched on the television.

"Hey, little sister, want to go out for dinner? My treat!"

Dockside Café is a small seafood restaurant on the bay. Cooper texts me he's already arrived and got us a table outside on the back deck. We cross the pebbled parking lot to the wooden planked walkway that leads to the side of the restaurant facing the water.

The Great South Bay is a smooth, dark mirror reflecting the brilliant orange rays of the setting sun. Sparks of light glint off the intersecting line of boats tied off at the wharf. The light acrid smell of motor oil and gasoline hovers in the air. Cooper stands near the metal and wire railing that separates the dining area from the boat dock, talking to a few guys I recognize from school. Noticing me, he shakes hands with the guys and waves me over to a small square dining table.

In contrast to the suit he'd worn at his father's funeral services, he's dressed down in jeans and a polo shirt. His hair, slightly unruly from the bay breeze, falls into his bright green eyes.

"Hello." I stop in front of the table, a ball of nerves, and motion behind me. "I have a tag-along. Hope you don't mind."

"Hey, Cooper!" Kara bounds forward, smiling.

"Kara, what a nice surprise." To his credit, Cooper doesn't flinch at the sight of the unexpected addition to our party. He sounds sincere and leans in to give her a quick hug and then me, leaving a soft waft of cologne lingering in his wake. "They make excellent margaritas here. Want one?"

"Heck yeah. I'm in." With a huge grin, Kara claims the seat next to him. "I like my rim salted."

"Ha-ha." I settle into the chair across from Cooper. "When you turn twenty-one, I'll treat you to your first legal drink."

We both know she's not an alcohol virgin.

"What-ev." She rolls her eyes.

With only inches between Cooper and me, it's difficult not to look at him. I prop the menu at an angle to give myself something else to focus on.

We're quiet for a few minutes as everyone studies the menu. When the server comes, we decide to order everything sharable: clams on the half shell, fish tacos, fried calamari, and a nacho supreme platter. Cooper and I order margaritas.

"How's your family? How's Jess?" Kara lays a hand on Cooper's forearm. It's casual, but I'm envious.

"Jess is doing okay. We're all doing okay." Despite his words, he sounds somber.

Our server brings us our drinks, and Kara raises her glass of iced tea.

"We should toast your dad," she says.

I'm proud of her for being thoughtful and mature. Cooper and I follow suit and hold up our drink glasses.

"To an amazing teacher," Kara says.

"To an amazing father," Cooper adds.

"To the man who gave us wings," I say, catching Cooper's eyes.

"Here, here," Cooper says, his eyes glossy with emotion. We tip our glasses until the three rims clink together.

The food is served and for a few minutes, conversation stops while we each grab what we want to eat.

"So Troy was weirdly incommunicado while he was home," Kara says once we've all tucked into our food. "Jayden said it was nothing, but he barely said two words to me. When Troy Murphy doesn't go out of the way to annoy me, something is definitely up."

"He has a lot on his mind. The show keeps him busy." I can't believe I'm defending him.

"Nah." She shakes her head. "It's because you guys are fighting."

Cooper stops chewing. I kick the side of her foot, immediately regretting bringing her along.

"Oww. You were the one who told us." Kara plunges a chip into a bowl of guacamole and eyes me. "I didn't know it was a secret."

"What's going on?" Cooper busies himself with squeezing lemon on his seafood, but the arc of his eyebrow tells me he's more than casually interested.

I think about how much I can say without revealing the truth.

"Things are different with Troy so far away. It's an adjustment."

"But you're going to Las Vegas soon, right?" Cooper lowers his fork.

"Not anymore. My plans changed."

"She bombed her audition and is staying with us for a while," Kara says, like we're doing a ventriloquist act.

"You decided to audition," he says.

I wither in my seat. "Yeah, you and your dad got me thinking, but it wasn't meant to be."

"I'm sorry to hear that. As my dad would say, better to have tried and failed than never try at all." He offers me a consolatory smile. "Headed back to law school in the fall?"

"Yes." Agreeing is the easy, expected answer, though I've not spared a thought about writing a mission statement to reinstate my scholarship or an alternate way to pay for school.

Cooper smiles as he leans toward Kara. "Can't you see her sitting behind the bench in a black robe, Judge Jones, smacking the gavel, and demanding everyone to order?"

"Yep. My sister is good at smacking things around. She's been doing that at the house all week."

"Shut up." I swat her arm.

Cooper appears intrigued, but Kara sidelines him with a question on a totally different topic.

"So, Cooper, tell me. Are you seeing anyone?"

I choke on a nacho, embarrassed by the question, but also, I'm annoyed at how much I want to know the answer.

Cooper laughs good-naturedly. "I dated this girl, Brittany, for a while, but not since I got home."

A moment of pure, hot jealousy rides down my back, the force of which shocks me. I cool the burn with a mouthful of icy margarita.

"Ooh, that means you're available." Kara rests her chin on her hand and stares at him. "What's your type? I know lots of girls."

I tip my glass, draining it, and again question my sanity in bringing her. She needs to stop hounding the guy on his dating status. Who cares? I don't. Seriously, *I don't.*

"I'm not in the best place for a relationship right now." He glances at me, and again, my cheeks warm. "My mother didn't like Brittany. Said she wasn't the one for me."

"I would never ever ask for advice from my mother." Kara waves her hand. "She hasn't a clue when it comes to guys. But you're lucky, Coop. Your mom is the coolest."

Kara's right. Mrs. McCaffrey is uniquely awesome—an everybody's mom. She brought batches of baked goods and coolers of sports drinks to every wrestling match. When Dad died, she'd brought food to the house. And when I needed a break, she and Jess stayed with Kara so I could have one.

"It's probably not cool to admit this, but my mom and I get along well." Cooper leans back in his chair, grinning as he tugs at his earlobe, plainly comfortable in his skin. "She has this weird psychic thing going on. I almost hate to admit it, but she's usually right about most things."

It was such an innocuous thing to say, bordering on good ol' mama's boy sweetness. It pulls at me unexpectedly. The wind catches his hair, the same caramel color as the candies I brought to his father at the hospital. A longer wedge of bangs flips across his forehead. Paying no attention to the wayward hair, he traces the curve of his drink glass with an index finger.

Warmth floods my lower half as I imagine what those fingers would feel like on my skin, trailing up the inside of my leg.

My heart wobbles when his eyes catch mine, and he smiles as if he's reading my mind. I suck in my bottom lip and look away.

Jurisprudence. Jurisprudence. Jurisprudence, I chant to banish my hot mess of thoughts. I cannot have them. Our strained friendship is the result of those kinds of thoughts.

"Got any plans for summer?" Cooper leans forward, elbows on the table.

"Find a job." I throw out. "And a gym. There's too much processed junk at my house. They're singing magical nymph songs."

"Muscle Makers Fitness," he says. "They have a separate MMA gym called Gloves. You could work there and train for free." Cooper arches his eyebrows in a hopeful expression. "I'm a certified trainer. We can work on getting you ready to try out for the next season of *Sin City Fight Club*."

"No, I won't be auditioning again. I'm over it." I busy myself tidying up my eating space.

"Really?" He tips his head, clearly not believing me.

"Really." I meet his gaze. "I want to stay in shape. Moreso, I need a paycheck."

"Ask at the gym. I know the owner. I'll put in a good word for you," Cooper says, and I nod my thanks.

The server collects our empty dishes, and we request the check. A flash goes off from a few tables over where someone is taking pictures.

"Are they taking pictures of us?" Kara asks.

Cooper and I look. A guy sitting at a table diagonally from us has his phone aimed in our direction. Seeing us, he puts it down and gives us a little wave.

"He probably recognizes you from your cameo on the show—as Troy 'Country' Murphy's girlfriend." Cooper twists back around.

He's probably right. The show requested permission to use images of me to tell Troy's story for the duration of the season. I appear on-screen for a few seconds here and there, Troy's voiceover narration explaining our small-town upbringing and friends-to-lovers story. It's not the first time I've been recognized.

"Here she is, romantically linked to Troy Murphy, who's like our town's Dwayne 'The Rock' Johnson." My sister slants toward Cooper and motions to me. "People are positively starry-eyed for the two of them, and she's oblivious to all the attention."

"That's not true. It's just that I don't like that kind of attention. Besides, in Brooklyn, I can blend in with the crowd. In a small town like this, everyone knows everyone's business," I say. "Anyway, it's really Troy they're interested in."

"Yeah, the same guy, a fixture at our house, burping and farting and eating us out of house and home—annihilating an entire box of our Little Debbie cakes in one sitting—is killing it." Kara shakes her head, but she's smiling. "Who'd ever thought that goon would make it big?"

"It doesn't surprise me," Cooper answers. "Even in high school, Troy had a showman-like quality about him that people loved. And girlfriends, he practically had to set up a turnstile for all of them. Right, Jayden?"

To the unaware, he almost sounds resentful, but I know it's not jealousy.

"Yes," I say because it's the truth. Cooper, with his looks and charisma, and being the son of a well-loved teacher, had twice the popularity at school as Troy did. But Troy was in a league of his own. Despite his hard work and dedication to wrestling, Troy had a mischievous playboy reputation, a true aphrodisiac to most women. For most of our history, though, I had never thought of him sexually. It wasn't until after my father died that I fell prey to a new, exciting awareness of him.

Cooper holds my eye longer than I'm comfortable with. I can't help thinking he knows something of Troy's infidelity, but he can't. The two of them obviously talked recently, but I'm certain Troy didn't confide in Cooper. Not about us. Not after Cooper ruthlessly condemned our relationship.

"*Excusez-moi*. Gotta use the facilities." Kara extracts herself from our group and heads toward the rear of the restaurant. I avoid Cooper's gaze and instead focus on the setting sun, which, surrounded by a halo of sherbet-colored clouds, has dipped into the surface of the bay.

"You doing okay?" I glimpse his way.

"As I'm sure you can attest, some days are easier than others."

Well acquainted with the ups and downs of grief, I slide my hand across the table to nudge his.

"Thanks for the daily texts and for coming out tonight. I needed this." Cooper returns the nudge. "And I'm glad you asked Kara to join us."

I draw my hand back and finger the stem of my glass. "She keeps things interesting. Thanks for not minding that I invited her."

"Not at all. I think we can both admit it was nice to have that third person to fill in the awkward pauses."

We exchange a knowing look before my regard returns to the bay, to a line of nearby boats bobbing in the water.

The first time I saw him across the floor of the wrestling room gym, stocky and confident, Cooper McCaffrey took my breath away. As sophomores, we were teammates, and wrestling together left no place for romance. Troy and I welcomed him into the fold of our friendship. The three of us were tight. It's depressing that we no longer talk. I miss him.

"I understand Sin City didn't pan out, but you planned to spend the summer in Vegas with Troy." Cooper interrupts my reverie. "Why aren't you there?"

"I didn't like it there." I shrug. "It's too hot."

"So, you're spending the summer at home, with *your mother* instead?" He looks incredulous. "Not buying it."

I shake my head and let out a hollow laugh. We were good enough friends once that he knows when I'm lying. "You're right, something's up. Like in a royally screwed-up sense."

"Troy?"

The unanticipated conversation catches me open. "There's some drama going on. As you know, we're not normally a drama couple."

"I wouldn't know. I haven't spent any time with the two of you as a couple." The truth sits a beat before his expression softens. "Want to talk about it?"

The urge to tell him rises inside me. How nice it would be to share the heavy burden weighing on my heart. People do it all the time, but I can't. Opening that door is too hard. Too revealing. I've already said more than I wanted to.

"I appreciate it, but no."

"I won't push, Jayden, but I need to know, that welt on your face. Did Troy have anything to do with that?" Cooper leans closer, waiting for my answer.

"If you're asking if he hit me, he didn't."

"That's a relief." He sits back. "Honestly, I can't figure out why you're still with him."

"Why do you say that?"

"Because you've always been too smart for him."

Normally I'd defend Troy, but I'm not in the mood to be charitable towards him. Besides, academically, Cooper's right. My GPA left Troy's in the dust.

"You have so many doors open to you," he says. "Troy has only one—competitive fighting."

I swallow and swirl my glass. "The one door closed to me."

"It's not closed if you don't want it to be."

"The show was my one opportunity. That's done, so I'm going back to law school."

"Is that what you really want? You don't sound convinced."

I stare out at the scene before me without really seeing it. "I don't know."

"Sometimes the right answer takes time to reveal itself. Have a little patience. It'll come to you," he whispers as Kara returns.

I nod at him and push away from the table. "Ready to go?"

There is no one I can confide in. I am neither Troy's girlfriend nor friend. I am nothing to him. And as kind as Cooper is, we aren't friends anymore. Not like we used to be. He's the last person I can talk to about Troy's cheating.

Then he'd know he'd been right.

Seven

I get up in time to have coffee with my mother in the kitchen before she leaves for work the next day. She seems delighted for the company and prattles on about this coworker and that one. She doesn't seem to notice I've been mostly silent.

"What are your plans for today?" She arches a brow. "All you've done since you've been home is loaf around the house."

"That's not true," I shoot back. "I went through the shipping boxes in my bedroom. All new stuff. Are you planning on keeping all of it?"

"Of course. I bought those things because I need them." With a snap of insincere laughter, she dumps her lip-stick-ringed coffee cup in the sink.

"When I came home, my room was like an Amazon warehouse. Neither you nor Kara will need more beauty products, body-slimming gadgets, bed sheets, or another piece of clothing for the rest of your lives."

"I'll get around to putting everything away at some point."

"It's done. I took care of it," I say. "All of it."

There's a moment of silence between us. She's about to blow, call my cleaning up meddling, but then she clears her throat.

"All right." She nods. "Thank you."

Grudging, but I'll take it.

"Do you know where Dad's law books are?"

"I haven't thought about them in years. I honestly have no idea."

Not surprised, I move past her and make myself another cup of coffee. "Anything else you want me to do around the house?"

"The lawn? You said you were going to see to the yard maintenance. Your contribution," she reminds me.

As soon as she leaves, I call O'Brien's Lawn Service to see what the holdup is.

"I've been meaning to call," Carol O'Brien says. "Honey, I'm sorry, but your family's account is in arrears. I'm sure it's just an oversight on your mom's part. We all get so busy, but unfortunately, we can't service your house until the outstanding payments have been settled."

Mrs. O'Brien goes over the account with me. Mom hasn't paid them since last July, though the company continued to cut the lawn for the rest of the summer. My mother owes them hundreds of dollars. Embarrassed, I tell Mrs. O'Brien I'll figure out what happened and try to get the payments up to date.

I pick up the mound of unopened mail on my father's desk and take it to the kitchen. I slice the envelopes open with a knife and make stacks while I wolf down a peanut butter and jelly sandwich.

The Impala's new registration card is among them, but the rest, one after another, are overdue statements and bills—each one demanding payment. I lean back in my seat and blow out a slow breath.

Dad was the one who did the family banking, paid the bills, and kept the finances on track. He left us in good financial shape. My mother, still working, should live a comfortable life, but she's gone off-track. Her finances appear as stable as a hollowed-out Jenga tower.

It's no secret that credit card debt is a major problem for the average American. My mother's mindless buying sprees of exercise equipment, kitchen gadgets, and an assortment of "As Seen on TV" junk excess disturbs me, but could they alone have caused this mess?

The overdue bills would have made Dad crazy with worry. I am my father's daughter. The state of the household finances has me concerned.

I almost reach for my phone to call Troy, but catch myself. I always called him at times like this. He let me vent, and he understood my mother and the nature of our relationship. Talking to him always made me feel better. But I can't call him. This is mine to deal with alone.

There's a dusty old electric lawnmower in the back of the garage, and I break it out to cut the grass. It's the only way I can help the situation until I find a job.

Once that chore is finished, I shower, braid my hair, and put on my best workout clothes. In the garage, I disconnect the electric charger from the Impala's battery and close the hood. A sheen of sweat layers my skin as I slip the car's new registration into the glove box and then slide the key into the ignition.

"Daddy, I need a job." I send up a brief prayer and, holding my breath, twist the key. She coughs a few seconds, trying to catch, then revs to life with a deep, powerful growl. I pat the dashboard. "Thank you."

Muscle Makers, the health club Cooper suggested the other night, sounded like a place where I might enjoy working. One town over, it's the first on my list of places to apply. The gym is state-of-the-art, with shiny machines and beautiful people sweating on them.

Past racks of free weights and rowing machines are another set of doors with a sign marked GLOVES, a mixed martial arts training center. I pass through the health club and head straight to the MMA gym.

As soon as I push open the door, the sights, sounds, and smells of the gym race through my bloodstream. The swishing sound of jump ropes slapping the floor, the smack of gloved fists against weighted bags, and the grunts of men and women straining to build muscle carry into the high vaulted industrial ceiling.

The place reminds me of the summer during high school when Cooper convinced me to try a new workout program with him to deal with the stress of my father's failing health. The classes had been a mixture of disciplines: karate, jiu-jitsu, kickboxing. When the trial week was over, there wasn't one part of me that wasn't sore. I could barely lift my arms up to pull my shirt on each morning. But I was totally addicted. I signed up for a membership and met Cooper there almost every day. The intense workouts cleared my mind and energized me.

I'm desperate to feel that rush now.

I approach the desk where a young woman is working on a computer. She looks up and smiles.

"Who do I talk to about a job?" I ask.

"You can start by filling this out." She slides an employment application form across the counter to me and goes into a sales pitch about the gym, a rote speech about how Gloves is independently owned and operated, separate from Muscle Makers. "Once you're done, I'll see if our manager, Van Abberra, has time to interview you."

Standard entry-level employment. Dad used to say, that when you need immediate answers, always go straight to the top person. That's how you get respect.

"Is Mr. Abberra here now?" I ask.

She points to a tall, buff, tatted older dude across the gym. He's giving punching tips to a brawny guy, slugging it out on one of several black heavy bags hanging from a steel overhead girder.

"Be right back," I tell her. My arms tingle with energy as I walk over to Van.

"My name is Jayden Jones, and I'd like to work here," I tell him. Cooper's name sits on my tongue, but I want to land this job on my own.

"Jayden Jones, huh?" Van cocks an eyebrow like my name is familiar. "And you've trained in MMA?"

"No, but I just finished up four years of wrestling at the college level."

He scrutinizes me with one long look-over. "You're a little flabby, but you still have good muscle mass."

The flabby comment stings. I'm in good shape, but I haven't maintained my workouts, and compared to the hard, muscled bodies surrounding us, it's accurate.

"We're always looking for sparring partners for our women fighters. Is that something you might be interested in?"

"I'm interested," I say. "What's the pay rate for that kind of work?"

I'm hoping it's not peanuts, but I don't care. The sounds, the smell, the energy. I need to work at this gym.

"A membership to the club and a stipend that depends on the level of the fighter. But we need to see what you got first. You got time to try out now?"

"Yes, definitely." The words fly out of my mouth. I haven't been this excited since scoring the Sin City audition.

"Alright." Van nods and calls to a young guy spotting a woman lifting weights and jabs a thumb in my direction. "Marcus, set her up for a sparring round with Dani."

The guy instructs the woman to rack the weighted barbell and motions me over to a low, roped-off platform, off to one side of the open floor space, the ring.

"Where's your gear?" he asks.

"I wasn't expecting to need gear today," I respond with a nervous laugh. "I just came to ask about a job, and here we are."

"No worries. You can borrow stuff for today." He smiles and bends over a large black Rubbermaid bin overflowing with an assortment of used gear. "I'm Marcus, by the way."

"Jay," I offer.

Marcus digs into the plastic bin, riffling through a hodgepodge of gear until he finds a mismatched pair of shin guards, a scuffed-up black head guard, and training gloves. They're a lot like boxing gloves with padded knuckles but leave fingers exposed for grappling.

"Suit up." He dumps the items into my arms. "You'll be sparring with our best strawweight, Dani."

The best? I drop the gear on the mat and start putting the pieces on, one by one, my nerves spinning. Maybe this isn't such a good idea. In fact, it could be my stupidest idea ever. Other than wrestling in school and a few underground fights, I have no significant MMA training, and, as Van validated, I'm not in top condition.

The borrowed gear smells of old sweat, and as tight as I pull the strap on the padded head guard, it remains too loose. Suited up, I follow Marcus's instructions and enter the ring.

"Hey." Dani nods toward me, shadowboxing in the adjacent corner, her wiry dark hair twisted into a tight French braid. She's the one Marcus had been assisting with bench presses, muscular but tiny—several inches shorter than me. At strawweight, she's two weight classes under my bantamweight division. I easily outweigh her by a good twenty pounds. Still, Dani is a trained fighter. My extra weight is an edge I accept with no regrets. With a sense of relief, I start a round of stretches to warm up my limbs.

As soon as we start mixing it up, throwing jabs at each other, it's obvious that my added weight and height make up for very little with taking punches. I watch her, though. I notice she leaves herself open after each punch she lands. Before she tires me out, and Van notices my lack of skills,

I decide to finish it. Dani swings and nails me in the head. The impact knocks me backward, but I flout the pain, lunge forward, and put her in a front headlock. I snap and spin until she goes down on her elbow, which allows me to reach under her back and lock my grip around her wrist. Muscle memory has me rolling fast and hard. I flip her onto her back, and finally, drive my weight on top of her.

"All right, that's enough." Marcus tugs me off Dani.

I sit back, jacked up by a rush of endorphins. It's been a while since I'd used that move, but I'm excited that, in the thick of it, I remembered.

"Hey, good fight." I stand and offer Dani a hand up.

"It was supposed to be sparring." Dani snubs my hand and springs to her feet. "Marcus, she's obviously untrained. I'm not getting in the ring with her again."

"Looks like I found my new BFF." I chuckle under my breath as Dani ducks through the ropes.

"Way to show off, Jay," Marcus says.

I catch Van Abberra watching. His face is tight, unsmiling. Maybe I went too far.

"She left herself open. Was I supposed to ignore that?"

"No, of course not." Marcus tosses me a water bottle. "We generally don't encourage sparring partners to take down our fighters, but you proved to her what we already know. Wrestling is a weak spot for her. You, on the other hand, blew me away. You ever think about fighting competitively?"

"I did… for a minute." I shrug. "Right now, I'm only interested in making some money, so I'll take whatever sparring work you can get me."

"I'm sure Van will definitely have more work for you." He crosses his arms and smiles at me. "That move you used to take Dani down, that was tight. Where did you learn to wrestle like that?"

I part my lips to answer, but someone behind us beats me to it.

"High school. The Flat Man was her signature move."

I recognize the voice, and my gaze swings past Marcus to find Cooper, a cocky smile etched on his angular face.

"That one move earned her top seat in her weight division and the title of All-State wrestling champion," Cooper says to Marcus, but that thick-lashed green-eyed gaze is aimed at me.

"All-State champ, eh?" Marcus nods his head in admiration. "Pretty sure you got yourself a job, Miss All-State. Leave me your email address, and I'll send you the employment forms. You can start Monday."

The sight of Cooper catches me off guard, and I barely register what's being said. Did he see me get hammered in the earlier part of the sparring?

"I'll get her info," Cooper tells Marcus.

I step down from the raised platform of the ring. "I forgot you work out here."

"You sounded ambivalent when I talked about this gym the other night. Imagine my surprise to come in and find you in the ring, doing MMA." He draws my hand toward him to help me remove my glove. "Or whatever you were doing in there."

Ugh. He saw the whole thing. I pull my hand away and use my teeth to release the Velcro closure on the gloves. "I won. Sure, my fighting skills are rusty, but it's the endgame that counts."

"Rusty? That thrashing you took, that's a lack of training." He crosses his arms, dragging my reluctant attention to those rock-solid limbs. "Wrestling rules don't apply in MMA. In the octagon, you're going to be kicked and punched, and if you don't learn how to protect yourself, your 'endgame' might be a serious beat-down with facial disfiguration."

The smugness makes me bristle.

"She got in a few lucky shots. It won't happen again."

"Okay, but stop by and see Becca at the front desk before you leave. She's a trained paramedic. Make sure you're not concussed."

"Don't need to. I'm fine." I yank the head guard off, my face flaring with heat.

"Okay, okay," he says. "I thought Troy might have worked with you, shown you some of his famous moves to get you ready for the audition."

"We didn't have time." And probably because Troy didn't really want me in Vegas.

"How about I work with you, then? I know a thing or two about boxing." He pushes. "I'll teach you some basics. Because getting pummeled for a paycheck isn't any fun."

Working with him would mean being in close quarters with him, and that worries me. As my runaway thoughts the other night prove, I'm still physically attracted to him.

"That's unnecessary. It's just sparring, not competition. I'll watch some training videos." I briskly wipe down the gear with disinfectant and toss them back into the plastic bin.

"Man, I forgot how stubborn you are."

"Yeah, well, I forgot how annoying you can be," I say over my shoulder.

When he doesn't respond, I turn to look at him.

"Touché!" He bursts out laughing, his lips curled into that same heart-stopping grin that made all the girls in high school swoon. "We're still good at busting each other's balls."

His laughter loosens the tightness in my body.

"Some things don't change," I say and even manage a small smile.

"Listen, Jayden, all I'm saying is no one should get into the ring unprepared. But hey, if getting your butt kicked is your thing, more power to you."

"You know damn well it's not *my thing*."

"After that beat-down, you might have to remind me." He moves to the free weights and loads plates to a barbell. "You want to work out, like old times?"

"Some other time." I'm too self-conscious to relax around him.

Wrestling is what I know best. But in the MMA world, where pretty much anything goes, I am sorely mismatched. I bragged myself into a job and went into the ring unprepared. I'd been impulsive. What's worse is, Cooper called me on it. And he is right, *as usual*. But I'm not ready to openly admit that, though I should have been nicer to him. His father just died.

The scene with Cooper leaves me ill-humored when I get home. My mother is on the couch beside Kara, their attention on some reality show. They gossip and giggle about the people on the show, chummy, like girlfriends.

"Isn't that cozy?" I mutter to myself.

It's approaching dinnertime, though the kitchen is vacant, and the house is void of any noticeable aromas of food cooking or having been cooked. Neither of them seems to care about eating. My rumbling stomach adds to my rotten mood.

"Hi!" Mom calls out, turning to look my way. "Good gravy! What did you do to your face!?"

Her squawk pries Kara's attention from the television screen to me.

"With your other bruise, it totally balances out your face," my sister says.

"I got a job sparring at a gym."

"You're too bright for that kind of work," Mom says. "Surely you can find a cushy office job as a paralegal or clerk at a law firm."

"It's just temporary, and I like it," I say, avoiding the stink eye she's giving me. She doesn't understand my desire to be involved in competitive sports. She never did. "You guys have dinner yet? I'm starving."

"There are takeout menus in the drawer next to the stove." My mother motions to the kitchen. "Kara, honey, what do you feel like eating tonight?"

I don't wait to hear Kara's answer. In the kitchen, I snap on the light and grunt at the mess: discarded shoes, pocketbooks, the day's mail, and several bottles of nail polish. They've probably been home less than an hour and messed up what took me a day to clean.

"What the hell happened in here?" I shout. No one answers. I'm tempted to leave, go out for something to eat—be away from this mess and this house, anywhere other than here. But I'm ravenous. And broke.

Growling, I ignore the clutter and check the freezer to see if there is anything I can throw together for a meal. I find a pound of ground turkey and put the meat in the microwave to thaw. Cans of tomatoes and string beans from the pantry firms up a plan for the turkey. An onion would make it better, but there's only a slimy one in the refrigerator bin, which I toss. I miss Brooklyn. There, I can shoot down to the market on the corner, where everything is fresh. Here, you need a car to drive to the store.

My mother strolls into the kitchen and takes a seat at the cluttered table.

"Oh, you don't have to make dinner. Kara wants pizza. I'll just order a salad," she says.

I remember the stack of unpaid bills.

"I've already started cooking, and besides, the two of you shouldn't waste money eating out so much."

"It's pizza and salad, Jayden, not caviar and filet mignon." Mom pulls out a credit card from her wallet. "Stop being such a martyr."

"I'm not a martyr. I'm concerned." I dump the vegetables into the turkey mixture, banging the cans on the side of the pot. She doesn't know I snooped and am aware of her debt. "I read that to avoid the temptation to buy on credit, you should cut up your credit cards and buy only with cash."

Mom holds her chin high. "I'm not cutting up my credit cards. That's ridiculous. I have good credit."

"So, you're not over-spending?"

"No, I'm not," she says.

"Well, I called O'Brien's. You haven't paid the lawn service bill since last July. The account is way overdue."

She shrugs. "I was busy. I forgot."

"If you pay the overdue amount, I'll cover any new billing."

"Sure, I'll leave you my new credit card. Call them back with the number."

More credit debt. I adjust the temperature on the stovetop to simmer and turn to face her. "Seriously, Mom, look around you. You've got all this brand-new stuff lying around—in ridiculous amounts—all unused."

"I'm going to use everything." Her tone sharpens and my mood flares to match it.

"You're maxing out your credit on garbage you don't need. How do you think Daddy would feel about what you're doing?"

Even as I say it, I'm aware of how that one question will unbutton her.

Her forehead crinkles with anger, and her lips tighten in a scowl.

"Don't you throw Daddy in my face!" Her chair scrapes the floor with a screech as she rises out of her seat. "How dare you come home after all this time and try to tell me how to run my life. I didn't invite you. Stay out of my business, or find another place to stay."

Mom fists her credit card and leaves the kitchen without another word. And just like that, the tentative welcome mat has been taken in.

I finish cooking and eating my meal, though my appetite is gone.

What did I think would happen? I've been in the ring with my mother my whole life. Screw it. I didn't come home to fix her problems — I came home to deal with mine.

Upstairs, I fill the bathtub and sink into the hot water, a pen and yellow legal pad on the tub ledge. Though my return to law school is uncertain, I will write the mission statement Dumfries assigned me. As the warm water soothes my aching muscles, I try to remember why, other than following in my father's footsteps, I decided to go to law school.

But there isn't an answer that doesn't include my father. Dad grew up on the East End of Long Island, where his own father was drawn into the suffering of the East End farmworkers. Grandpa Jones, also a graduate of Brooklyn Law, spent his retirement years fighting for decent pay and working conditions. Dad worked as a public defender, but he continued Grandpa's work pro bono, serving the network of low-income farming communities in his free time. He could've gone corporate and raked in serious dough, but money didn't drive my father, and I respected him for this.

We talked about his most challenging cases. Although I didn't envision myself as a public defender, I found the concept of advocating for those in need quite appealing.

I still loved the idea of practicing law, could picture myself passing the bar, arguing before the court, but being forced to say goodbye to the sport I'd loved and excelled at for nearly ten years has cast a long shadow over that vision.

I tap the pen on the blank page. How am I to convince others of a future I, myself, am no longer focused on or excited about? I let the pad and pen fall to the floor and submerge myself in the water.

EIGHT

I wake sore. Muscles I haven't used in a while make themselves known. Despite the aches, I feel good. The kind of good that comes when you're doing something you're meant to do. And my face looks a lot better. I'd iced the sparring session injury while I ate dinner alone. Today, the swelling is barely noticeable. The bruise from Zoe has faded, too.

I brought my legal pad to bed last night and tried to brainstorm ideas. Having not come up with any earth-moving revelations, the pad lies on the floor beside the bed, blank but for some doodles.

My cell beeps with a group text from my mother and Kara. Mom has plans and will be home late. Kara is going shopping with a friend for a gift, reminding me Mother's Day is this weekend.

After I submit the online employee form for Gloves, I make a brunch reservation for Mother's Day hoping to make Mom happy. I flip on the TV and sit on the floor to stretch and work out the kinks and soreness in my muscles.

With not much else to do, I clean my room, run a few loads of laundry, and organize the pile of clothes from my suitcase into the dresser drawers. My attention catches on the deep mahogany-stained wooden trunk at the foot of my bed. I kneel in front of it and lift the lid with a surge of optimism that I'll find Dad's law books. The hinges protest with a groan. The unmistakable scent of cedar tinged with other faded scents emerges like an uncorked bottle of perfume.

Awash in sentimentality, I brush my fingers over a photo album, a baby doll, and other trinkets from the earlier stages of my life. A pink and white blanket my grandmother crocheted when I was little still holds the faint scent of the lavender sachets Nanny kept tucked in her dresser drawers.

Under the yarn blanket, I dig out a framed photo of my father and me on the day of my high school graduation. I'm in my cap and gown, holding my diploma. Dad has one arm slung around my shoulders. The two of us are broadly grinning at the camera.

It's years later, and still, it's impossible to fathom my father won't be a part of anything in my future. I keep hoping I'll wake up and realize his death is only a bad dream.

I run a finger over my father's face, the familiar pointed chin and high cheekbones. Everyone said with my thick dark hair, brown eyes, and the straight slope of my nose, I looked like a female version of him. People especially noticed our resemblance when I'd cut my hair short during wrestling.

My father was a people person, a natural conversationalist. I liked it when people looked at me and saw him. I wanted to be just like him.

For a long minute, I stare at the photo, experiencing a mix of emotions, happy and sad. Mom, Kara, and I don't talk about Dad. When he died, he slipped out of our lives and off our tongues. I set the photo on the dresser where I'll see it every day and where it'll make me think about and remember him.

I dive back into the trunk and move things about, searching for the law books, but they aren't there. I find instead another framed photo, this one of Troy, Cooper, and me, taken at the last high school wrestling tournament before going to the States in our sophomore year. I'm sandwiched between the guys, their arms around my shoulders. It was the first season I could formally compete. All three of us, the best of friends, glow with pride because along with them, I'd made it to the top of my weight division.

Underneath the photo is a laminated newspaper article. I trace the bold print of the headline with my finger and smile.

South Shore's first female wrestler suits up for competition.

The article tells how I, with the support of the high school wrestling coach and the boys' JV and varsity teams, took on the school board to become the first girl wrestler in our small rural town. A place where male-dominated sports have reigned supreme since the school opened in the late 1920s.

I sit with the newspaper on my lap and close my eyes, remembering the journey. I'd wanted to wrestle because Troy did. As best friends, we did everything together, and it made little sense that I couldn't also wrestle. My defiance against leaving well enough alone caused a lot of commotion. I'd worked my butt off—not just fighting the district's outdated, small-town attitudes about gender and sports but also to win the respect of the boys on the team.

And I'd done it.

Once I competed, I quickly rose through the ranks, outmaneuvering a few girls but mostly boys, to the top of my weight class. Dad encouraged me to study Title IX law, which made it illegal for any schools or educational programs that received federal funds to discriminate against someone based on their sex. We both agreed my firsthand experience would be valuable. I was all in.

Back then, the door to life was wide open. Cooper, Troy, and I had a strong friendship. The three of us were, as Coach said, like the Three Musketeers. High school had been full of challenges, but with those guys at my side, and my future drawn in detail, I felt invincible. I soared.

My rise never would have happened without Mr. McCaffrey's help. Coach spent a year working alongside me, using his school position to speak out on my behalf, fighting for my right to wrestle competitively. When I started looking at colleges, Coach helped me narrow down my list to the top five. With my high GPA, I had the pick of the best. Coach had suggested North Central College in Illinois. I can still feel the warmth of my father's pride when I received my acceptance to North Central. The university had both women's wrestling and pre-law studies. Because most wrestling careers end in college, as mine did, at least I'd be set to start law school.

After graduation, the guys and I headed off to different colleges in different states, but we'd agreed to stay in touch, *no matter what*. None of us would have suspected then that just a few years later Cooper and I would barely be speaking to one another, and my relationship with Troy would be fractured beyond repair.

I gasp for air as the reality of Troy's infidelity strikes me once again. As close as I had been to Cooper, I've known Troy longer. We'd grown up alongside one another, could complete each other's sentences. But there's nowhere to go from where we are now. I lost Troy, and that realization plucks me raw.

My mind combs through our conversations over the last few months. We'd been happy together. All right, happy-*ish*. We didn't see each other much, but when we did, it was casual, comfortable—without airs. We talked about everything—or I believed we had. Now, I see that's not true. He'd been hiding his involvement with Zoe. How had I not seen his disconnect? How could I be so totally and utterly clueless?

I shoot to my feet and slam the trunk closed. I need to get out of this house. I take a bike from the garage and pedal through the streets of the neighborhood. Before I'm consciously aware of it, I'm in the vicinity of the McCaffreys' house.

I steer the bike onto their street. I promised Cooper I'd pay his mother a visit after I freaked out at Coach's wake. Resigned, I pump the pedals harder.

Coach's family lives on a cul-de-sac, an idyllic suburban street, the kind where kids play ball and ride their bicycles on the road without fear of cars. Their house is pale gray with white trim and hidden behind a massive pine tree that takes up most of the front lawn. It's smaller and less stately than the surrounding homes, but the McCaffrey residence always struck me as comfortably homey and welcoming.

The velvety green lawn has fresh uniform mower stripes, and big pots of bright flowers sit on each of the porch steps, angled to face the driveway. An American flag posted on the front porch waves gently in the breeze. I coast up to the driveway, brake, and hop off. Loose blue stones crunch noisily underfoot as I walk my bike to the front of the house. I rest the bike against the porch railing, take a deep breath, and climb the steps. Before I knock, a portly beagle appears at the windowed storm door and begins barking his little head off.

"Hey there, who's a good boy?" I talk to the beagle, but the attention makes him bark more.

From inside, Cooper speaks to the dog before he appears at the door. I had hoped he might not be home. For a fleeting moment, I'm tempted to turn around and leave. But the stronger part of me resists.

I need to do this. I *can* do this.

"Wow. This is a shock." Cooper pushes the storm door open. "I figured you'd either forgotten or decided not to come."

I shrug. "To be honest, I kind of surprised myself."

"You should've texted me." He steps aside to let me enter the house. "I just finished doing yard work and I'm drenched."

"Don't sweat it." I step past him and scrunch my nose. "Oops, too late for that. Anyway, I didn't come to see you. I came to see your mother."

"Ouch, that hurts." He puts a hand on his heart, grinning. The motion draws my gaze to the red T-shirt that clings to his chest. He's sweaty all right.

I look away and inhale the scent of onions, warm oils, and spices.

"Obviously not you, but something smells great."

"That's dinner. Eat with us."

"I can't." I shift from foot to foot.

"You have plans?"

"Well, not really. Kara and my mom are wing-it kind of people when it comes to dinner."

"It's settled then. They'll wing it, and you'll have dinner with us." He moves away from the front door. "You catch up with my mom. I'll hop in the shower."

"Sure. Thanks." I follow him as a ball of tension grows in my stomach.

The interior of the house is exactly as I remember, much like the outside, bright and cheerful, welcoming.

"Mom!" Cooper's booming voice reverberates through the house. Her answering call comes from somewhere in another room. Cooper and I continue through a series of doorways until we find Mrs. McCaffrey in a room at the back of the house. The petite matriarch, with her wavy, dark chestnut hair and patrician features, sits on a loveseat, feet curled under her.

"Someone's making good on her promise," Cooper says.

Liz McCaffrey glances up at me, dark-framed reading glasses perched on the end of her nose. Her brown eyes are intelligent and at first, she lifts them to us with a stern countenance, but her smile washes it away.

"Jayden." She stands, grasps my hands, and openly gives me a once-over. "You've grown even lovelier with the years."

Emotion coats my throat.

"Mrs. McCaffrey, I'm so sorry about Coach."

She envelops me, holding me tight to her slight frame, and whispers, "Thank you," before releasing me.

"I invited Jayden for dinner if that's okay," Cooper says from behind me.

"Perfect. We'd love for you to join us. I'm always prepared to feed an extra mouth or two whenever my son is home." Mrs. McCaffrey, a candidate for sainthood in my eyes, casually drapes an arm across my shoulders. "Coop, honey, please shower. Your scent is *quite* pungent."

"I've been saving this rank for Jayden specifically. She loves it. Reminds her of the wrestling gym." Cooper winks at me.

He isn't wrong. Weirdly, I do like his musky, sweaty smell.

"Cooper Kellan McCaffrey."

"Mom's bringing out the middle name." Cooper shifts closer and raises his brows comically. "Jayden, take one last whiff before I go neutralize this memorable scent."

"No, thanks. I already got a nose full." I push him away.

When Cooper finally goes off to shower, Coach's wife invites me to sit. I perch on the cushion edge of the loveseat perpendicular to her on the matching couch, our knees nearly touching.

"He was—" I stammer. "He was just the best, an inspiration to me and so many others. I couldn't have gotten to where I am without him."

Her cool, thin hand with long, delicate fingers slides over mine. "Teaching and coaching meant the world to him. He loved what he did."

I'm too emotional to do anything but nod.

"You probably don't know this, but Kellan visited your father in the hospital, about a week before he passed." She pauses when I look up, my face registering surprise. "He promised your father he'd keep an eye on you."

"*He did?*" My voice crumbles as my heart expands painfully in my throat.

"Nothing gave him more pleasure than to watch his students grow up and succeed in life, but Jayden, you had a special place in his heart."

Coach, oh Coach.

I didn't think I could cry anymore, but as Mrs. McCaffrey holds my hands, tears spill down my face. We sit like that, hands joined, for several long moments, until I can speak again.

"I didn't know about the visit," I say, my voice shaking. "Thank you for sharing that."

She meets my eyes, hers flooded like mine, and squeezes my hands. Her grip, though firm, trembles slightly, and I sense the fragility behind her courage. With a final squeeze, she releases my hands to grab tissues from a nearby box and presses several into my palm.

"I need to check my roast. Let's get some iced tea." Tears blotted, Mrs. McCaffrey leads me into the family's kitchen. "How's your mother doing?"

"Good." I stand at the kitchen island, glad for the change of subject and the emotional reprieve, watching as she dons oven mitts and opens the oven to baste the hunk of meat inside. A burst of mouth-watering aroma fills the kitchen. "Got into the online dating thing."

"Please tell her to be careful. I've heard some nightmares involving those dating sites," she says.

Except my mother doesn't listen to me. Maybe I can get Liz to talk some sense into her.

"Cooper says you're working at the gym. How do you like it?"

"I haven't started yet. Just had a sparring interview with a boxer, hence the bruises." I motion to my face. "But I'm looking forward to working there. Don't tell Cooper, but if I didn't need the money, I'd probably do it for free."

"I heard you plan to go into mixed martial arts competition." She pours us glasses of iced tea complete with lemon wedges and a sprig of mint. "Cooper sounded quite excited about it."

I shake my head. Cooper can be aggravatingly stubborn.

"No competition. Unfortunately, those days are behind me. The gym is simply a summer job. It's back to law classes come fall."

Well, if I get that mission statement written.

Our conversation is interrupted when Jess McCaffrey enters the kitchen, the family's beagle at her heels.

"Jayden!" She rushes to hug me.

Jess is a slender reed of firm muscle. Like Cooper, she's athletic and into competitive sports.

"J-bird, honey, feed Toby before we eat." The nickname softens Mrs. McCaffrey's command.

"Toby? Why does that name sound familiar?" I ask.

"It's the name of our *really hot* neighbor. Mom said we should come up with a nickname for our Toby. But he was here first, weren't you, boy?" She ruffles the dog's fur affectionately and smiles at me conspiratorially. "My friends and I used to drool over Toby—neighbor-Toby, not dog-Toby. Just to get his attention, we'd yell out 'Toby!' and then pretend we were calling the dog."

"Jessica Eleanor McCaffrey," her mother chides, but her veiled grin contradicts the reproach.

Jess chuckles, her eyes bright, and I laugh along with her.

"Tell me." I turn my full attention to Jess. "What are your plans after graduation next month?"

"I'm working at Fire Island for the summer, checkout girl at the Pines Pantry. Then I'm headed to Chapel Hill in the fall." Jess pulls out a rolling bin of dog food from a cabinet and unceremoniously dumps dry kibble into Toby's dog bowl. The beagle dives in without being invited. "I got a lacrosse scholarship."

She fills me in on the impending start of her freshman year of college, an exciting event, especially for small-town girls like her, like I used to be.

"That's amazing. Congratulations," I say when she's done.

"Thanks." Jess beams. "Hey, maybe next time you come over, you can bring Kara with you."

"Sure. She'd like that." I'm in awe that this girl who recently lost her father seems good, happy even.

The atmosphere in the room changes when Cooper struts into the kitchen. His wet hair has a glossy sheen and his skin, scrubbed clean, glows.

"Feel like a million bucks." He stretches his arms over his head, and his shirt rides up, exposing his flat, toned abs.

I drag my eyes away.

"Well, you look more like a hundred." Both Jess and Mrs. McCaffrey sing in unison.

"You guys need some new material." Cooper rolls his eyes. "That one's older than dust and twice as lame."

I chuckle at the exchange. The nicknames and teasing lend an air of comfort, of being with your people. They are the ideal family. Minus one.

Jess asks me to help her set the table while Cooper fills our water glasses. She places the dishes around the table as I follow with napkins and silverware. She lays down a plate at one end of the table but screws up her face for a moment and moves the dish to the side of the table, leaving the spot without a setting. I don't need to ask why. I lay a hand on Coach's place at the table and wallow in another tough moment of missing him.

Mrs. McCaffrey motions me to sit to her right, next to Cooper, with Jess across from us. Once she sets the roast and side dishes on the table, Mrs. McCaffrey takes my hand and bows her head; her children do likewise. Cooper clasps my other hand.

"Father, thank You for this food, for our family." Mrs. McCaffrey's voice is strong and calm as she prays. "And for the gift of Jayden's company." At the mention of my name, Cooper squeezes my hand. "Lord, we are coping with an empty seat at our table. Be with the one we are without, and help us to trust in Your timing, purpose, and great love for us all. We pray your blessing over us, and the strength to endure the months ahead. We thank You for all the gifts you've given us. Amen."

For a moment, we sit in quietness until Mrs. McCaffrey lifts her head and noticeably pushes out a smile.

"Let's eat, shall we?"

I kind of want to hang onto the moment longer, but they release both of my hands, and the family passes the plates of food.

The dinnertime prayer moves me. I can't remember the last time I prayed, or spoken to God of my own volition. With the emotional toll of this visit, it's more comforting than I expect.

Dinner—a roast with baby carrots, potatoes, and a side dish of asparagus with bacon—is the best home meal I've had in a long time.

"Mrs. McCaffrey, this is absolutely fantastic," I say between bites. "Thank you."

"Yeah, with meals like this, Mom makes it hard to leave home." Cooper leans back in his chair and pats his stomach.

"You're welcome, Jayden," his mother replies. "And Cooper, dear heart, I thank the good Lord every day that you survived that horrific car accident, and that you are home to enjoy my cooking. Despite your injuries, you have a whole life ahead of you to start a new path."

Injuries? In the hospital, Cooper had said he'd healed and was fine. I glance at him, but his frown suggests his mother is exaggerating.

"Thought I'd stick around to help out." His tone remains respectful, but there's an edge of frustration there, too.

Surprise, surprise. Cooper and I share common ground—both getting pushback on being home.

"Thank you, my darling, but I'm perfectly fine to manage on my own." She turns to me. "Jayden, where are you living these days?"

"I was in Brooklyn—" I start to say.

"Brooklyn?" Mrs. McCaffrey cuts in. "What a coincidence. Coop plans to go to Brooklyn College to finish his teaching degree. He's thinking of commuting. I keep telling him he'll enjoy it more if he rents a place near school, you know, to socialize and network." Mrs. McCaffrey smiles at her son. "Do you need a roommate? I can vouch that he's fairly neat and pretty good in the kitchen, too."

Her sales pitch would be funny if things between Cooper and me were easy like it was in high school before the blunder in his Mustang.

"I gave up my apartment." I force myself to smile. "I'm also living at home for the time being."

"Mom, can we talk about this later, please?" Cooper says.

This little crack in the family's veneer is the first uncomfortable moment I have witnessed between them.

"Who's up for dessert?" Jess bounds to her feet and starts collecting dishes. "I made cheesecake."

"I'm sure it's delicious, but no dessert for me," I say, grabbing some dishes. "I'm gonna get going."

"Leave those. I want to show you something."

Cooper brings me up the main stairway near the front door to the second story. A wooden-floored hallway leads to a bedroom converted into an office. A large mahogany desk with a banker's lamp sits before a window that looks over the front yard. The tall, green pine tree takes up most of the view. Two bookshelves line one wall, and on the other three walls are rows and rows of framed certificates and team photographs—Coach's office.

From the leather chair to the stub of a cigar still sitting on a glass ashtray, to the many team photos, trophies, and pennants from county and state championships, it's like he's still using the room.

On the floor next to the desk is his beat-up leather briefcase.

"That's Rupert!" I reach out to the case like an old friend and run my fingers across the aged leather.

Cooper laughs and shakes his head. "I can't believe you remember."

"When a teacher gives his briefcase a name, especially a funky one like Rupert, you don't forget it. Your dad was always fun. His class was my favorite period of the day."

"If you remember Rupert, then you'll remember this little guy." He reaches behind him to grab a small multi-colored stuffed bear sitting on the shelf next to a row of wrestling trophies.

"Champ!" I snap the bear from him, grinning at the cheap eight-inch stuffed animal pulled victoriously from a coin-operated claw game. "We won him at the restaurant after we swept William Floyd junior year."

"Champ came to every competition after that." Cooper nods at the bear. "Dad used to get some funny looks with that bear hanging out of his pocket."

"He was our good luck charm." The bear's fur, once bright spirals of color, like a tie-dye T-shirt, is faded and the sheen of its black plastic eyes worn down, but his green stitched smile is exactly as I remember it.

"Yep." Cooper cups my elbow and draws me toward the wall of photos of the teams his dad coached over the years.

"Bet it's been a while since you saw this photo." He points to one midway down, and I bend to look at it with him, overly conscious of how close he's gotten to me.

The heat of his body radiates a clean citrus and cedar scent of soap from his recent shower. The scent curls in the back of my throat and continues a luxurious slow roll across my chest and through my limbs, making me loopy. Powerful pheromones. My lips pop open to draw in a steadying breath.

Squeezing the bear with both of my hands, I force myself to focus on the image in front of me, our wrestling team, junior year.

"There you are," he says, pointing.

A lone girl dwarfed by a wall of youthful male bodies and testosterone. The team and I are in royal blue singlets with "Phantoms" across our chests in yellow lettering. Unlike that of my brawny-chested male counterparts, the bold print does not sit straight and flat on my chest. The letters curve over the roundness of my breasts. Distinctly. Despite wrapping myself tightly with elastic bandaging, there was no hiding the fact that I was a girl.

Before the picture was taken, I'd been messing around, grappling with Troy and Cooper who were standing on either side of me. A smile on my face suggests I'd just been laughing, that I had been happy.

"And here." Cooper points to a photo to the right of it—our senior year of wrestling. Compared to the earlier photograph, my mouth is pressed together, in a semblance of a smile.

Dad had been diagnosed and started chemo and radiation treatments that year. I'd been feeling overwhelmed, emotional. It was rough going, and I decided it'd be best if I didn't wrestle that year, but Coach called me to his office after school one day. We talked for a long time about the challenges my family and I were facing, which I appreciated. Before I left, he insisted I come to wrestling practice, even if I didn't feel like wrestling. And I did. He guided me with a gentle hand and didn't force me to compete. Being with the team helped me get through those days, but I wrestled differently, more aggressively.

"Not that you weren't always a good wrestler, but senior year, you were hell on wheels," Cooper says with a tone of respect.

"Got a few ref warnings that season." I study my younger self and the rigidness of my stance.

"He nicknamed you Courageous Cat because, off the mat, you were reserved and quiet like a kitten, but on the mat, facing an opponent, you fought like a big cat." He glances sideways at me. "Only the students my father truly cherished got dubbed with a nickname. You were always bright and energetic. Talented and smart. When your father got sick, you changed. My dad was worried about you." His voice softens. "All he ever wanted was for you to have a shot, a chance to show the world what you're made of."

My eyes swim. Of all the people I've let down, Coach is one of the hardest to bear.

We fall into silence with our gazes resting on each other. His tender expression makes me remember those moments in the car, after my father's funeral. How thoughtful, sweet, and gentle he'd been with me—holding me while I cried. I'd thought he wanted me like I wanted him. I took my top off and everything came to a screeching halt. Talk about being ashamed. The familiar coil of embarrassment permeates my face.

There's a tick of awareness in his eyes, and before I can back away from the moment, he grabs hold of my hand.

"Don't run away," he says.

That's exactly what I want to do.

I stare at my hand in his and wrack my brain for something, anything, to defuse the moment. *Injuries.* His mother's comment at the dinner table jumps into my mind.

"Why haven't you told me the truth about how badly you were injured in the car accident?" I pull my hand away and jab the bear in his direction.

"Don't change the subject." His jaw tightens as he takes Champ from me.

"Then answer the damn question."

"Got banged up a bit, but, as you can see, I'm fine." He raises his arms wide, inviting me to look.

I look at him hard, then turn away. He looks better than fine.

"Jayden." A floorboard whimpers as he moves closer. "This thing, this tension between us. I'd like to get past it. I don't want to fight with you."

I spin around. He's closer than I thought. Raw energy hums between us, making me remember the feel of his soft mouth on mine, the urgency of our kiss.

My face heats and I slip past him, putting several feet between us. "I don't know what you're talking about. We are *not* fighting."

"You have a distinct edge to you. Hard to miss it, especially yesterday." He pauses, lips in a rigid frown, as he waits for me to respond, but I don't. "Sports is a good way to expel pent-up energy, but if your head isn't in the game, someone is going to get hurt. From what I saw yesterday that someone is likely going to be you."

"It was one lousy sparring session, Cooper. One. And I bested her." My ears burn. "I wasn't angry. I was competing. Stop thinking you know me. You don't."

"I haven't spent much time with you recently, but I do know you, Jayden." Facing me squarely, he anchors his hands on his hips. "I appreciate you came home for my father's services, but why are you *still* here? After your father died, you kicked this town, and everyone in it, to the curb. You never looked back. Why the sudden change of heart to reconnect with this Podunk town? What are you running from this time? Troy? Life? Maybe it's none of my business, but you're wound spittin' tight."

Fresh on the heels of my mother's criticism, Cooper's judgment makes me see red.

"You haven't changed. Still so opinionated. You think you know it all."

"Well, some people have a hard time seeing things, *and themselves*, as they really are."

That familiar little righteous snap of his chin eviscerates the last of my control. A big fat F-U burns my tongue, but that's too simple, too indiscriminate.

"Maybe you should leave me the hell alone and mind your own damn business." My eyes are wet even as I fight to keep my curled fists at my sides. Without another word, I leave the room and tramp out of the house.

I grab my bike and pedal hard, steering south, toward the water. The intimate moments between us in his car years ago play on a loop as I pump my legs. Embarrassment fuels my anger. I drop the bike on the pavement that edges the beach and take my first deep breath.

"You're a grownup. Just stop it. Stop thinking about him," I shout across the bay.

I don't want to remember him and me together. I don't want to remember how his lips felt pressed to mine, how his arms felt around me. I don't want to feel anything about Cooper McCaffrey.

NINE

When I get to the gym for my first day of work on Monday, Van and Cooper are at the front desk, seemingly awaiting me. Cooper slides a packet of papers across the countertop.

"What's this?" I ask.

"A sparring contract," Van says.

"Contract? You mean, an indemnification provision." I move closer, ready to sign.

"That, and a promise to work on a professional level," he says.

"And that means what?" I look at Cooper through narrowed eyes. This has something to do with him. I just know it.

My former classmate rests his hands on the counter and meets my gaze. "It means, if you want a job sparring, you need to be trained. Otherwise, you're out."

I step back. "It's the owner's call to decide what I need to do while in their employ."

"Yes, as part owner, I agree with this contract," Van says.

"As the other part owner, well, you know how I feel." Cooper crosses his arms.

My gaze flicks at him. *Part owner*. Great.

"Fine." I hastily grab a pen and scrawl my signature across the bottom.

Cooper collects the paperwork and hands it to the employee working the counter.

"Keep that in a safe place." When he turns to me, he's grinning, like he's won something. "Okay, let's get started, shall we?"

"You didn't tell me you were a part owner of the gym," I grumble.

"Part owner of the MMA gym," he clarifies. "It was my father's idea. We invested together. If you'd bothered to keep in touch the last few years, you'd know."

That truth keeps me silent as we walk to the center of the workout space of the gym. The place is a blur of motion and sounds, the whirl of jump ropes and smacks of fists pummeling boxing bags. In a corner covered with wrestling mats, guys do core work, torso twists, crunches, and planks. The sounds of ongoing, hardcore training forces Cooper to speak louder.

"You used to know how to channel your energy. I'm going to remind you how that works. You'll train with me for the next few weeks."

When I release a noisy breath, he flashes another grin. Cooper knows he's won this round. I'm done resisting, for now.

He wastes no time, running me through a series of warmups, lunges, squats, and burpees, making notations on the clipboard as each set is finished. Though I complete every exercise, I'm tested and winded by each set.

"Today, we're gonna teach you how to stand properly," he says.

"Stand? I know how to stand." I squat, assuming a wrestler fighting stance, hunching low, elbows bent, and hands ready to grab.

"For now, I want you to forget that you know wrestling. Let's figuratively strip away that knowledge." Cooper pulls me out of the stance. "Here, watch me."

I cross my arms and observe.

"Put your left foot in front of you, at a 45-degree angle from your opponent. Your left heel should line up with your right toe. Most of your weight should be on your back foot. Keep your elbows in and your hands up, with your left hand under your cheek and your right under your chin. Keep your chin down at all times. Whatever you do, never be a stationary target." He raises his fists, shifts his weight, and throws a right cross. "Every time you punch with your left fist, I want you to tap with your left foot. The same goes for your right. Got it?"

"Yeah, but when do I get to put on gloves and hit something?" I ask.

"In time, Rocky. As a wrestler, you've always had good upper body strength, but we need to build up your core and leg strength. From what I've observed, your balance needs work."

"I'd rather work on my boxing skills. They suck."

"And yet, that didn't stop you from doing underground fighting?"

The reference to that night sets my teeth on edge. "I won that fight."

"A sloppy win."

"A win is a win."

"Not in my book."

"You're just upset that I avoided you that night."

There's a hostile silence as our challenging glares bounce off each other.

"I suppose you had your reasons." Dismissing the matter, he checks his clipboard and tosses it aside. "I'm going to try to push you off balance. Don't let me."

Forty minutes into the hour-long balance training lesson, I've fallen on my ass too many times to keep track of. My butt aches, and my patience is thin.

"Reset," he orders and waits for me to stand.

"You're angry with me."

"I'm not," he replies sharply. "I'm *trying* to teach you to fight, to protect yourself. Now, reset."

He comes at me before I'm ready, his fists raised, but suddenly changes course, and cocks his leg for a sidekick. Forced to retreat, I stumble backward.

"Hey!" I snap.

"That's what happens when you're on your heels," he barks. "Do it again. Reset. Feet together, step forward."

I'm still scowling at him when he rushes me like a football player, arms up and shoving me with more force than before. I land on my backside, *hard*.

"I wasn't ready." Grimacing, I rub my butt.

"Opponents don't wait. They strike. Every time you step onto the mat, you *need* to be ready."

His haughty tone shreds my patience. Gritting my teeth, I get up and re-center, leaning into the stance, arms at the ready. If he wants a fight, I'll give him one.

I crook a finger at him. "Bring it."

This time, when Cooper shoves me, I don't budge—not an inch—and I push back.

"Better." He steps away and throws a towel at me. "Hit the machines. Personal training is done for today."

I wipe the sweat off my face as he walks away.

"*Better?*" I rush to catch up. "That's it?"

"Yeah, better. You want a medal?"

"What's with the attitude?" I scowl at him.

He stops short, and I brace for a verbal throwdown, but when he looks at me, his expression softens.

"Sorry for being short with you. You pulled out a win that night in Brooklyn, but before that, I watched you get pummeled. You could've gotten hurt. I don't know what you'll do with this training, but if you're going to keep climbing into the octagon, you need to take your training seriously." With that, he walks off in a waft of cool politeness.

I'm completely thrown—landing somewhere between embarrassed and disgusted with myself. Because once again, he's right. Other than a paying gig that allows me to get in fighting shape, I don't know why I took this job. It won't amount to anything. But I'm not a martyr. I don't want to get hurt. If I'm going to put on gloves and fight, I need to learn how to do it correctly. He's willing to teach me. I need to trust him. And trust myself around him.

At home, I plop myself in front of my laptop, remembering what my father had once told me. When called to represent a new client, to present the strongest defense possible, the first step was to prepare. Put in the due diligence to understand the situation and its perimeters. I intend to be prepared for my next day of work, researching what it takes to be a good fighter and sparring partner. Once I get started, though, I can't stop. I don't want to. I spend hours upon hours watching sparring videos and reading online articles, taking notes, and absorbing all I can.

The number one priority in sparring is to try not to win. I failed that on the very first day with Dani. Number two is to check your power with the fighter. Are your punches too hard? Too light? You want to give the fighter a real workout but not beat them up.

The information makes me understand why Cooper and Van take my training seriously. I can help make those I spar with better fighters. Something I can do and take pride in. Since positivity as of late has been in short supply, I decide helping others is a respectable motivation for this job.

I start running every day, steadily adding distance, aspiring to run a minimum of five miles without gasping. I meet Cooper at Gloves by six a.m., where he puts me through different routines, rotating squats, and hoppers, bouncing onto my toes from a squatting position. Mobility drills, switching footwork, pivoting left-right, left-right. Punches, rolls, and pivots. I don't tell him, but I'm impressed with the level of his physical training knowledge and his ability to teach me more than I know.

The following week, wearing the new padded headgear that Cooper ordered for me, I spar with a few new fighters. Marcus gives each fighter instructions and steps back to watch. I weave and jab as Cooper has taught me: gloves up, chin down, elbows in. Marcus often asks me to grapple with them. Apparently, it's the weakest aspect of all the fighters he works with. When I pull a move that locks up the fighter I'm sparring with, Marcus has me explain what I'm doing and how the fighter might avoid being trapped.

Two weeks in and I've fallen in love with my job, with the routine of my days, pushing myself to improve and grow stronger. I settle in nicely, getting to the gym every morning, warming up and going through workout routines with fighters readying for sanctioned competitions, spotting them on the free weights, and then sparring with them.

From the moment Cooper walks through the door, I'm aware of him. Besides training me and working with other athletes, he's likely to be at the front desk, on the computer, or on the phone talking to vendors, handling the business end of things. The hostility between us from that first day vanishes and watching him work, I'm super impressed. He tackles everything with a steady, sure-footedness that reminds me of his father.

He arrives and leaves with a smile. We've engaged in friendly banter, almost like old times. My time here is limited, as this is only a summer job, but I could get used to this, working with him every day.

I'm out running the last mile of my five of the day when a small blue car beeps and pulls up alongside me.

"Hey, Jayden!" Jess McCaffrey calls out, slowing the car to keep pace with me. "I'm having a graduation party at our house in a couple of weeks. We're going to have music, food, and dancing. Please say you'll come!"

She stops the car, and I walk over to the passenger window.

"Sure. Wouldn't miss it," I say.

A smile lights up her face. "I'll text you an invite."

I give her a thumbs-up and start jogging again. She beeps a few times and leaves me in her rearview. Across the street, the handholding, speed-walking couple I had rolled my eyes at when I first arrived home waves to me. Before I consciously plan to, I wave back.

When I get home, things are looking up. The front lawn has been mowed, the gardens edged, and the hedges trimmed. My mother got the lawn service here. Inside is another surprise. The house smells crisp, of lemon and pine. The carpet has fresh vacuum lines.

My mother kisses my cheek.

"You're happy," I say. "From the looks of things, you had a good day?"

"A fantastic day." She glows. "You'll be happy to know I made some headway with my finances. I made payments on all my past due accounts."

"How did you manage that?" I fill a glass with water and drop into a chair at the table.

"Alejandro helped me."

I nip my bottom lip to keep from groaning out loud. "Do you think that's a good idea? You barely know him. Did he make you sign anything?"

"For Pete's sake, Jayden. You worry too much." Mom waves a hand at me. "I know him plenty. I talk to that man every single day, more than anyone, probably more than I ever talked to your father."

I hate that she compares whatever this is to her marriage to my father.

"Where are you going to get the money to pay him back?" I ask.

"You let me worry about that."

Of course, her saying that makes me worry. I want to know how much she borrowed and what his payback expectations are, but I keep my mouth shut.

The following day, I'm the first one home and snoop, once again looking through the credit card statements. Her online passwords are predictable: a combination of the cat's name and house number or our birthdays. I scroll through her accounts and estimate Alejandro gave my mother about fifteen hundred dollars. She divided the money, paying just enough to each account to keep collectors from calling.

Kara is at the kitchen table on her laptop when I put dinner in the oven.

"So, what's Mom's boyfriend like?" I lean against the counter and wipe my hands.

"Dunno. Never met him."

"Have they met in person?"

"Nope." Kara shrugs. "He lives out in Silicon Valley. Probably why she's hung onto him this long. Mom said they plan to get together the next time he does business in Manhattan."

"How serious of a relationship can they have without having met face to face?"

"You live under a rock, sis? Haven't you ever watched *90 Day Fiancé*? People meet and hook up online *all* the time."

Until now, it wasn't the way of things for our mother. I'd never pictured her willingly participating in such an unusual relationship dynamic. She used to like to be out and about, a face-to-face person. She and Dad were always doing something. Weekends commonly meant a new adventure, even if it was just a day trip to take a walk and picnic in a nearby park.

I feel a sharp twinge of loneliness, of losing someone so close you can practically finish each other's sentences.

"Any idea what *kind* of banking work this guy does?" I ask.

"Mommy said he works for Harvey and Sloane. They have that jingle: *When you need a loan, call Harvey and Sloane!*" Kara sings. "Some kind of money lending company."

"But don't you think it's odd that no one has met him?" I push.

"Mom had me say hello to him online a few times." She shrugs. "I don't bring anyone home to meet her."

"If you started seeing someone steady, you would. And she seems really into this guy."

Kara sits back and thinks about it. "Yeah, I suppose so."

The front door opens and closes.

"Hello!" Mom calls from the foyer. "Smells good. Someone cooking?"

Kara and I exchange a look.

"I'll ask. Back me up." I hand her a stack of dishes and silverware.

"Okay." My sister takes the dinnerware and starts setting the table.

Our mother strides into the kitchen, jiggling her keys. The scent of her faded perfume, Elizabeth Taylor's *Gardenia*, enters with her. Her curls have a little less bounce, and her eyes are a little less bright, but she looks almost as fresh as when she left the house.

"Kara and I were just talking. Do you have plans to meet Alejandro? Because we think we should meet him, too."

"I didn't think you girls were interested." Her hands are still as she looks from me to my sister, gauging our sincerity.

"I think two people who're serious about each other should meet in person," I say. "I mean, you believe he considers this relationship serious, don't you?"

"Yes, and we talk about getting together." She shifts a hand to her collar to stroke her neck. "But I wanted to lose a few pounds. And he has an important job. He's an executive and has two young children from his first marriage."

"You don't need to lose weight. You look great, and surely, even an executive can take a few days off to meet the woman he's serious about."

"Yeah, Mom. Tell him to get his butt out here," Kara chimes in. "We need to check him out, and give our seal of approval."

Mom blinks—we've caught her off guard—but then she recovers and smiles.

"You're right, absolutely right. I'll call him now." With a firm nod, she pulls out her cell and dials her boyfriend.

"Alejandro, we need to make plans to get together. My girls want to meet you, too. And I won't take no for an answer," she says, beaming at us. "When can we make this happen?"

Turns out Alejandro is more than agreeable. Mom ends the call flushed, practically levitating.

"He's looking into flights to New York to take me on a date next Friday! And then—" She pauses for a punch of drama. "On Saturday, he'll rent a boat and take us all out for a day on the water!"

"Woot!" Kara squeals, fist-bumping my shoulder. "Can we rent a float to go tubing?"

"And water skis? I haven't been water skiing in years." I ask, drawn in by my sister's excitement.

Mom texts Alejandro, who assures her that he will be more than happy to rent any equipment to do whatever activities we want.

"Way to go, Mom, landing a guy with beaucoup bucks!" Kara says.

Mom's cheeks burst with color.

Kara paints Mom's nails Thursday night, and the two of us fuss with her hair and weigh in on dresses and shoe choices for her date with Alejandro. It's so "girlie" and different for me, but also fun, and despite my reservations about Alejandro, I jump in, enthusiastic for Mom's first date, and sharing in a bit of her nervousness, too.

Friday, though, Mom comes home from work frowning.

"Alejandro's flight was delayed. A weather situation. He's not coming until tomorrow. He doesn't want to let you girls down, so we decided to skip our private date and go straight to the boating trip."

"You okay with that?" I ask.

"It's fine." Face pinched, she twists to look at her reflection in the dresser mirror. "But his first sight of me in person is going to be in a bathing suit, with no way to conceal these hips. What if he doesn't like the way I look?"

My back stiffens. "Tell him to go f—"

"Jayden!" Mom intercepts my f-bomb.

"She's right, Mom," Kara says. "If the guy's that shallow, kick his butt to the curb. You have a rockin' figure, a little rounded and soft, a little cushion for the pushin'."

"You girls!" Mom throws her hands up. "I have no idea where you learned to talk like that."

Laughing, Kara and I high-five each other.

When I open my eyes Saturday morning, the first thing I see is my father's face looking at me, his bright eyes and classic full-toothed smile frozen in the framed photograph on my dresser. As I trace the memorable lines of his face with my eyes, I wonder if the script were flipped and Dad had been the surviving spouse, what he'd be doing. I imagine him ceaselessly and quietly grieving Mom while outwardly being more focused on Kara and me and the health and happiness of our family.

I roll out of bed and stand in front of the picture. "I know, I know, Daddy. We all handle things differently." I kiss two of my fingers and press it to his face.

Next to Dad's photo is the notepad I'm using to write my mission statement, half a page filled with vague notes, more doodles than sentences. I pick up the pen, tap it against my lips, and then, pressing pen to paper, I write *Strive to be a source of optimism and support to everyone I meet–like my father.* A lofty goal but achievable. Certainly worthwhile. I add a few swirly doodles and toss the pen aside.

Downstairs, Mom is already running around, picking things up and putting them down, and forgetting what she's doing. First-date nervous giddiness. I join in making sandwiches with Kara and packing a cooler with drinks, slices of watermelon, and an assortment of snacks in hopes we have something that Alejandro will like because not even Mom knows. In our swimsuits, we bump into each other, laughing, collecting towels, and lathering each other's backs with sunscreen. We haven't been this buzzed about an outing together in many years. I'm ambivalent about meeting Alejandro, but Mom is serious about him. He lent her money, showing he's invested in their relationship. In keeping with what I'd written earlier, I pledge to remain open-minded and will support my mother, no matter what.

"That's him," Mom sings when her cell chimes.

I watch her as she talks to him, curling a lock of her blonde hair around a finger, like a teenager. She looks great in a new red one-piece strapless, an eager, sexy cougar ready for action. Part of me wants to cover her up, lock the door, and take a sledgehammer to her laptop.

Damn you, Alejandro, you better be worthy.

"Oh, Alejandro, no," I hear her say, pulling me from my thoughts. She turns her back to us, her volume dropping to a whisper, and leaves the room altogether.

Kara and I look at each other. Mom shuffles back into the room a few minutes later, cell phone dangling at the end of a limp arm.

"I'm sorry, girls." Her expression melts into a sulk. "Alejandro's flight was canceled. Wildfires in California. They basically shut the airport down."

Mom shows Kara and me the news page weblink Alejandro sent her. The headline reads *Turbulence and reduced visibility near SFO. Flight cancelations growing.*

"Alejandro is so disappointed. He was looking forward to this weekend. He promises he'll come to New York as soon as he can and make it up to us." Mom rubs her arms as if she has a chill.

"Why did he wait so long to tell you?" I ask. "We're ready to go. He was supposed to be here already."

"His flight was only delayed before they canceled it. He was at the airport early, hoping he'd get out," Mom responds, indignant.

I resist saying more and instead ask, "He's safe, though?"

"Yes."

"Couldn't he drive to another airport?"

"No, that's inconvenient. I wouldn't want him to be put out."

I think, yeah Mom, he *should* put himself out for you. Troy didn't put himself out for me. If only I'd been paying attention, maybe I would have been better clued into where we were at, where we were heading, *before* I attempted to reposition my future around him.

"Okay, well—" I glance at the two of them. "We have an amazing, sunny day, all this food, and these great bathing suits. I say we reclaim the day and head for the beach."

"Yes, beach day!" Kara jumps to her feet.

"You girls go on ahead," Mom says.

"You're coming with us." I hook an arm around my mother's shoulders. "We're not taking no for an answer."

Mom takes some prodding, but she eventually puts on a brave smile and joins Kara and me in loading the car. I need to rescue this day, to make it better for her. To keep her from dwelling on Alejandro and the fires. That might be asking too much, but I'm going to try anyway.

With Mom in the passenger seat of the Impala and Kara in the back, the three of us coast down Sunrise Highway, headed east for Smith Point County Park. The windows are down, and the wind is whipping all our hair around like crazy. And we don't care. We're too busy singing along to Mom's favorite Neil Diamond song, "Sweet Caroline," at the top of our lungs, pumping our hands in the air, *buh, buh, buh.*

We swim, eat, gossip, and sunbathe, and come home sun-kissed and tired. All in all, a great day. Mom is smiling until we walk in the door. She slips into her bedroom. I hear her talking on the phone and know it's Alejandro.

I want to follow her, tell her men aren't worth our tears. I consider sharing with her what Troy has done and why we aren't together anymore. But my phone pings with a message. Speak of the devil—it's Troy.

I need to talk to you. It's important.

We haven't communicated in weeks. I can't imagine what could be so dire that he suddenly needs me, out of the blue.

Me: *About what?*

Troy: *The show. They want to talk to you.*

Sin City Fight Club? Maybe they had second thoughts and want me to audition? Now that Troy and I aren't together, do I even want that?

I repeat: *About what?*

Troy: *Too much to text. I'm about to take off. I'll call you later.*

I squeeze my eyes shut and slowly count to ten. Tossing the phone aside, I put Troy out of my mind and help Kara clean up from our beach day.

Ten

My day at the gym finishes up before I know it, but I stay longer to get in an extra workout. Outside, the sun is bright in the sky, and for the first time in a while, I feel sunny inside. Being home isn't as bad as I expected. Life is leveling off, with Mom, Kara, and Cooper, too. Things are becoming more balanced, more enjoyable.

As I'm throwing my stuff in the back seat of the Impala, a woman behind me calls out, "Jayden."

She doesn't look familiar, but the use of my name holds my attention.

"I'm Kate Wheat with the *Beacon Times*. Could I interest you in a cup of coffee ... or better yet, a protein smoothie? I'm writing a story about you and Troy Murphy," she says with a friendly smile. "And Zoe Bocek."

"Zoe?" I blink. "How—"

"There's talk, just a murmur, really, of an incident between the three of you," she rushes to say.

How could she know? Who told her? Oh my god. *This* is what Troy wanted to talk to me about. Someone shot their mouth off. The press knows. And soon, everyone will know Troy cheated on me and that Zoe kicked my ass.

"No comment." I push past her and get into the car. The interior is sweltering, though, and I roll down the window.

"I'll tell your side of the story. I'll be fair." Kate's still talking as I start the engine and put it in reverse. "Think about it."

Before I pull out, she flings her business card through the window, and it lands in my lap. At the traffic light, I toss the card aside and check my phone. I have three missed calls from numbers I don't recognize.

Already tense entering the house, I hear my mother talking in the living room. Her high-pitched, upbeat tone is in sharp contrast to the deep timbre of a male voice responding to her in conversation. I stay, frozen to the spot, hidden by the short wall that separates the foyer from the living room.

"Jayden, is that you?" my mother calls out.

When I don't answer, she marches to the foyer and finds me.

"What are you doing?" A brief flash of impatience shadows her brow, but she doesn't give me time to answer. "Come see who's here."

She grabs my arm, her demeanor changing instantaneously to one of delight as she tows me into the living room.

Just by his voice, I already know who it is.

Troy is sitting on the couch under the front window, his lean face tilted toward me. He runs a hand over the top of his stylishly cut blond hair and rises to his feet. He did mention he was on a plane. He just never said where he was going. I didn't suspect he'd show up here, at least not in this house.

"Jay." He says my name with a soft, expressive lilt.

The familiarity of his voice rings in my ears and settles heavy on my heart. He waits for me to say something, but with all that has transpired between us, seeing him again here, in my home, renders me speechless, and for an agonizing moment, we simply stare at each other.

"Troy was just telling me that the show is on a break while they put the season's final episodes together. He flew home to spend some time with his father. Isn't that nice?" my mother says breezily.

She might be oblivious to the tension between Troy and me, but the twist of his mouth, the way he shifts his weight and has difficulty meeting my eyes, says he knows he's not welcome. At least not by me.

I fold my arms across my chest. "Why are you here?"

"Jayden, that's rude," Mom says. "Troy doesn't need a reason to visit us."

"Oh, so this is a social visit?" I give him a pointed look.

"Not exactly. I have some stuff I need to talk to you about like I said in my text." He shoves his hands in his pockets and smiles at my mother. "But I haven't seen your mom in a while."

To my left, someone clears their throat. An older, gray-haired man stands in the hallway that leads to the bathroom. In leather loafers and dark jeans with a dark sports jacket, he looks like a trendy grandfather. Except I know Troy's one living grandfather and this guy is not him.

For a moment, I think it's Alejandro, until the man says, "Ben Davids," introducing himself with a nod. "I had to use the little boy's room."

"This is Jay." Troy steps next to me. "Ben is my promoter."

"Nice to meet you in person, Jay. Troy's told me a lot about you." Ben grins broadly with a set of large, overbright teeth, too perfect to be natural. "Got big things planned for everyone's favorite new MMA celebrity."

Ben has a salesperson-like vibe. Whatever he's selling, I'm not buying.

"Cool." Unsmiling, I keep my arms crossed. "Well, I'll leave you to your visit. I have stuff to do."

Troy and the promoter exchange a look.

"Jay—" Troy opens his mouth, but I fly upstairs before he can say more.

Of course, he doesn't leave it there. He follows me up to my bedroom door.

"A reporter wanted to talk to me about you and Zoe." I twist around, clenching my fists, and find him staring at his feet. "You knew this got out, and you didn't even have the decency to warn me about it?"

"It's why I came home. To tell you." He looks up but has enough sense to keep a safe distance. "Right now, Ben needs to talk to you."

"Me?" I tap my chest. "What for?"

"This is much bigger than you know. The team condo in Vegas." He swallows audibly. "It's wired with video cameras."

I'm about to tear into him, to demand why I should care, when it hits me.

"Our fight?"

He nods. "They caught the whole thing on video."

A phantom ache blooms in my jaw where Zoe struck me. I've been trying so hard to erase the scene from my memory.

"They want you to sign off on permission to use it—to air it," he says.

"Do you even need to ask me this, Troy? I'll *never* give them permission."

Troy blows out and leans a shoulder against the wall. How many times had he done that over the years, waiting for me to finish getting ready for school, to practice, to hang out?

"I told them you wouldn't agree." Chin low, he raises his eyes to me. "I don't want it out there either."

"Bad for your celebrity image?"

He holds my gaze. "You know that's not the reason."

"With you, I know nothing anymore."

He twists, his broad back now fully against the wall, and scrubs a hand through his hair. "I'm sorry."

"*Stop* apologizing. It doesn't help." I struggle to control a powerful compulsion to punch him.

"How do we get past this, Jay?"

"Make me understand what happened." I cross my arms. "When did you start to feel it was time to end our relationship?"

Gaze lowered, he shifts his feet. His hesitation stills the air in my lungs and heats my face. "Pretty much right after we slept together."

I suck in a breath. I wanted him to answer, to be truthful, but his response is unbearably worse than I could ever believe.

"You've felt this way since the very beginning?" Was it possible the last four years have been a sham, a make-believe relationship, and I didn't see it? Unshed tears burn at the back of my eyes. When he looks down at his feet, I have my answer. "This must be the greatest snow job of all time, Troy. You fooled me. Fooled me for years."

"Jay, I wasn't trying to fool you." He raises his hands, palms up, beseeching. "I'm sorry. I realize I should have told you sooner."

"*Ya think?* Telling me now doesn't absolve you. Not by a long shot. You should have had the balls to tell me the truth that morning." My sharp voice carries through the house.

"Jayden, is everything all right, honey?" Mom calls up the stairs.

"Yeah, Mom. Everything is fine." I punch the molding in the doorway. Pain zips through my knuckles, branching through my hand.

"Can you please come down? Mr. Davids requires a few minutes of your time." My mother's tone is polite, but I hear her annoyance, loud and clear.

Flustered, furious, and nauseous all at the same time, I push past Troy and return downstairs. Troy follows. I sit stiffly as Ben Davids details the show's request to air the footage of my brief visit at the condo that day, highlighting the producers' desire to use the tension to ramp up the end-of-season ratings before the last fight.

Mom listens on, knowing enough to remain silent through most of the conversation. She catches my eye every so often and raises a hand to her mouth as she puts the pieces together on her own.

"Troy and Zoe's contracts don't give them much of a say," Ben informs us. "The show can use any footage filmed in the general area as per outlined in the production agreement. And, to a lesser degree, you're included as well."

"I signed off on my image for Troy's storyline," I assert.

"Yes, and that includes permission to let them use footage of you, past and present."

"This is different. What happened is"—my gaze swings to Troy's face. He watches me, hands clasped on his knees— "extremely personal. My private life is not for public consumption."

"The producers understand the delicacy of the situation and are prepared to compensate you." Ben presses a number into his cell and holds the device out to me.

On the screen, there's a five-digit number, half a year's decent salary.

I raise my eyes to his face. "And if I refuse?"

He pockets his cell. "Without your consent, you'll get a check for a nominal fee, and they'll digitally blur your face."

"They can't do that. I'll sue."

Unruffled, Ben stands and adjusts the sleeves of his sports jacket. "I suggest you reread the contract you signed last June. You'll see it's fully within their legal rights."

As much as I hate to admit it, I know he's right. Last year, when Troy was hired, the production company sent out permission agreements to Troy's family and friends so they could use our likenesses to tell Troy's story for the duration of the season. Everyone was excited for Troy and cheerfully signed off. He was our hometown hero. We were best friends, in love. What could possibly go wrong?

"They'd really prefer to have you on board." The promoter moves toward the door with Troy following, like an obedient dog. Ben looks back a final time. "There's talk of doing a special episode interviewing the three of you with a nice paycheck for all."

When they leave, I sit there, wooden and flat, with no emotion left in me.

"You had a fight with a woman on Troy's team," Mom says from her seat across from me. "You've been prickly since you've been home. You were just arguing with Troy—who's not only your boyfriend but your best friend. All this fighting, lashing out at people. It's not healthy. Your anger is out of control. Maybe you need to talk with someone."

"Yes, Mom. Your eldest daughter needs mental help." I get up and text Cooper to see if he wants to go out for a drink.

When the episode airs, the world is going to know more about me than I care for anyone to know. Will they be able to tell that Troy didn't really love me? That I was completely unaware that our relationship was not just in trouble, but over?

God, I cringe. I'll look like a total loser. Maybe because I am.

"Hey, glad you texted," Cooper greets me forty minutes later as I climb into his pickup truck.

"Needed to get out of the house," I reply.

"Well then, I'm doubly glad you called me." With a grin, he pulls out onto the road. I don't know how it's possible, considering the day's events, but his smile immediately coaxes me into a better mood. "Docksides, right?"

It's a perfect summer evening, and the restaurant is busy. The only table left is in the middle of the floor, near the bar area, which is crowded and loud.

"Your mom getting on you?" Cooper asks, eyeing the menu before him.

I shake my head. "No, we're getting along okay. It's Troy. He's home."

"Oh." He meets my eyes.

"It's not good," I hurry to add, not wanting him to misunderstand. "We're still... fighting. This show stuff is getting out of hand."

"How so?"

I hold his gaze, sensing it's time I level with him about Troy. After working with him for the last couple of weeks, I'm sure he won't rub it in my face and say *I told you so.*

"I've been meaning to tell you—"

I'm interrupted by a boom of boisterous voices. All heads turn toward the entrance onto the open back deck of the restaurant. Troy strides in with Ben Davids at his side, followed by a handful of muscle heads I recognize from high school.

"Oh, perfect," I mumble and drop my head low. "I can't get away from him."

Ben steps ahead of Troy's entourage and addresses the restaurant. "Here he is in the flesh, your own Troy 'Country' Murphy." Ben claps Troy's shoulder. After the applause dies down, he adds, "I have another surprise for y'all."

He gives Troy an irritating wink and steps aside. There's a high-pitched hyena-like shriek, and a woman launches herself into Troy's arms. The restaurant utters a collective gasp, followed by a frenzy of picture-taking.

"Ladies and gentlemen, Zoe Bocek!" Ben announces.

Restaurant and bar patrons, many now on their feet, erupt into applause and whistles.

"I can't believe this," I hiss.

Cooper gapes. "She's the Canadian bantamweight on Troy's fight team."

I grit my teeth. Of course he knows her. By the response of everyone in the restaurant, smiling and clapping, approaching for pictures and autographs, they all know her.

Cooper lifts his chin in my direction. "Ooh. You really don't like her, do you?"

I lean back in my seat and blow the bangs out of my eyes. "You have no idea."

Cooper's eyes perceivably darken, making me think he senses what I haven't had a chance to say. There's no pity or ridicule though.

"Come on." Without warning, he pushes to his feet. He throws down some cash for the server who has yet to greet us. "Let's blow this place."

To leave, we must pass the crush around the TV celebrities. I'm swift to my feet and hustle past the mob but stop when I realize Cooper isn't behind me.

He's standing in front of Troy, his body in a defiant stance he rarely displays.

I push closer to hear the exchange.

"I don't know exactly what you did, but I would've expected better of you, man. Jayden is the best friend you've ever had." Cooper's hands are curled at his sides.

Troy, quiet, looks at me. I'm done feeling ashamed. This is his circus, his monkey. With one last glance, I square my shoulders and turn to leave. At the same time, Zoe advances, whacking me with her shoulder. It's no accident, not with her.

Elbow up, I shove her back. Her eyes grow dark and freakishly wide.

"You got a death wish?" She seizes a handful of my hair.

Before I can react, she yanks my head back with a hard snap. My eyes sting with the pain. I twist around, blindly swinging a hand in her direction. My balled fist connects with the side of her face. My second punch strikes empty air. In an instant, my arms are pinned to my sides, and Troy is dragging Zoe away from me. She lets go of my hair with one final, painful tug.

"Let. Me. Go." I thrash against the arms imprisoning me.

"Calm down," Cooper commands in my ear. His arms, like bands of steel, have me locked down. "We're leaving."

Flashes, like lightning bugs, illuminate the darkening scene. Zoe jeers, her raging eyes narrowed on me. I return the look until Cooper twists me away and, with a guiding arm, prods me toward the exit.

In the parking lot, Cooper holds open the passenger door of his truck for me, but I'm too wound up to get in.

"You see what she did?" I pace the length of the truck. "She was goading me, on purpose."

"Clearly. The question is, why?" Cooper leans against the side of the truck, tension rolling off him. "The fight you had with Troy, does Zoe Bocek have something to do with it?"

I pause my agitated pacing to look at him. It's way past time to come clean about Troy and me.

"Troy and I broke up. Because of her." I crack my knuckles and look down at the pebbled parking lot. "I flew out to Vegas and found them together."

"He cheated on you." Cooper clasps the edge of the truck bed. "Why didn't you tell me?"

"We've barely talked in the last few years. I suppose the story is a great icebreaker. 'Hey, you know how you predicted Troy and I wouldn't last … well, you were right!' It's humiliating."

"I wish you'd have trusted me. You have nothing to be embarrassed about," Cooper says. When I don't respond, he bumps the underside of my chin with his knuckles. "Seriously, this is not on you."

"Maybe not, but…" I raise my eyes. "Troy wasn't just my boyfriend. He was my friend, the only one I have."

Cooper takes my hand. "I know we have some baggage, but in case you hadn't noticed, I *still* am, and will always be, your friend."

Despite what went down between us years ago, Cooper remains the most judicious, good-natured guy I've ever known.

"Thank you." Overcome with gratitude, my voice shakes. "The show plans to air footage of me confronting Troy and Zoe in Vegas. And now, with her getting up in my face and everyone taking pictures, I fear this is about to blow up on me. We'll be all over social media. My private life on display... I don't know if I can live through that."

"I'm here for you." He squeezes my hand. "Whatever happens, we'll get you through this mess."

Simple words but somehow, they comfort me. He's so close, it'd be easy to bridge the space separating us, to burrow into him and absorb a little bit of security. But I can't. Being lonely and upset, I'm afraid I'd want more. That's a line I tried to cross once with him, and it was a mistake, a mistake I regret and am still paying for.

We're friends, and right now, a friend is what I need most.

After tonight's drama, I don't feel like going to another restaurant. We go to a taco drive-thru, eat in his truck, and then he drops me off at home. This situation with the fight show is only going to get worse. Ben Davids sprung Zoe on Troy — and me. I sense he knew exactly what he was doing. He lit a fuse and watched it explode. I take out my laptop and type up a strongly worded email to the production company, stating my objections to using the scene and the possible damage the airing of such will have on the mental health of those involved. One semester of law school has armed me with a litany of legal jargon, and I wield phrases and words of contest throughout the letter. It's satisfying to read from a legal standpoint. Dad and even Professor Dumfries would be proud, but it probably won't do much.

To my horror, the next day, Troy, Zoe, and I make the online editions of the local papers. Our faces are strewn across all formats of social media, accompanied by the hashtag #girlfight.

I scroll through the images, studying not Zoe or me but Troy and his expressions. There are photos of him and Zoe hugging, kissing, and her gazing up at him adoringly. All that PDA. Why is he doing stuff we swore as a couple we'd never do? I'm embarrassed for him.

Going to the gym is the only break I get from the coverage. There are no televisions in the gym, and Van doesn't allow employees to carry cell phones while on the clock.

"I got an interesting phone call this morning," Van says as I gear up to spar with Marcus's new trainee. "You've been offered a sanctioned fight for September."

My gaze pivots to him. Marcus's does, too.

"Not surprising after all the coverage you've received," Van continues. "You're all over the place. Guess they got wind that you trained here."

"It's all hype based on misinformation. It'll die down when they realize I have no fighting credentials." I wave it off.

"That's selling yourself short by a big margin." Marcus clasps my shoulder. "Do you know how many fighters would kill to be in your situation, to get this kind of publicity? You should consider taking advantage of this spotlight." He turns to Van. "Did they say who Jay will be up against?"

"That Canadian newcomer, Zoe Bocek."

The blood drains from my face. I glance around, searching the floor for Cooper, but it's early, and likely he hasn't come in yet.

"Was the caller's name Ben Davids?"

"Yeah, that's the guy," Van replies.

I stab my hands into the grappling gloves and stand to shake out my arms and legs. "Forget it. I'm not doing it."

"Marcus has a point. It's a rare opportunity. And all along, you've been doing the same workouts as the fighters," Van says. "We can train and get you where you need to be to qualify for the fight. Think about it."

This is too easy. Nothing has come easy for me. I've always had to bust my ass to get what I want. I don't trust it. Even with the weekly sparring, I'm no match for Zoe and her extensive MMA training. She would run through me in a few minutes. There's no way I would put myself in that position.

"I appreciate the offer, but I don't think so." I move past him and Marcus to start my warmup routine.

I ride the new girl a little rough and Van, displeased, dismisses me for the day, proving my point that I don't belong in a professional arena.

Eleven

The producers respond to my letter with sympathy but stand firm that the footage of the fight in the condo is their property. And it's their right to use it.

The episode airs prime time. They ramp up the drama, showing Troy and Zoe's budding friendship, the two of them flirting playfully. Troy giving her fighting advice, upbeat and happy, and then they cut to him on the phone, sounding tired, distracted, purportedly talking to the old girlfriend, the burden holding him back. Me.

There are shots of me from behind, and when they show my face, it's blurred out. It's pointless, really. Anyone who knows me or is a fan of the show already knows it's me. I should have taken the money.

Living life in hindsight. I excel at that.

My mother and sister watch with me, quiet as the episode reveals what I haven't told them. When the scene of the fight in the condo kitchen starts, Kara scoots a little closer, brushing her arm against mine.

Seeing the brawl on the screen in front of me is like watching someone else's outlandish drama unfold. It's hard to believe it's my life. *My drama.*

The only part that doesn't make me cringe is watching me tackle Troy in the kitchen after he'd gotten out of the shower. I hit him like a bulldozer, my strength evident. Frankly, I'm impressive, if I do say so myself.

The facts are artfully spun, though. To their credit, no one is made out to be the antagonist of the story, *not even* the cheating boyfriend. Troy is just misunderstood, disconnected from his old life, seeking a higher good, a tale of fame and glory they twist to resonate with the audience. They wouldn't malign Troy. He's the hero of the story.

The episode ends with Troy and Zoe sharing a secret smile as they work out together in the show's gym. Their relationship is intact. I am the odd woman out.

"It's true then," my mother says, looking at me with a furrowed brow. "You broke up with Troy."

I blink at her. "After watching what happened, that's your conclusion? That *I* broke up with *him*?"

"He must have been lonely out there. He's under so much pressure," she says, lifting the blame off Troy as if this happened *to* him instead of *because of* him. Mom pats my hand in sympathy. "When he's done with the show, you'll get him back."

I yank my hand away and rise to my feet.

"So, I'm just a casualty of Troy's victimhood? Poor, poor Troy. No consideration for me and what I've been through—what Troy put me through?" I cross my arms tight over my chest. "Whatever. You've never, ever been on my side about anything."

"And you've never been on mine," she throws back, her gaze heated.

"Maybe because we're not each other's blood." The words come out angry, but voicing those feelings rips into me. Tears fill my eyes.

She jolts to her feet. "Jayden! That has nothing to do with anything."

To me, it has everything to do with it. I sweep past her, grab the Impala keys, and leave the house.

I drive without a destination, discouraged that two important people in my life have failed me. Troy is proving he's not only untrustworthy but also a traitor. And Mom, the woman's willfully ignorant of my situation. When my father died, she'd been too caught up in her own pain to offer any kind of shelter for Kara and me, leaving us on our own to figure out how to cope with our grief. Right now, I'm experiencing a similar feeling of isolation.

My cell rings, and I pull over to answer it, putting the phone on speaker.

"Just calling to see how you're doing." It's Cooper.

"You saw the show?"

"Yes, and I worried about how you're taking it," he says.

His sympathy wrecks me. I'm silent as I try to catch my breath, letting the clanking sounds of the gym through Cooper's phone fill the void.

"Listen, I'm at Gloves if you want to come down," he offers.

"Be right there."

I'm at the business a few minutes later. This evening, maybe a dozen people are working out, running on the treadmill, using the training equipment. No one takes notice of me slipping in, crossing the main gym to Gloves.

My phone vibrates in my hand with incoming calls and messages from numbers I don't recognize.

It's even quieter in Gloves. Cooper is at the desk, doing paperwork when I walk in. He drops his pen and comes around the counter to greet me. We stand in front of each other in an awkward moment. I think he wants to hug me or something, and I kind of want to be hugged, but it's like neither of us knows how to initiate it or if it's the right thing to do.

"How're you?" he asks.

"Pissed off." I shake my arms out, too edgy to be still. My phone rings again. A number unknown to me. I send it to voicemail, but a second later, it rings again. Another unknown number.

"These calls are from the last hour, since the episode aired." I hold up the screen and show him the long thread of unknown calls. "This is a freak show, and I'm the main attraction."

He takes the phone from me, toggles the switch to silent mode, and puts it under the counter.

"Come with me," he says and leads me across the mats to the lockers.

"Did Van and Marcus tell you about the offer—to fight Zoe?" I ask.

"They did."

"Ridiculous, right?"

"No, not really." He pulls out a pair of boxing gloves and motions for me to put my hands out. "Isn't this what you wanted, to go on the show and fight?"

I wriggle my fingers into the gloves and let him secure the Velcro wrist strap.

"Yeah, I wanted to fight. But even if Zoe hadn't ruined my chances, my life wouldn't be a spectacle like this. This is way and above the notoriety I would have had."

Listening, he pushes my pink padded headgear down on my head and fastens the strap under my chin.

"Hard to know if that's true. You're a good fighter. If you had the chance to showcase your talent in the octagon, you could spark that kind of fame." With a second set of gloves tucked under his arm, he puts his own headgear on and motions me to follow him to the boxing platform.

"But this episode has little to do with my ability to fight. It's all about Troy and Zoe making me look stupid."

"I guarantee no one thinks you're stupid. You knocked Troy 'Country' Murphy on his butt!" He chuckles and holds out a mouthguard for me. I part my lips and let him pop the plastic into my mouth. With a gloved hand, I push the guard into place. He pauses before putting his own mouthguard in. "I thought we'd do a little sparring. Get some rage out of your system. Sound good?"

I nod and smack my gloves together.

We warm up for a few minutes, jumping in place, stretching, and swinging our arms. I'm limber, having worked out a few hours earlier.

"Earn your name, Courageous Cat. Come on, show me what you got," he eggs me on, bouncing around, shuffling and weaving.

I spring forward and hit him with a series of uppercuts, crosscuts, and jabs. Cooper shields his face, not returning any blows.

"Come on." He shoves me backward forcibly. "Stop being a girl. Hit me like you mean it."

The girl comment lights my fuse, as I'm sure he knew it would. I hit like a fighter; I always have. That I'm a girl has nothing to do with it. I charge him, back him into a corner, and go at him with everything I have. I'm slamming him with punches, most of which he deflects. But when I hit him with a right cross to his side, he lets out an audible grunt of pain.

"Hold up!" he yells.

Sweaty and breathless, I pull back. Cooper bends over, holding his side.

"Oh, my god." I yank my gloves off with my teeth and put my hand on his shoulder. "I hurt you. Sorry, sorry."

"No, no, it's all good," he says through gritted teeth, his complexion pale. "Just a little sore in that area."

"Let me help you get those gloves off." I grab his hands and whip the Velcro straps free. "Do you need to sit down?"

"I'm fine. You knocked the wind out of me." He accepts help to remove his gloves but refuses my help to get out of the ring. Clutching his side, he winces as he steps down from the platform.

"Cooper, damn. I'm so sorry." I want to help, but because he's resisting, I hover, not knowing what to do.

"Don't sweat it. Just an old war injury." He tries to joke, but I can tell he's in pain. "You put the gear away, and I'll go grab some water."

I quickly gather the equipment, watching over my shoulder as he hobbles over to the desk area, using the counter to support himself as he takes water bottles from the glass-fronted refrigerator behind the worktop.

When I get to the counter, he's holding an ice pack to his hip, but his color has returned, and he looks much better.

"Thanks for letting me get some punches in." I lower my eyes. "But I feel really bad that I hurt you."

"That's what I get for calling you a girl. You've got a decent right cross." He pushes my phone across the counter toward me. "Listen, I was thinking. What do you say to getting away, going dark for a few days, give the spotlight on you a chance to dim?"

I pick up the phone. More missed calls and text messages from people I don't know.

"Getting away will not help when everyone else is still plugged in."

"We'll go where people are not plugged in."

"What, like Mars?"

He grins and tips his head. "The great outdoors. Camping."

"Like in a tent?" I scrunch my face. "Sleeping in the woods, with bugs and without electricity?"

"That's generally how it's done." He chuckles. "And the 'without electricity' is the whole point."

"I've never gone camping. I wouldn't know how to plan that kind of outing."

"No worries. I come from a family of proficient campers. I have everything we'll need."

"You're coming with?" I arch a brow.

"I wouldn't send you off into the woods by yourself," he says. "Because of my car accident and my father's health, I haven't had the chance to go the last two seasons. I'd welcome the opportunity to get away. There's nothing like the solitude and tranquility of a few nights under the stars to put life back in perspective."

He hangs, waiting for a response. My eyes take a quick inventory of him, the broad shoulders, muscled chest, and solid arms straining the sleeves of his T-shirt. The thought of a few nights alone with that body in the woods causes a wiggle of heat to stir in my belly.

"Okay." I raise my eyes to him and smile. "While I wouldn't say fun, it at least sounds like a good distraction."

"It's likely Jess will want to go. She loves camping." Looking away, he slides off the stool and moves behind the counter, making a show of putting the ice pack away but noticeably putting distance between us. "We'll ask Kara, too."

Our sisters. Not the type of weekend I'd been envisioning. And obviously not what he was suggesting, either. Especially with that quick shimmy to get behind the counter, away from me. Message received, Cooper.

"All right." I pick up my cell. "As long as no one talks about Troy or the show."

"Not one word." He mimics twisting a key, locking his lips.

I go to leave but turn back.

"Cooper." I put my hand on his arm, and he looks up. "How are you holding up?"

He twists his mouth and shrugs. "I'm doing okay."

"If you ever need to talk, I hope you know you can call me, anytime," I offer, and he nods. "And thanks for tonight. I appreciate it."

"Did it help?"

"Yes, both the exercise and talking with you. I feel much... lighter."

"Good." He pats my hand. The corners of his eyes crinkle with his smile. "That's what friends are for."

I'm saddened that friends are all we are, all we'll ever be. Years ago, in contrast to my otherwise rational outlook, I believed Cooper and I would have a storybook romance, the only time I believed in happily ever after. Even so, I know how lucky I am. Cooper McCaffrey is the kind of thoughtful, amazing friend some people only dream of having.

Cooper texts me later to say Jess is in and ecstatic about camping. But when I ask Kara to come, she looks at me like I've lost my mind. My sister does nothing that resembles manual labor for fear of ruining her manicure. I've never seen her make a bed or push the vacuum around. Camping is outdoors, with dirt and flying, crawling bugs, but when Cooper pitches a spirited spin on the outing and says Jess will be there, she agrees.

The producers of *Sin City Fight Club* hit pay dirt. The episode's ratings skyrocket to an all-time high. Drama is a covetous beast. It craves more. Just as Ben Davids said, a representative from the network calls me the following morning on my way to work to talk me into doing a half-hour follow-up special, featuring interviews with the three of us: Troy, Zoe, and me. They promise, along with a bundle of money, that I, the jilted ex, will have the opportunity to tell the world my side of the situation.

I turn it down, flat. I don't want any part of that. But the gym is buzzing, and I can't go anywhere without someone mentioning the episode, or worse, pointing at me and murmuring. Requests for interviews flood my voicemail and email inbox by the hour. The weekend can't come soon enough.

We set out on Friday afternoon, the bed of Cooper's pickup truck filled with camping gear, supplies, and coolers. The hour-long drive takes us through the north shore of the scenic East End. The roads curl back and around, lifting our stomachs, and making us laugh.

We register at the campground office and drive slowly through the wooded campsite with our windows down. In the dense canopy of trees, the sound of traffic and people fades. I look around and think, this is exactly what I need.

When we pull into our numbered campsite, I am relieved to see that there's a restroom station with running water and electric outlets a short walk away.

Seasoned campers, the McCaffrey siblings orchestrate the setup of our camp. They've brought two tents—sibling tents. A green one for Kara and me. A second, blue, for Cooper and Jess.

Once we've got our tents up and bedding situated, Cooper gives Kara a lesson on how to light the campfire. He oozes patience and authenticity, a natural teacher. My sister is surprisingly attentive as he explains how to teepee twigs to start the fire and carefully add wood in increments that allow the flames to breathe.

Once the fire is crackling and blazing, we pull up camp chairs around it. Kara is taking selfies, posing with the fire and us in the background.

"Round 'em up." Cooper nudges Jess.

There's a moment where brother and sister exchange a look of challenge. "You're sticking to Dad's barbaric tradition, huh?"

"You betcha," he says with a snap of his chin, conjuring a strong likeness to Coach.

"Then you'd better explain to them." Jess motions to us.

Kara is busy texting, but the siblings have my full attention.

Cooper clears his throat.

"As I explained to Jayden when I suggested coming here, these next few days are about getting away from the news, social media, and email. Basically, unplugging from all electronic distractions. When Jess and I were old enough to have cell phones, my father started a rule that we relinquish our phones the days in between camp set-up and take-down. He collected them and locked them in the car." He rises to his feet. "In keeping with that tradition, I am going to collect all phones."

"Not going to happen." Kara shoots Cooper a steely defiant glare. "I'm not giving up my phone."

Cooper stands before me, hand extended. "It's liberating to not be controlled by a minicomputer, 24/7."

Our eyes meet, and I can see from his gentle smile he expects me to set an example. While I will not balk at the request like my sister, I understand her resistance. The thought of not having my phone stresses me.

"This will be good for you," he whispers. "It's exactly what you need. And what we came here for."

I inhale and surrender my last digital connection to the world to his awaiting hand. Jess follows suit, her expression imbuing no reluctance, but when Cooper moves to Kara, my sister holds her phone to her chest with both hands as if he might wrestle it from her.

"Kara, I know it seems really hard, but I promise you, you'll survive."

She shakes her head. I brace my arms on the camp chair, a need to intervene niggling in my chest.

Cooper hunches low to talk to her. "Just think for a moment: Who or what holds the power here. Do you have control over your phone, or does your phone have control over you?"

"I'm in control," she replies with a sharp edge of rebellion.

"Great, then it's within your power to be away from it for a few measly days. Show it who's the boss." He touches her knee. "We're doing this for your sister. This is important for her."

My sister glances my way, and just when I'm sure my welfare is not a selling point, she lowers the hand clutching the phone.

"I'll give you my phone, but I want regular visits with it," she tells Cooper.

"How about once before lights out?"

"And once in the morning," she counters.

"Deal," he says.

Like handing over a beloved child, Kara slowly relinquishes her phone to him. He rounds the fire and locks all our devices in his truck. I settle back in my chair and breathe a sigh of relief, thankful for my sister's compliance.

We pass out prepared sandwiches for a quick meal. As sunlight dips behind the tree line and darkness slowly creeps in around us, Jess, a former Girl Scout, breaks out the chocolate bars, graham crackers, and marshmallows and gives us a lesson on how to make s'mores.

While we're munching on our gooey chocolate marshmallow sandwiches, Jess starts a word game where we go around in a circle, adding to the story. All the fresh air makes us crawl into our tents, grateful even for the minimal comfort of our sleeping bag-covered air mattresses.

Kara tosses and turns. The air mattress under her groans with each twist.

"Stop fidgeting," I say.

"It's too dark, too quiet," she replies. "I want my phone."

I slip out of my bedding and shift my mattress to butt up against my sister's bed. After I crawl back in, I feel around until I find Kara's hand.

"Since I've been home, I noticed a big difference in that little sister I left behind. You're so independent. Brave," I whisper. "Thank you for coming on this trip with me—for giving up your cell phone. These last few weeks have been hard. I need strength like yours."

"I know you came home because of the B.S. with Troy, and I feel bad about what happened with him. You deserve someone way better, but it's been cool having you around." She yawns and rolls over. "I think I can sleep now. I miss my phone, though. You owe me big time for that."

Her words make me smile. I shift to lie on my back, looking up at the tent ceiling. I had never intended to be with Troy. Except for an experimental kiss in middle school, which we decided was too weird to enjoy, we'd sidestepped all feelings of attraction. Until the night of the funeral.

Fresh from Cooper's rejection, I'd come home to find Mom alone with a coworker, a guy who often flirted with her, an empty bottle of wine between them. I called her out on it. She denied it meant anything. We shouted at each other, and in a rage, I ran to Troy's house.

Losing my father was a blow to Troy, too. Dad and he had been buddies. The two of us commenced on our own pity party. I'd ditched my dress and borrowed his yellow Adrian Bulldogs sweatshirt and a pair of drawstring shorts. A six-pack and a few shots of bourbon later, I'd grown warm and asked for his help to take the sweatshirt off. The removal of clothes didn't stop until there was nothing left to take off.

I remember waking up next to him the following morning, looking at him as a woman instead of a friend, the swirl of warmth in my belly. For the first time in weeks, this exciting desire overshadowed my sorrow. I'd wanted it to continue. I'd needed it to continue.

But now I know the ugly truth. Troy had wanted to stop right then and there. A prickly rush of shame washes over me, though I'm not sure who I blame more—him for pretending, or me for being ignorant of the truth.

The sound of people quietly rustling around the perimeter of the tent wakes me the next morning. Without my phone, I can only guess the time. Jess and Cooper, dressed and ready to start the day, stand outside the unzipped tent doorway.

"Shorts and sneakers, Jones," Cooper says. "We're going for a run."

Jess joins us, but she's a gazelle, a natural runner, and she leaves us in the dust after the first mile. On our way back to camp, we stop for water near the comfort station. After I take a good, long drink from the water fountain, I yield back to him.

"You haven't really said what you think about the offer to fight Zoe," I say, watching him drink and admiring the way his T-shirt hugs his broad, muscular back.

He stands upright and swipes a hand across his mouth. "It's a bad idea."

My back stiffens at his quick, dismissive reply.

"Why don't you say what you really mean — that I don't have a chance?"

"All I'm saying is you're not in competition-ready shape."

I don't like that answer any better.

"You can train me. We have three months. Women's MMA bouts are only three five-minute rounds."

"Less than three months, and *a lot* of damage can be done in five minutes. Zoe's coming off nearly a year of high-level training and fighting. You're not anywhere near that." He pauses, hands on hips, and tilts his head. "Besides, what's your motivation for taking the fight?"

"You saw the show and the way she went after me at Docksides." I wave a hand. "She's a bitch. She deserves to be taken down a notch."

He shakes his head. "That's exactly why you shouldn't fight her."

I arch a brow.

"The other night, that promoter guy brought Zoe there to see what would happen. He was banking you'd have a strong reaction. And he nailed it. You fed right into it. It's too personal for you," he says and jogs off toward our campsite.

"Jerk," I mutter and run after him.

We eat a chicken barbecue dinner and play several rounds of campfire games. As the unfed fire begins to wane, Cooper asks, "Anyone up for a walk on the beach?"

We extinguish the fire, and all go, the four of us strolling along the wooded trails until we reach the beach. The sun has slipped past the horizon, leaving a glowing mist of orange and pink hues in its wake. We walk along the water's edge, where our steps create rigid impressions in the pebbled, damp sand, picking up shells and unusually shaped rocks, as the night's rich, thick darkness overtakes the last tinge of the sunlight. Behind us, the water rolls forward over our footprints and the waves lick away the evidence of our passage.

I inhale deeply. The serenity and mere simplicity of the day eases the tightness within me. To my left, Cooper stops to point out summer constellations in the early evening sky, so clear without all the usual light pollution. After that, though, he falls silent. As we walk, the silence pulls him away.

Kara, distracted, swats at her arms and legs. The tiny mosquito-like no-see-ums that come out at dusk seem to have a taste for her.

"I've had enough," she grumbles. "Can we head back?"

"You guys go. I'm going to sit out here for a while," Cooper says. "I'll see you in a bit."

Flashlights leading the way, Jess, Kara, and I climb the embankment that leads back to camp, but once we hit the mouth of the wooded trail, I stop.

"You girls okay to go back to camp alone? I want to make sure Cooper is okay," I tell them.

"He is being a little quieter than usual," Jess says. "Maybe because Father's Day is this weekend."

Something we all know, but until now, have not mentioned.

"I'll go talk to him. We'll be back shortly."

"Okay, but don't go swimming. Remember, *Jaws* attacked at night," Kara says.

With a laugh, I start back down toward the water. "Now that you put that in my head, I won't even dip a toe in the water."

"If you're not back in an hour, I'll call rescue," Kara yells after me.

Back on the beach, I switch off the flashlight. The moonlight illuminates Cooper sitting on the sand, facing the water.

"Hey," I call out.

He turns his head at the sound of my voice.

"Jayden, don't. I need a minute." He puts up a hand to halt me, but the distress in his voice has me moving to him faster.

"Cooper?" The sand cushions my knees as I drop beside him. "What is it? Are you okay?"

When he turns his face away, my alarm grows. I sit beside him, our arms touching, and follow his gaze out onto the water. The only sound is the steady lapping of docile waves rolling forward and retreating.

"Thinking about my dad." The catch in his voice unseats me. Cooper has always been strong and composed. This is the first time I've seen him crack.

I stir the sand between my feet with my fingers and wait for him to continue.

"Every now and then, it hits me that there's going to be all these milestones in my and Jess's life that he won't be around for. He's going to miss her graduation. That's just the start. He won't be here to see either of us get married, walk Jess down the aisle. My father will never meet or hold my kids."

He sucks in a deep lungful of air before his shoulders pitch forward. His breath staggers unevenly, weighted with a low decibel of pain. My chest aches, but my silence is no longer enough. I move behind him, to straddle his back, and wrap my arms around his torso. Bracing him, I press my cheek to the ridge of his spine.

"I'm sorry," I whisper. "I'm sorry you have to go through this, too."

His chest expands with his deep breath, briefly tightening my hold on him. After a bit, when I sense he's calmer, I release him and flop back onto the sand. He moves over and lies down next to me. The roll of the waves mingles with the night air and sends a refreshing cool breeze over us.

"If anyone knows how it feels, you do." He finds my hand on the sand between us and rests his over mine. "How do you move on?"

"I don't know if I'm the best person to ask," I say with a strangled laugh. "At our house, we're still kind of a big mess. Your family is solid."

"We have our moments."

My father wasn't like Mr. McCaffrey. Still, there was one thing I knew for sure—that he loved me. I haven't ever felt that sure of anything else. A little of that surety would go a long way, especially now.

"There are times I'm doing great, and then, bam, I'm dragged down all over again. Like when I got accepted to law school. He would have been so proud. You know?" Tears immediately fill my eyes and spill down my face. "Maybe it'd be better if my mother and I were close, but even then, there's no one who can take the place of your dad. Not dads like ours, anyway." I turn to give him a gentle smile. "It helps to think my father is still with me, that he's just over my shoulder, cheering me on."

"Thank you for being honest." He sits up and stares out at the water. "I never imagined I'd be going through this time in my life without him. He's irreplaceable. We were fortunate to have fathers like ours, who cared and loved us. Not everyone has that kind of relationship with their dad."

"Yeah, we were lucky, for sure."

With Cooper, this type of forthright conversation is typical, reflective of our relationship. From our years as friends and teammates, to when my father was in the hospital and through his memorial services, my conversations with Cooper were often very much like this one, thoughtful and affecting.

I've missed him and his steadying, comforting quality. It bubbles in my throat, and I'm about to tell him when he reaches behind his back and peels his shirt off, backward the way guys do, revealing our friendship tattoo on his thick bicep.

"I'm gonna go for a swim. You game?"

The moonlight plays across his muscular shoulders and chest, spurring a flutter of energy between my legs.

"You go on ahead," I say over the lump in my throat. "I made a vow to never take my clothes off in front of you ever again. I did that once, and it pretty much ruined us. Only a fool would chance that a second time."

He crumples his shirt in his hands and leans down, elbow in the sand, drawing closer to me. "To this day, I feel bad that I never got to explain my reaction."

He lays a hand on my upper arm and meets my gaze. Tingles race up my throat and spiral in my chest. I pull my eyes from his and look up at the sky.

Jurisprudence. Jurisprudence.

"There wasn't a need." I shift my arm and his hand falls away. "It was my mistake, an error in judgment."

"Jayden, when I suggested going for a ride, I had no ulterior motive other than to get you out of the house," he whispers. "You said your last goodbye to your father that day. You were vulnerable. I didn't want to take advantage of your emotions. You threw me when you took off your top. I should have said something. Anything. I messed up, and I'm sorry."

The soft pleading in his voice pulls at me.

"You didn't mess up anything." I sweep my hand across the sand, unable to look at him. "You were great. It was me. I got it wrong. We were friends, but I thought—hoped, I suppose—we were becoming more."

"You didn't get it wrong." He turns onto his stomach and inches closer. "I was into you."

"Shut up."

"Not kidding. I had every intention of asking you to senior prom in high school, but..."

"My dad's health took a turn for the worse. Troy mentioned you were going to ask me." I twist my lips. "Even though it was a pity-ask, I appreciate the thought."

"My ask wasn't driven by pity," he says, sternly. "I wanted to go with you because I liked you. I always liked you, Jayden, but we wrestled together. And there was Troy and your relationship with my dad. It never felt right to act on those feelings. Prom wasn't a pity ask. It was my do-or-die ask."

Everything feels warm. My chest, my face, my hands. Cooper liked me. Really liked me. All those times when the air swirled between us and spiked my pulse, it hadn't been one-sided.

"Then everything happened with your father. You needed a friend more than anything else." He drags an index finger through the sand. "But then you kissed me..."

I lower my eyes as my face burns anew with the old embarrassment. "So, you were being sensible?"

"I suppose, but I knew immediately by your reaction that you didn't see it that way."

I fist my hands. "No. I needed to feel something else. Something other than pain—just for a little while."

Even now, I'm too proud to say it was a mistake. When I bring my eyes up, he's looking at the water.

"I was nineteen, Jayden. It wasn't easy to turn you down, especially because I really liked you."

His confession pulls at my belly.

"I'm sorry I put you in that position." I dig my heels into the sand. "How can you stand to be so nice to me when I acted so terribly?"

"Despite what you thought of me all these years, I have never stopped thinking of you as my friend." He turns. "I was hoping we could get back to that place again."

"You mean a place of friendship?" I hold his gaze. "So, you're not attracted to me anymore?"

He laughs and shakes his head. "Considering your history with the wrestling team, your forwardness shouldn't surprise me, but it still amazes me how you voice stuff most keep to themselves."

I shrug. "I like answers. I like to know where I stand."

He anchors a hand in the sand and twists toward me. The moon highlights half of his face and the expanse of his hard, wispy-haired, bare chest. The sight of the raw maleness muddles my thoughts, but his silence draws my eyes upward. His intense gaze hangs on my legs and slowly moves up my body, to my stomach, chest, and neck. Under this singular focus, my body warms as if his hand, instead of his gaze, moves over my skin. When his eyes meet mine, he's unsmiling. The pressing seriousness of his expression makes my breath catch.

"Does that answer your question?" he asks.

My heart is beating so hard it might burst out of my chest. "I think the only question now is why haven't you kissed me already?"

He blows out a breath. "You and I are a complicated dynamic."

"It doesn't need to be complicated." I curl an arm around his shoulders and lean forward.

I'm pleased when he doesn't resist my touch, and more so when he leans in, his bare chest brushing up against me, scattering my thoughts. I close my eyes, afraid he'll pull away, but then his lips move against mine, soft at first, exploring, questioning, and then with more pressure, more certainty.

Little explosions shoot off inside me straight down to my toes. Arms around his shoulders, I tug him closer. He complies, moving over me, his weight pressing me into the sand. He cups my face and deepens the kiss. Strong lips and tongue. I feel the kiss all over. A long pent-up hunger is unleashed, and my hands wander, palms gliding over the smooth, hard contours of his back to his butt—round, tight, fantastic. I want him to touch me, but no matter how much I murmur encouragingly under him, his hands remain sweetly stagnant on my face.

Suddenly, he rolls off me, and the two of us pant, lying side-by-side under the smooth velvet sky.

Boo-yah! Cooper McCaffrey just kissed me breathless.

And I so want him to do it again.

I roll onto my side and smile at him. "We have the beach to ourselves."

In one fluid motion, he's on his feet. He shakes out his shirt and stabs his arms through the sleeves. "We should get back."

I sit up with a start. "What? Ww... why?"

He grabs my hand and yanks me to my feet. "'Cause it's getting late. Our sisters are probably wondering what's happened to us."

"They're fine. Your sister is practically another Anne LaBastille."

"Who?"

"A famous woodswoman." I tug his hand. "Let's stay on the beach a while longer. It's not *that* late, and we have a lot of catching up to do."

He shakes his head. "It's not happening, Jones. Put it out of your mind."

"My mind wasn't where I was hoping you'd put it." Pouting, I dust the sand off my butt. "Cooper McCaffrey, are you a virgin? Or a Mormon?"

Laughing, he scratches his brow. "I'm just a decent guy who respects you."

"Oh, wow. I got nothing."

"C'mon." He ignores my teasing and offers me his hand.

We hold hands and follow the dark trail in the direction back to our campsite. Except for the murmurs of families and groups around fire pits, it's quiet. I'd much rather be butt-naked with him on the beach, getting sand in uncomfortable places, but his warm, solid hand holding mine is unexpectedly nice, a nod to closeness, to shared affection. Maybe that handholding, speed-walking couple in my neighborhood isn't so ridiculous. Handholding is rather enjoyable.

Twenty feet or so away, the flames of our site's campfire cast the girls sitting around the pit into sharp relief. I tug Cooper's hand to make him stop walking.

"I want to thank you for this, for bringing me here," I say, turning toward him. "I'll still have to face the craziness when we get back to civilization, but this little reprieve has been great. I feel calm, re-centered, ready to take on whatever I need to."

"Good." He smiles. "I'm glad to help. And I'm glad you trusted me to help."

"I've always trusted you."

"Not always."

My face warms.

"Do you ever wonder about the years of friendship we missed, how different things would be between us if it weren't for that night?" He sounds more curious than regretful.

Through the screen of darkness, I see his face, the angular jaw, the defined cheekbones. Training with Cooper the last month and a half has given me time to study him up close, to appreciate the man he's become. He is part comfortably familiar, part excitingly unknown, and I'm feeling like I want to stick around and get more familiar with the unknown parts.

I grip his hand a little tighter. "We can't get those lost years back, but I'm glad we reconnected. Glad we're friends again... Or whatever we are."

"Yeah, me too." He leans in to brush my lips with a chaste kiss and then starts walking toward the campfire, where our sisters are chatting and roasting marshmallows, their faces glowing in the firelight.

I fall asleep that night on my blow-up mattress overheated with provocative thoughts of Cooper. A future with him feels inevitable. With the misconceptions of our youth and Troy out of the way, nothing is stopping us.

My eyes flutter open at the soft hum of the tent zipper. I barely register the brightness of the morning light when my ankle is seized in a vice-like grip. Cooper leans into the tent, a smile on his face. I twist and try to pull my leg away, but he grabs both my ankles and pulls me off the mattress. My butt plops on the cool, hard ground, but I'm laughing.

"Oh my *god*," Kara grumbles and rolls over. "Will you two get a room already?"

Cooper and I catch each other's eye.

"Shorts and sneakers, Jones. Last run through the camp before we pack up." He releases me and backs out of the tent. "And head back to loud, messy civilization."

If I had the choice, I might prefer to stay in the woods, but since that's not feasible, I'll put my game face on and try to hold onto a bit of the Zen-like calm the weekend has given me.

TWELVE

"What do you think?" I spin around in the kitchen, dressed for Jess's graduation party.

Mom found a cherry red dress in her closet for me to wear, tags still attached—no surprise. She gave it to me when we returned from camping, and said she had a feeling I would look amazing in it. It felt like we'd come to a truce of some sort. For now, the animosity between us is a burden off my shoulders.

"You look wonderful," my mother says, and I warm to the rare compliment.

The dress fits me perfectly. The straight-cut neckline, daringly low for me, shows off a tempting hint of cleavage. The tight skirt, a long expanse of leg.

"Not fair. With you wearing that, no one will look at me." Kara narrows her eyes.

I know I look good. Working out five days a week, my body is toned and tight, but my sister's envy is the supreme compliment.

My sister insists on changing and makes us late for the party. I invite Mom to join us. I know the family wouldn't mind, but she makes excuses. After parking the Impala in front of the McCaffreys' house, I switch off the ignition.

Kara flips the visor mirror down for one last makeup check, and satisfied, she snaps it back into place. "Ready?"

The party is an end to a good week. We returned from camping to a full-blown media whirlwind, the town buzzing with the commotion between Troy, Zoe, and me. Eyes followed me the moment I walked into the gym right until I left. However, the time tucked away strengthened my armor. I kept my chin up and got to work. Focused, I could ignore the unimportant stuff. If people wanted to waste their time on such matters, so be it.

Music spills out from the yard as we walk up the driveway. Kara is a step ahead, eager to get to the party. Despite my confidence in how I look, my stomach is doing flips, because of Cooper. The night on the beach turned a corner for us. The cat's out of the bag. We not only like one another, but we're also attracted to each other.

A light breeze from the bay travels down my bare back, cooling my heated skin as Kara and I stand at the entrance to the yard and take in Jess's night sky theme. Earlier weather threatened to ruin the town's high school graduation, but it held out and the overcast cover has turned into a creamy sherbet-colored night sky. The backyard, dimming with twilight, is decorated with countless strings of glittery star lights, candles, and bamboo torches. Glow-in-the-dark stars are scattered across the tabletops, and a strobe light that throws white specks across the grass has the effect of a meteor shower. The thumping beat of music infuses the party with a dance club vibe. Hired wait staff dressed in black and white zip around and in between people, picking up the empty cups and plates.

I scan the crowd for the new graduate and find Jess in the center of a makeshift dance floor surrounded by a pack of girls her age, bopping to the music. Mrs. McCaffrey is standing nearby, and I drag Kara with me to say hello.

"Jayden, Kara, so glad you could make it. You both look wonderful." She hugs each of us. "Jess is on the dance floor, and Cooper is... somewhere around here. Please have something to eat, and enjoy yourselves."

Kara spots a few girls from school and leaves me to wander the party alone. At the buffet table, I run into the neighbors who I had met at Coach's wake, Toby and Claudia, with their adorable kids. Three of them, two girls with long silky hair and a boy, just a toddler.

"Having Jess right next door has spoiled us. She's our go-to babysitter, fantastic with the kids," Claudia says. "I don't know what we're going to do when she goes off to college in the fall."

I point out Kara and tell them she's a good kid, an experienced babysitter, and that she'll be a senior next year.

We are chatting breezily when a hand catches mine. The scent of Cooper, his clean soapy smell, his soft musky cologne, permeates the air around me, and my pulse bumps up. I turn and he kisses the side of my face.

"My mother just chased me out of the house to come and find you. She said you look beautiful." My body warms under his lingering, appreciative gaze. "She totally got that right. Coming up from behind, I thought Jess invited a supermodel."

My lips curl upward with the compliment. Classic Cooper, a charmer, quick to make just the right, thoughtful comment—a characteristic I've always liked about him.

I skim a palm across the fabric, stomach to hip. "The crafting of this body is owed in part to your meticulous training in the gym."

"Man, oh man." He tugs me into the throng of bodies gyrating to the loud music and begins moving to the beat. "I do good work."

"Laugh if you like, but you're an excellent trainer. Mean sometimes, but good," I say, mirroring his movements. "You're going to be an amazing teacher, coach, and mentor. Just like your dad."

He stops dancing and gawks at me. For a moment, I think I've said the wrong thing, until he pulls me to him and hugs me so hard, I'm sure he'll squeeze the life right out of me.

"People often say nice things to me." He's smiling, big and goofy. "But Jayden Jones, that's definitely the nicest thing you've said to me, ever."

"You make it sound like I never give compliments." I laugh.

"You don't. It's not your style."

"Hey." I pull back. "I do. It is, too."

"Name one nice thing you've said to me. Or anyone," he prods.

I swallow. "Well, I can't think of one on the spot, but I totally remember thinking nice things."

"You're a straight shooter, Jones." Laughing, he draws me to him, pulling me until my nose is buried in the crease of his collarbone. "That's what I love about you."

My heart leaps, but I tamp it down. The guy is happy, likely had a few drinks, and is loving on everyone.

"Jayden!" Jess swoops in and pulls me away from her brother. I let her drag me into the middle of a large group of girls, Kara one of them. We start bopping along to the chorused steps of the "Cha Cha Slide," followed by "Cotton Eye Joe." Cooper grins as he watches on, but eventually, I lose sight of him.

Several songs later, the line dancing ends and the DJ announces Jess is needed before they can serve the graduation cake and open the dessert bar. A mass exodus of the dance area ensues until Jess's whoop draws all attention. Heads turn to the tall lone figure who has come through the entrance gate.

Troy's graced us with his presence. Jess is ecstatic, and from the looks of it, so are all her friends. They rush up and mill around him, taking selfies and gawking at him. He's brought along a bag of MMA gloves and T-shirts branded with his name and image and hands them out.

I watch, noting his perfected role of celebrity, magnanimously giving each charmed party guest a few moments of his undivided attention, throwing his arm around their shoulders when they request a picture, flashing his newly whitened smile as he leans in, just enough, but not too much to be creepy. He looks directly at each face, his lips moving, probably asking their name, likely forgetting it as soon as they answer.

Troy has a new, synthetic existence. I am suddenly grateful to have flubbed the audition. What a relief that I'm not required to play a part in that world. As far as I'm concerned, Troy can keep it. I don't want any of it.

When the fanfare dies down, Troy ambles over to Cooper to shake hands, and the two of them appear to engage in friendly conversation. Out of the limelight, and without Zoe and his entourage, he acts a little more like the Troy we used to know. Maybe we haven't completely lost him.

Inside the McCaffrey house, I find the downstairs bathroom occupied and head up to the second-floor bathroom, sure Mrs. McCaffrey won't mind. I freshen up and shut off the light. The sounds of the party waft up from the yard through an open window at the back of the house, in Cooper's bedroom. I wander into the room, remembering the few times I'd been in it when we were still in high school. In the dusky light from the yard, I can see the room is neat, the bed made. A hint of his cologne lingers, and I inhale deeply.

"Turned on by the smell of his room. Girl, you got it bad," I whisper to myself.

Movement near the doorway makes me look up.

"Find anything you like?" Cooper prowls toward me.

My legs turn to jelly. "I forgot how much your room smells like you."

"Is that a good thing?" He brushes against me, pushing me up against the wall next to the door.

My hand snakes up his chest and curls around the back of his head, playing with the short hair at the nape of his neck.

"Mm mm," I murmur. "I always liked the way you smelled, even right after wrestling practice."

His hands, warm and large, take purchase of my waist, tilting me toward him. Our pelvises bump together and in unison, we both emit throaty sounds of pleasure.

He lowers his head toward me slowly, his eyes on mine, giving me time to move away. If he thinks I'm going to stop him, he's dead wrong. I arch into him, meeting him, eager to feel his mouth on mine.

Cooper tastes like the smoky scent of bourbon he's been drinking. Our kisses hit me like a drug, and I feel myself coming apart under his lips. His hand flexes, laying claim to my hip, and slides warmly up my ribcage. I hum approvingly, and he skirts around the underside of my breast, caressing the outer edge with his thumb.

"You're so beautiful, Jayden," he whispers against my lips.

"Cooper?" an urgent male voice barks from somewhere downstairs.

He slumps, pinning me against the wall, and growls into my hair. He tips his forehead to mine. "Jayden, I want us to do this the right way."

"What's considered the right way these days?" I ask, deliberately shifting against the hard ridge along the front of his gray chinos.

"Ummmph." He squeezes me tight and trembles. "The right way is alone, with lots of time to explore."

"Cooper?" the voice comes again.

"I'm coming!" he yells over his shoulder. Turning back, he locks eyes with me and inhales deeply. "I haven't stopped thinking about you since camping. How about we meet up after the party's over? I'm dog-sitting for a friend down the block. They have a nice private yard. I'll bring a blanket."

"Sounds perfect." A huge smile dominates my face.

He cups my chin and kisses me again. With a sigh, he steps into the doorway but turns to let his gaze drag over me one last time before he returns to the call of duty.

As I slowly make my way downstairs, back to the party, my cell buzzes with a text from Cooper, an address and a request: *Wear that dress.*

I press a hard fist to my lips to stifle my laughter—otherwise, I might shriek with joy. Cooper McCaffrey wants me. This is going to happen. Finally!

Outside, there's a chorus of regret because Troy has announced that he's leaving. He hugs both Jess and her mother and waves goodbye to his adoring, hormonally driven, cherub-faced fan club. I am in the direct line to the exit. He can't avoid me.

"Hey, Jay." His eyes dance over me, up and down and back again. "Wow, you look amazing. Seriously."

"Thanks." I lift my chin, my body still flush from kissing Cooper. "I've been sparring and training with Cooper at his gym."

"Oh yeah?" He licks his bottom lip, a nervous tick. I'm tempted to remind him that doing it makes his lips chap. "Jay, about what happened at Docksides, I didn't know Zoe was going to be there. Ben planned the publicity stunt without telling me."

"I figured as much," I say. Despite what's happened between us, Troy's never been intentionally cruel. Stupid maybe, but never cruel.

"Ben was practically foaming at the mouth at the way it went down. Figured the more riled up you got, the more likely you'd take the fight." He shakes his head. "But you're going back to law school in the fall, so it's a moot point."

"That's the plan. But they've made it clear—the offer still stands. I can still take the fight." I smile and cross my arms. "Wouldn't that be interesting?"

"Yeah, that'd really be something. Zoe's going places. Her first professional fight is going to be a big draw," he says, all brag. "I can train with you, see what you got, and let you know if I think you're up for it."

"Train me to take a fight against your girlfriend? You're kidding."

He reddens under his tan. "Zoe's got plenty of trainers, and I just figured, being that we're friends and all."

"After everything that's happened, do you honestly think we can still be friends, Troy?"

"I hope so." His expression softens.

The DJ pumps up the volume, and Troy leans closer, his hand on the small of my back. "Listen, I'm staying with my dad for a while. If you want to stop over, that'd be cool. He'd be happy to see you."

He's trying to smooth things out between us and not be a dick. My anger at him loses its edge. Maybe partly because I'm still tingly from the sexy interlude in Cooper's bedroom, and that I'm filled with anticipation of being with him later tonight. The bubble of happiness makes it easier to be magnanimous toward Troy.

"Sure. Maybe."

"Great." His smile is hopeful. "Call or stop by anytime."

"Okay," I say.

As Troy exits the yard, I turn back to the party and find Cooper's eyes on me from across the way, his expression curiously somber.

Kara appears at my side. "You picking up where you left off with Troy?"

"Not on your life. He's just angling to be friends again."

Cooper's eyes fall away as he converges into conversation with a table full of middle-aged couples, likely parents of Jess's school friends.

"Back when you guys were in high school, I always thought you'd end up with Cooper." My sister is watching me, aware I'm tracking him. "I mean, you and Troy were close, like goofball buddies. But when Cooper walked into the room, you used to light up. He was the same way."

I swing my gaze to her. "You noticed that?"

"It was hard not to," she replies.

"You never said anything."

She shrugs. "You're my big sister. You were like crazy smart in school. I figured you knew."

"I didn't, and I made a lot of mistakes." I glance at Cooper again and take a deep breath. "But I'm getting it right, finally."

Over the din of the partygoers, the DJ calls Mrs. McCaffrey and Jess to the dance floor.

"This is a special request by the graduation girl for her mother," the DJ says.

The first few notes of "The Time of My Life," the theme song from *Dirty Dancing,* begins.

From beside the DJ, Jess announces, "This was my parent's wedding song." Everyone stops to watch the new graduate walk toward Mrs. McCaffrey, take her hand, and escort her to the center of the dance floor. Jess kisses her mother's cheek, both sets of eyes wet with emotion, and the two slowly sway to the music.

Over her shoulder, Jess beckons to Cooper. He hesitates for only a moment before he heads toward his mother and sister. Spreading his arms wide, he embraces them both, and then, hands joined, he twirls Jess and Mrs. McCaffrey slowly around the dance floor. The DJ invites everyone up to join the family, and soon they are surrounded, encircled by their closest friends. My vision is blurred by my tears when Kara presses her shoulder against me, her hand finding mine. I lace my fingers in hers, knowing she feels exactly what I am feeling—we are missing our father while we witness the McCaffreys missing theirs.

After the dance, Cooper gets swept up in the needs of guests preparing to leave. I can't get a moment alone with him.

"I'll see ya later," I call out to him, which he acknowledges with a hasty wave.

Kara and I say our goodbyes and drive home. I put the car into Park and leave it running.

"Going out again?" Kara asks.

"Yep. Meeting up with Cooper."

"You covered in the BYOC department?"

"I have zero idea what you're talking about."

My sister sighs dramatically and unzips her clutch. "BYOC: bring your own condoms. With that dress, I have a feeling you're going to need them."

My jaw nearly hits the floor when she pulls out not one but a string of prophylactics. I want to balk because my baby sister is carrying Trojans, but I can't lecture her. We haven't been all that close the last few years. At least she's being safe.

"Here's three." She separates a few from the cord and holds them out to me. "Underneath that mild-mannered politeness, I'm willing to bet Cooper's got some stamina in the sack."

I slap a hand to my forehead. "I'm not even sure I'll need one, let alone three."

"Better to be safe than sorry." She shakes the packets at me.

I push them away. "Sure way to look desperate, like I'm begging for it."

"Begging?" She cocks an eye at me and grabs my clutch. "I've never met a guy who turned away an opportunity to get laid."

I chuckle. "I used to think that, but that's not been my experience."

"Seriously? Are you saying you had to beg Troy for it?"

"Not beg," I retract. For most of our time together, Troy and I had been on different college campuses. After months apart, sex was expected, part of our reunion, but my appetite for sex proved greater than Troy's. "I had to initiate most times."

"That's nothing to be ashamed of," she says. "But most guys are horn-dogs. It's like their radars are tuned to pick up on any whiff of action, actual or perceived."

"High school boys are different." As Troy's best friend, I witnessed him go through a gamut of girls. We never got into explicit details back then, but I knew who he was sleeping with. He'd been different with them. More engaged. Quicker to blow off plans with me to see them. "Guys your age are more hormonal and have much less responsibility."

"Maybe, but there definitely won't be any begging on your part tonight." She tucks the condoms inside my wristlet and hands it to me. "When the action starts, believe me, your boy will be glad you have these."

"He's not *my boy*," I mumble, even though the thrill of possibility bubbles inside me.

"Yeah, sure," she throws over her shoulder and exits the car.

I wait until Kara enters the house and then head back toward the neighborhood where Cooper texted me he's dog-sitting. The small, meticulously kept home is on the east side of the channel that leads out onto the bay, the last residence before the ferry service. The front door is open and interior light spills over the front steps. Cooper sits in a rocking chair on the open front porch, stroking the fur of a small white dog on his lap. He's changed out of his party clothes into tan shorts and a yellow polo shirt.

"Nice house. Is the dog friendly?" I ask as I climb the short set of steps to meet him. The dog wags her tail and raises her snout to encourage interaction.

"Luna's a sweetheart." He holds her as I pet the dog's soft white head. "I didn't think you'd come."

"Why?"

"I don't know." His expression unreadable, he puts Luna down and motions to me to follow him and the little dog inside. "Figured you changed your mind."

I blink, wondering if I've missed something. "Well, I'm here, aren't I?"

"You are." With a shrug, he cruises around a counter to the small galley kitchen and opens the refrigerator. It's filled with rows and rows of green and brown bottles of beer. "Joe's into craft beers, but Gabe's into wine. They keep a few bottles of wine chilling. Red or white?"

He pulls out two bottles and shows them to me.

"Red." I need something to settle my nerves. "You have a few drinks at the party?"

"Yeah. With Jess's lacrosse coach. Good guy. Likes to drink. I made sure his wife drove them home." He pours me a glass and puts the bottle away.

I reach for the wine, my nerves jangled with what's to come. "You're making me drink alone?"

"Oh, I had enough. Switched over to water." He points to a glass of water half full on the counter. "Alcohol dehydrates."

This makes me think of high school keggers. Cooper would drink beer, just like one of the guys, but unlike Troy and many others who drank until obliterated, Cooper protected the body he'd labored for by interspersing water and food between his beer consumption. The guy is nothing if not responsible. I have long appreciated his confidence in being himself, in being Cooper McCaffrey, uninfluenced by peers. That confidence is crazy sexy.

He finishes the glass of water and sweeps by me on his way further into the house. Luna's nails click-click on the hardwood floors. The house is modest, decorated in a modern Scandinavian-Ikea style—understated fussiness. Cooper tells Luna to place, and she obediently goes to her doggie bed. We pass through a den to a set of French doors that lead out to a multi-leveled wooden deck that faces Brown's River, the narrow body of water that empties into the Great South Bay. The small yard, bathed in the pale glow of the moon and filled with the flickering dots of light from a network of lightning bugs, carries the unmistakable scent of brackish water, a salty, musty bog. Except for the distant hum of an outboard motor and the chorus of chirping bugs, it's quiet.

Down three steps to a small built-in pool, another short set of steps leads to the grassy landing that ends in a bulkhead. There's a small watercraft tied to a mooring. Tall pampas grass sways in the evening breeze as the waves slap against the bulkhead wall. Off in the distance, the homes on Fire Island, the strip of land off the coast of Long Island, glow like a string of lights.

"Great view, right?" Cooper sweeps his arms upward with comical the-atrical flair.

"Yes, it's a pretty sky." But I'm more interested in checking out his butt, and the way his twill khaki shorts hug the hard roundness of each cheek.

In his room earlier he'd said: *The right way is alone, with lots of time to explore.* I can't wait to explore that body, naked. I silently thank Kara for making me take the condoms.

Cooper has a slow and tentative approach, but that's never been my speed. I'm more than ready to move forward. And, thanks to my sister, I am well-prepared, and for three rounds. Three! That's a personal record I wouldn't mind setting with Cooper, though right now, one solid shag would appease me.

I toss my wristlet onto a wooden outdoor dining table and reach for his hand, but he moves again, and I miss my target.

He lopes down the steps, heading toward the water, but the last step messes him up and he stumbles. I try to smother a laugh but don't succeed.

"It's a wonder you could make the walk down the street without falling."

"The last step is crooked," he says.

"Clearly." I give the expensive wooden deck a stern look-over. "Definitely the steps and not because you're drunk."

"I'm not drunk," he says. "I'm … under the influence. There's a difference."

"And the difference is?"

"All my faculties are functioning normally, but the edges are less defined." He picks up the line mooring the boat to the dock and undoes the knot.

I take a sip of wine. It tastes amazing, but I put it down on the edge of the deck and wander closer to watch what he's doing. He grew up around boats. Most kids around here did.

"Cooper under the influence—an unusual occurrence." I rest my hands on his back, feeling his muscles move as he efficiently refastens the knot. "I don't recall you ever getting plastered in high school. Why was that?"

"I don't like not being in control of myself," he says, and satisfied with his knot, he stands at his full height. "It was good of Troy to stop by tonight."

"Well, your sister and her friends certainly enjoyed his visit."

"From what I saw, seems you did too."

I nearly snort. *Enjoy his visit* might be a little too overzealous of narrative.

"It's the first time we've had a civil conversation since Vegas."

"What did you talk about?" Cooper asks, continuing to face the water.

"We covered quite a bit," I say. "He apologized for the scene with Zoe and told me I looked good, for which I gave you credit. Then we talked about law school and the fight offer."

His arms go stationary. "What did he say about the fight with Zoe?"

"I don't know. That Zoe's first professional fight is going to be a big draw. He was being nice. Trying to get back into my good graces, I guess." I rub his back in slow circles. "Offered to train with me, see if I'm anywhere ready to compete against her."

"Really? And are you taking him up on that?"

"Hmm." I press up against him, wrapping my arms around his waist.

"What's that *hmm* mean?"

"Sounds like you're trying to change the subject away from your fascinating, rare state of inebriation. I'm much more interested in getting a peek at what makes Cooper McCaffrey tick." I slide my hands up under his shirt, feeling the musculature of his stomach and chest, distinctly punch-drunk with lust.

He turns and captures my hands, ceasing their movement. "Are you trying to take advantage of my fascinating, rare, inebriated state?"

"Maybe." I sway into him. "Is that okay?"

Without letting him answer, I arch up against him and press my mouth to his. His lips and breath hold the sweet residue of liquor and spearmint gum. His hands slide up my back to hold me to him. Our kiss explodes with an edge of desperation. Resisting each other has wound us tightly, and now, the walls are knocked away.

His hands are in my hair; my fingers are digging into his back; our tongues do a mating dance. I bend my knees, and we sink down onto the damp, grassy embankment. Cooper's solid weight falls atop me, fanning the flames of want and searing off any thought past physical sensation.

He tilts his head back slightly, allowing me to trail my mouth down his neck. His soft moan spurs me forward. I push a hand inside his shorts, but he catches my wrist before I can touch him and pins both of my hands to the ground with one of his.

The tall grass sways around us like a curtain. I don't move, don't resist. I stay still, tingling with anticipation. His scent fills my nostrils.

He is catnip. And I am the cat.

His eyes darken as his attention scrapes over my face and down to my chest, rising and falling with my rapid breaths. His free hand caresses my face, but the force of his touch grows stronger as it moves lower to cup my left breast. Leaning in, he presses his weight into me, letting me feel the strength of his desire. He releases my hands to hold my face as he kisses me harder, grinding up against me in a way that hurts so good, that I simultaneously want him to stop and never want him to stop. His kiss deepens, his tongue demanding my response while his hands trail down my dress, slow and thorough, familiarizing themselves with my curves.

His lips move down my neck, stopping to pay homage to the top half of my cleavage exposed by the low cut of the dress. He cups one breast and squeezes. Sensation rockets to my core and a sob-like moan jumps from my lips. He's barely touched my erogenous zones, and already I'm a hot mess.

I'm disappointed when he shifts away but much more excited when he kisses his way south, down the bodice of my dress. Through the satiny fabric, the heat of his mouth claims my body with each drugging press of his lips. The heat intensifies when he reaches my pelvis. His large hands fight the resistant hem of my dress, caressing and teasing the sensitive skin of my thighs. Not far from his mouth, the space between my legs clamors for his undivided attention. My underwear is a scrap of fabric that won't get in the way, but once he gets there, my dress will be a major encroachment. For the main attraction, an event years in the making, I want it off.

I'm ready to get naked and busy but remember the condoms in my purse—on the outdoor table, yards away. After my breakup with Troy,

I stopped taking my birth control. Frustrated, I push softly at Cooper's shoulders hitting the pause button for this necessary step of safety.

"I saw a nice big chaise lounge on the deck," I whisper. "It'll be more comfortable than this ground."

I stand and hold out my hand to him, my upper thighs tingly and slick with want. His face and shoulders, the hardness of his body, command my awareness. I have to take a deep breath because I am shaken by how much I want this guy, how much I want to know every inch of his well-built masculine body. He sits up and slowly brings his gaze up to meet mine. Those green eyes are hooded and somewhat out of focus like I've awoken him from a deep dream. Clearly the effects of the alcohol capped by the unmistakable scent of our sexy foray.

"Cooper," I call to him and wiggle the fingers of my outstretched hand. Once we're armed with the necessary precautions, I'm certain the clarity of our objective will return. We have time, privacy, and three condoms to put the world in focus again.

He slides his hand into mine and climbs to his feet. Impatiently, I haul him back onto the deck but am forced to slow down as he climbs the "crooked" steps.

I rush ahead of him to grab my bag and sit on the wide, blue-striped cushioned lounger.

"Come here, Cooper." I pat the cushion next to me. He hasn't moved past the steps. Clarity has returned to his eyes, and with it, a tight set to his jaw. Anxiety rises in my chest, but even so, I get up and approach him, pressing against him to brush my lips over his. He doesn't respond.

The interruption to change location was a mistake. The magic is falling away.

"Let's sit down." I wind my hand around his and try to lead him to the lounger, but he's an anvil at the end of my arm.

"Are you taking Troy up on his offer?"

"What?" I turn to look at him, confused as to why we're still talking about Troy.

"To train. Are you going to train with him?"

I blink. "Train with him? I haven't thought about it."

He tugs his hand away and turns his back to me.

"What's happening?"

"I'm sorry. I thought I was ready for ... this." His voice is detached, far away.

"Cooper, you want this to happen," I coax. "You sent me the address. You said to wear this dress."

"Because I enjoy looking at you *in* it."

"I look pretty fantastic out of it, too. Let me show you." I reach behind me, but he captures my hands before I can touch the zipper.

"Don't." There's a vibration in his hands; he's trembling. "There's only so much a guy can take."

"We had to change location to be safe, not to stop." I move closer, pressing up against him. "I brought protection."

He grabs my waist and sets me a few inches away from him.

"Jayden, stop," he says with a terse breath.

"Just lay back on the lounge. I'll do all the work."

"You are relentless." A short, harsh laugh accompanies his smile, but he shakes his head and sets me farther away.

"If this is because you're grieving, I get it. Just tell me."

"It's not about my grief."

"Well then, I don't understand why you're making this so difficult." Irritation rises inside me. "Don't you want to be with me?"

"I do and I don't."

"What does that mean?"

His gaze slips low, and he inhales. "When you really want something, you work hard to get it."

I stare at him. "Is this some kind of game?"

"No." He lowers his chin and pins me with his eyes. "Just maintaining a safe distance from those momentary urges of yours."

Humiliation burns my lungs. I cannot believe after all these years that Cooper McCaffrey is once again refusing me. And worse, I willingly put myself in that position. It's a repeat of our car scene, only now I've added more footage to the reel. He's the keeper of this nightmare, free to haunt me at will.

"You're an asshole." I bite out, my cheeks blazing.

He doesn't seem surprised by my anger. And I hate him just a bit more for that stupid self-control of his.

"You know, Jayden, sex isn't the answer to everything," he throws out as I march through the house, on my way back to my car.

I glance up as I get in the car and find him leaning in the doorway, arms crossed, calmly watching me leave.

Kara is wrong about guys and sex—at least when it comes to me. Apparently, I can be prepared and present a clear invitation, and still, it isn't enough.

Fighting for every inch with Cooper is exhausting. No more. I'm done chasing him.

THIRTEEN

Monday morning, I report to the gym as usual. Cooper is already there, clipboard in hand. He tells me of the day's schedule, the sparring and drills I'm to undertake with the fighters in training. He's all business, avoiding the weirdness between us. I mirror his attitude, listening and nodding. After he's finished, I put on my sparring gloves and start warming up on the bag, but he lingers.

"About Saturday night," he starts.

"Not doing this with you, Cooper. Whatever you have to say, keep it to yourself." With my eyes trained on the punching bag, I throw a combo of hooks and jabs. I prefer to never ever speak of this updated editor's cut version of my worst nightmare.

"Jayden." He stands between the bag and me, forcing me to either stop or punch him. "There's a lot of stuff going on in both of our lives. It's best if we don't rush blindly into something neither of us is ready for."

"But you started it! Remember, in your bedroom?" I raise a fist, tempted to hit him.

"I know. I'm sorry—"

"Wow. You sound *just like* Troy."

The comment lands exactly how I expect, silencing him for a measure.

"I *am not* Troy. I would never do what he did."

"I suppose you're right. You play at wanting sex. Troy didn't. We had sex, *a lot of it*, and it was very satisfying."

He pinches the bridge of his nose and breathes out my name, "*Jay-den*," slowly, like a teacher trying to retain composure after being unbuttoned by a disobedient student.

"There's nothing left to say. I'm done. Over it. Now move, so I can avoid the *momentary urge* to hit you."

He steps aside, a new wall up between us, and I refocus on my warm-up.

Van interrupts a moment later to say my mother is on the phone. I automatically assume something isn't right. She never calls the gym office phone.

"Did you take my car this morning?" she asks.

"No. I took the Impala, as usual," I say.

"My car is not here. Maybe your sister took it?"

"Kara has her own car. Why would she take yours?"

"It's due for an oil change. I've been distracted lately. She probably told me she was bringing it in for an oil change and I forgot." She laughs at herself.

"Do you need a ride to work?"

"No, no," she says. "I'll call a coworker."

The house is quiet after I return home from the gym. I'd made a quick stop at the corner farm stand, and now, with a grocery sack of fresh peppers, zucchini, and tomatoes, I head to the kitchen to make myself a three-egg veggie omelet and a protein shake.

The floorboards creak overhead. Someone is upstairs—though neither my mother nor Kara is supposed to be home. Seized with a rush of adrenaline, I grab the only weapon readily available, a broom, and stealthily climb the stairs. This dude's come to the wrong house.

As soon as I step into the hallway toward the bedrooms, I hear my mother's voice. I loosen my grip on the broom.

"When you get this message, please call me back." She sounds frantic.

Her door is open, but I rap my knuckles on the frame so as not to frighten her.

"Oh, honey," she says with a start, then eyes me curiously. "What are you doing with that broom?"

"Thought I was about to take out a burglar." I lean the broom against the wall. "Is everything all right?"

"Kara doesn't have my car. It was taken."

The hair stands up on the back of my neck. "Did you call the police?"

She nods. "They called back about an hour ago. It wasn't stolen. It was repossessed."

It takes several seconds for me to process what she's said.

"You're late on your payments?"

"I'm not," she counters with an indignant tone. "At least, I wasn't. The monthly payment is on autopay with my credit card."

"So, it's a mix-up. Call the credit card company."

"I did. They said my credit is over-extended."

"Oh, Mom, how could you let that happen? All this stuff you keep buying, you don't need any of it."

She presses her fingers to her mouth, anxiety in her eyes. There's more to this.

I sit down beside her. "Mom, what's going on?"

"I gave some money to Alejandro," she says.

"Doesn't he work for some kind of investment company? Why is he borrowing money from you?"

"He didn't borrow it. I *gave* it to him. To invest. He's working on a major overseas deal—a side deal—a retirement hotel for wealthy seniors. In Malta. He showed me photos. It's beautiful."

The starry-eyed look jars me.

"How much?" I ask.

"Five thousand ... at first."

I take a deep breath to muster patience. "How much did you give him, all together?"

"All together?" Her gaze arcs up and across the room. "I'm not exactly sure."

The answer decimates my semblance of patience. "*Oh my God*, Mom! Can't you see he's scamming you?"

"He isn't, Jayden, he isn't," she says forcefully. "After the hotel is finished, he's going to build a special convalescent wing for cancer patients, so family members can stay with their sick loved ones while they fight to rebuild their health. His mother died of that awful cancer, just like Daddy. This project is important to both of us."

Her brown eyes brim with tears she's trying hard to control. It takes everything I have not to argue with her because her heart was in the right place. She was thinking of Dad, thinking of families suffering through his disease as we did. It softens me, even though from where I'm standing, it's apparent she's caught up in a scam of some type. All I want to do is rip the veil off Alejandro. Expose him for the lowlife cretin he is and go after him.

That's how I'd handle it, but if there's one thing I now understand, my mother and I handle problems differently.

"Mom." I take a calming breath and reach for her hand. "Will you please let me look at all of your bank account and credit card statements since you met Alejandro?"

"You don't know him like I do." Her moist eyes are wide, pleading. "He did nothing wrong."

"Maybe you're right." Even as I say these words, I doubt them. "Let's just make sure. Let me see those statements."

A few hours and several phones call later, I'm convinced Alejandro is a fraudulent online dating scammer. His online profile is a series of professional photos. A reverse Google search of the emailed photos he sent to my mother of this supposed retirement hotel in Malta reveals an up-and-running resort that has nothing to do with seniors and isn't even in Malta.

I find the number to a special Online Crimes unit, but my mother isn't ready to give up on Alejandro even though, by my quick estimations, she's sunk three times the amount of money than what she's aware of or owning up to.

I'm ready to file a complaint, but Mom stops me.

"It's a mistake. A misunderstanding is all." Despite the conviction, she cries. "I want to talk to him first."

I make tea and pull down the blinds in her bedroom, hoping she'll rest. I search the internet for a number for Harvey & Sloane Investments. When I call, as I suspect, they don't have an employee by the name of Alejandro Flores. Whatever his real name is, he must have some financial background. He figured out how my mother could borrow against the equity in the house to give him money for his so-called investment. The mortgage, nearly paid off when I left for college, has new statements that show there's now a substantial amount owed. She's borrowed heavily on the equity. With her office job salary, she'll never get ahead of this new debt.

The grim numbers rattle me, and even more so when I research legal compensation for such cases. I pull up the number for my academic advisor at Brooklyn Law, Professor Dumfries, and hit the call button. We'd last talked when she gave me that pep talk, trying to save me from a nonexistent abusive relationship. While she'd misread that situation, she'd rightly perceived that I needed to be called out and redirected to save my GPA. Though my future in law is uncertain, her support and genuine interest in my success during my time at BLS brand her a discernable ally.

Dumfries, surprised by my call, has an upbeat tenor to her voice that suggests she is happy to hear from me. After a few moments of pleasantries and assuring her that I am perfectly okay, home with my family, I explain my mother's situation, hoping her studied, professional knowledge will yield a route, a loophole to explore, to recoup some of the money taken and maybe even punish Alejandro for his cruel dishonesty.

"She should immediately stop all communication with this man and report him to the dating site. She can also lodge a complaint with the Federal Trade Commission and the FBI." The sounds of her typing on her keyboard carry across our connection. "I'll email you a link to the form where your mother can explain the details of her experience, but unfortunately, other than those few steps, there's not much law enforcement and these agencies can do. Likely, the money will not be recovered. Federal agencies rarely track down perpetrators of these types of crimes," she says. "With how prevalent this crime is, it's clear these guys know exactly how far they can push and still stay untraceable by the law."

Exactly as I had thought.

"My mother thought she was doing good, helping this guy. She doesn't realize how easily people can pretend to be something they're not, especially online," I say stiffly, aware of how this colors my mother unsophisticated, naïve.

"It's not her fault. These people are predators who know exactly how to appeal to and manipulate lonely individuals, those desperate for a connection, as so many are."

Lonely. Desperate for a connection. It's difficult to connect my mother with that description.

"I appreciate your time, professor."

"My pleasure, and Jayden," she pauses. "How are you doing with the mission statement? I went ahead and scripted a letter of recommendation to go along with your statement to send to the scholarship board."

"I'm working on it," I say. Nothing says fraud like lying to people who only want to help you.

I miss her and dare I say, I miss my classes. The work and the deep, philosophical conversations challenged everything I thought I knew and believed in. But law school seems like a distant thought. Another life. Right now, my mother—who is lonely and desperate for a connection—needs my help to get out of this mess.

The payout for the fight with Zoe would easily absorb Mom's money woes and then some.

I stare out the front bay window, blowing the bangs out of my eyes. Diagonally across the street, a sleek white Lexus SUV is parked in the Murphys' driveway next to an older sedan. Troy is home as he said he'd be. Without consciously knowing what I'll say, I cross the street and walk up the driveway, as I've done thousands of times. After all these years, I can still make out the rut in the grass where Troy and I used to cut across the lawn with our bicycles. The same doorbell chimes, *bing-bong*, when I push the button next to the front door.

"Jay 'The Bruiser' Jones!" Mr. Murphy's face beams with delight. We embrace. It's been so long since I've seen him. My eyes mist over. As Troy told me, Mr. Murphy looks much the same, but the hair atop his head is thinner, and the lines around his eyes are more profound. His belly is rounder, too.

"I've seen you coming and going this summer. I've been hoping you'd stop in and say hello," he says.

"I'm sorry I haven't come over sooner." I wonder how much he knows about what's happening between his son and me.

"No need to apologize. I know you're busy. We're all busy," he says, but his dismissive wave humbles me. I stay put and take a few minutes to ask him questions and catch up with him. When I decline an offer of something to drink, he motions to the back of the house. "Troy is out in the yard. You remember the way?"

"Sure do," I say, and he leaves me with a wink.

In the kitchen, the angle of the late sun illuminates an accumulation of dust and long-abandoned crumbs clotted against base moldings. Slowing my stride, I take in the old stained wooden cabinetry, already outdated when Troy and his father first moved into the neighborhood, the room's bare white walls, the distinct lack of color and personality. No tossed clothing or pocketbooks, mislaid bottles of nail polish, or hair bands. A simplicity that was a comfort to my younger self.

Now though, it feels a bit sad, ignored, a place I'd dodge rather than seek.

Past the kitchen, a sliding glass door opens to the treed backyard and an in-ground lap pool. The yard is a startling shock of color and texture one wouldn't expect after the shabby front yard and stark interior. A single man with one grown child, Mr. Murphy has a lot of time on his hands, and clearly, he spends a lot of it in the backyard. It's an oasis. Bushes of every shape and height are bordered by arresting colors of flowering annuals. Hydrangea bushes, heavy with melon-sized flowers, catch my eye. The mowed grass is like a carpet that surrounds a line of gray polished stepping stones leading to the pool, where the pristine water gleams under the summer sun. The top of the water ripples with swells as Troy cuts through it with smooth, even freestyle strokes. I stand at the edge and wait for him to bring his head out of the water.

The Murphys' backyard holds years of memories, of summers spent in bathing suits, running back and forth between our houses, swimming in each other's pools, catching fireflies, and eating at each other's picnic tables.

"Hey." Troy splashes water at my ankles and ends my reminiscing. All six-plus feet rise out of the water in one fluid motion. He is built like a warrior, wide at the shoulders, tapering down to a distinct row of muscled abs and long, powerful legs. Time, focus, and coaching have changed his clumsy former gait into one that is lithe, sure-footed, graceful even.

"Feel like swimming?" Troy towel-dries his face and hair. "The water feels great."

I shake my head.

"Jay?" He approaches. "What's wrong?"

I don't say a word, and yet, he knows something is up. That's how it is when you've spent as much time together as we have. It hurts to think he's thrown us away, but right now, I need him.

"It's my mother. She messed up, big time," I say.

We sit on chaise lounges, facing each other, and I tell him about my mother and her swindler boyfriend.

"Wow, that sucks. How's your mom taking it?"

"She's in denial. She thinks if only she speaks to him, he'll be able to explain where all the money went. That this is all a mistake. The woman is delusional."

"Don't be so hard on her," Troy says. "This guy's intentions might seem obvious to you and all of us outside the situation, but like it or not, he must give your mother something she needs, something she isn't getting elsewhere."

A near repeat of the professor's summation. Troy knows my mother, and despite the issues between him and me, with my mother, his concern is sincere. He's always had a soft spot for her.

"I just don't know how we're going to get her out of this. Her savings are gone." I wring my hands. "And this morning, her car got repossessed."

"The cops *have to* find this guy," he snaps.

"It's unlikely they'll ever catch him. The money is gone. For good," I say. "She'll be in a significant financial hole for the foreseeable future."

That reality quiets me.

"Sin City offered you a sizeable payout to do an interview," he says. "Do it. Take the money."

"You're giving me the green light to trash you and our relationship on TV?"

"I can handle it." There's an earnest look to his expression. "And I understand if you want to. I messed up. I deserve it."

"You'll get no argument from me about that. But open my life up and feed this media frenzy? No, thank you. Not even to get back at you. My privacy is too important." I slide my gaze to his face. "But I've been thinking about taking the fight."

Troy jerks back. "Go up against Zoe?"

"Yes, it's a lot of money—even if I lose."

"Jay, that's not a good idea." He reaches across to hold my hand.

I stand, breaching our contact. "Why? Is Zoe too precious to you?"

"That's not it. I just..." He stands, too. "You're a good wrestler, and you look amazing, but Zoe, she's been fighting at a professional level for the past year. Out of your league."

He shoots an arrow directly into my heart.

"I don't know why I came here." I turn away before he sees tears of frustration burning my eyes.

Troy grabs my arm and forces me to turn toward him.

"Zoe's roundhouse kicks. They're lethal. In her last two show fights, she fractured one fighter's orbital socket and gave the other a concussion."

Having already been on the receiving end of Zoe's footwork, I don't have to imagine the pain and damage.

"It wigs me out thinking that could happen to you." His gaze softens. "I have money, Jay. I'll give you whatever you need. Let me help you. Let me help your family."

He pulls me into a hug. I don't resist. In fact, I burrow into his arms and press my face to his chest. It's been months since I've been in contact with Troy's tall, rigid frame, and I can't help but notice how our bodies fit differently, more awkwardly. And the carnal attraction we once shared is nonexistent. Other than the comfort of being hugged, I feel nothing.

"I miss you, Jay," Troy whispers.

As much as I don't want to admit it, I miss him, too. I tighten my arms around him and feel the solidness of him, the durability that got me through those dark days and nights after my father died.

"Why did you have to go and ruin everything? If you had told me how you felt, we could have stayed friends."

"I never meant to hurt you. Will you ever forgive me?" The pain and guilt in his voice mirror the emotion in his blue eyes.

"You really hurt me. I need time," I say.

"Of course. Take all the time you need." He brushes his lips against my forehead, continuing to hold me. "For now, please let me help your family."

Considering what Troy's put me through, letting him slide in to save the day instantly raises my hackles. Throwing his money about won't absolve him.

I remember my father, years ago, advising poor but proud East End farmworkers: "When times are tough, don't be too proud to accept a hand up."

If I let Troy help this one time it won't be charity, just a helping hand. Help that my mother needs and help that will allow me to refuse the fight offer, take a breather, and re-evaluate where I am and where I'm headed, wherever that is.

Even so, I reluctantly accept his offer and saunter across the street thinking about what comes next. I love working at the gym, but is that the future I want? Then, there's the tension between Cooper and me, knowing he knows I want him but still refusing me. Once he finds out Troy is going to help me, things are bound to get uglier.

With a sigh, I enter the house and head upstairs to retrieve the unfinished mission statement sitting on my dresser. It's time to shift gears and get back to reality.

FOURTEEN

Outside, the sky rumbles with a summer thunderstorm. I'm shoveling a spoonful of sugary breakfast cereal into my mouth with one hand. With the other, I'm searching on my cell for work as a paralegal assistant. My screen switches to an incoming call. Cooper. I take a deep breath and swipe to answer.

"Where are you?" His agitated voice hits my ear.

I skipped this morning's training and am still in my pajamas, but I'd been expecting his call.

"I took the day off. Marcus knows. I messaged him. My mother needed my car." Without a preamble, I continue. "To be honest, I'm not sure I'm coming back. I'm looking for other work."

"You're quitting the gym?" His tone bristles with annoyance.

"It's not working out for me."

"Is this sudden decision because of me—and what happened the other night?"

"Contrary to what you might believe, Cooper, not everything is about you," I snap and hang up.

Fifteen minutes later, the doorbell rings.

Not in the mood for the lecture that's sure to come, I drag myself to the front door and tug it open. But even with the challenging set of his jaw, in his shorts and tight T-shirt and hair, wet from the rain, the sight of Cooper jacks up my hormones. And I despise him for it.

I lean against the door frame and cross my arms. "Yeah?"

Pushing the door open wider, he lets himself into the house. I step back. He closes the door, shutting the rain out, and turns to face me. "Jayden, what's going on?"

"I told you—"

"Halfway through the summer, you up and quit your job, a job you love?"

"It was only ever meant to be a temporary job, something to hold me over until I went back to law school."

"No doubt," he replies. "But the summer's not over. What's driving your decision?"

I glance away, unable—or unwilling—to tell him. It's one thing to tell Troy, who knows my family and whose own family has issues, but it's another to tell Cooper, whose family is ideal and unblemished, of our gossip-provoking troubles. "There's some stuff going on."

"What kind of stuff?" he pushes.

"Family stuff I'd rather not get into." I rub my shoulder. "But I talked to Troy and—"

"Troy?" He pivots, pinning me with his glare. "What's he got to do with this?"

I pinch the inside of my wrist to resist snarling at him.

"I told him I needed money and was thinking about taking the fight against Zoe. Like you, he's against it." I wrap my arms around myself and proceed prudently. "He's going to help me out, so I don't need to take the fight."

"Troy's giving you money?" Tension, like waves, rolls off his shoulders.

Unable to look at him, I press my lips together and nod.

"What, so like, all's forgiven now? You take him back, take his advice and bailout money, and he gets to play hero—*again*?" He might as well have drawn a sword.

"Again?" I grit my teeth, brandishing my own sword. "What's that supposed to mean?"

"You know what I mean," he says. "After your father died, you ran to him. Right into his bed."

I bite my tongue to keep myself from lashing out. I blow out slowly, eyes slanted at him. "You sound jealous, Cooper. Surprising for a guy who out-and-out refuses to have sex with me."

"So, the only way I can show I care about you is to have sex with you?" He shakes his head. "I'm not jealous of Troy. I'm protective of you. There's a difference. It's not right what Troy did to you. Don't let him off the hook."

"That's not for you to decide. Troy's been my friend much longer than you. Most of my life," I say. "You don't know what it's like to cut someone out of your life who's been through so much with you."

He looks at his feet. "You're right. I don't know what that's like."

The tension in my shoulders eases. Sword sheathed, I head to the kitchen. "You want something to drink?"

He follows me, but when he doesn't answer, I look back at him.

"Take the fight."

I narrow my eyes. "Now you want me to take the fight?"

"Yes. Call that promoter and tell him you'll fight."

"There's no future in fighting for me." I set out two glasses and grab the water pitcher. "The Fight Club gig didn't work out. I'm heading back to law school in a couple of months. That's my future. It's time to move on."

"You can move on *after* this fight." He steps closer. "I really think you won't be content going back to law school unless you close this chapter in your life—on your terms."

"You said there wasn't enough time for me to get ready." I'm rattled and my hands shake as I fill the glasses with water. "And you said it was too personal. Remember?"

"Before this, you didn't have a good enough reason to take the fight."

"It's still personal, Cooper." I hold out a glass of water to him.

"Of course it is, but remember the speech my father gave at the beginning of wrestling season every year. 'Each competition requires a thoughtful, reasoned approach. You don't go into any match just to smash heads.' This fight has now become personal for different reasons—not a spiteful showdown over a bruised ego. Forget Zoe. This isn't about her. This is about *not* giving up on yourself. You go into this fight focused on your personal strength." He ignores the water glass and puts his hands on my shoulders. "Don't sell yourself short by taking Troy's handout."

A blaze of irritation zips up my spine.

"I don't have to sell myself short. You and Troy already have." I pull back and slam the glass on the counter. Water splashes over the rim. "You both think I'm not capable of taking on Zoe."

"I won't lie. The odds are not in your favor. Not because you're not capable, but because you haven't had the preparation. If you train every day for the next two months, no days off, you'll give Zoe a run for her money." He lowers his chin and meets my gaze. "You don't have to compromise... Or take handouts."

His words are an adrenaline rush that sends my pulse racing. It lasts ten seconds before I grip my drinking glass and shudder. Zoe is a well-trained martial arts fighter. I hear Troy's warning, the injured fighters left in Zoe's wake. I've watched her punch and kick the snot out of her opponents. *She's going professional*, Troy had said.

"Jayden—" He takes a step toward me, but I turn my back to him.

"Stop talking, Cooper. Please." With a hip against the counter, I sip my water while my eyes drift to the gray, wet day beyond the sliding glass doors. Fear hums loudly, drowning out all other sounds. "The truth is, I don't know if I want this fight. It'll be easier to take the money Troy's offering and figure out how to pay him back later."

"You don't run away when something scares you. You lean into it."

His father's words. Cooper knows full well the weight they carry with me.

He circles around, moving into my line of vision, impelling me to look at him.

"Jayden, you've fought underground. You know how to do this. I've seen you fight, seen what you're capable of. I can and will get you ready for this."

I'm not convinced, but I'm distracted by a faint jingle of keys. The release click of the front door lock follows the soft hiss of the door swinging open.

"Kara?" I call out, but it's my mother who comes through the kitchen doorway.

Her eyes are red and swollen. When she sees Cooper though, she steps back and hides her face under the curtain of her hair.

"Mom?" I step toward her.

"Oh, I didn't know anyone was home. I'm not feeling well. I'm going upstairs to lie down." She does an about-face and ducks out of the kitchen. The thump, thump, thump of her feet follows her exit as she rushes up the stairs.

"Is everything all right?" Cooper whispers.

I wait to hear her bedroom door snap shut before I answer. "She's been out of sorts lately."

"I'll get out of here." Cooper's eyes are full of questions he doesn't ask. He takes my hand and holds it. "What do I need to do to convince you to take the fight?"

I look at my hand in his, inhale, and slowly raise my eyes. "Tell me why sex with me is such a hard pass."

"It's not—"

"Sometimes, I think it's Troy," I interrupt, tipping my head to look at him. "But we're not together anymore."

He releases my hand. "You weren't 'together' the first time you had sex with him, either."

I prickle at the implied accusation. "Why don't you say what's really on your mind, Cooper? That it still bothers you all these years later that I chose him over you?"

He doesn't respond, and the silence sucks the air out of the room. He draws a key lanyard from his shorts pocket and pauses.

"Let's stay focused on the situation at hand. Promise me you'll consider taking the fight. *Really* consider it."

I inhale, fighting the itch to stay on topic. I want out of this hole he keeps me in, but my mother is upstairs crying, and right now, she is more important than untangling this exasperating situation with Cooper.

"Fine," I say.

"I'll call you later. Hope your mom is okay. If you need something—anything—call me." He pecks my cheek with a chaste kiss and leaves.

I don't owe Cooper any promises, but I agreed anyway. A faint smile slips across my lips as I think about how much he's like his dad. Coach used to line up my choices before me like that, nice and easy as you please, making me promise to think about what I was resisting and why. Under Coach's tutelage, students and athletes learned that the power of our futures was in our own hands. Making decisions might be hard but being able to choose gave us control. And though some decisions might not turn out well, there would be the opportunity to make a better choice at the next juncture.

The fight, however, is a pipe dream. A wish to have back what had been taken from me before I'd been ready to let it go. I have a perfectly good plan in place, having accepted Troy's help, and now my attention is needed elsewhere. I climb the steps to deal with today's episode of my mother's heartbreak.

FIFTEEN

Alejandro must suspect someone's talking to my mother and that she may be about to pull the plug because there's a flurry of activity on her credit cards. Mom is beside herself about it.

"Call your bank." I hand her the cell phone. "Tell them to put a hold on your account right away. I'll go online and cancel all your credit cards."

She takes the phone but lowers it to her lap.

"Pull yourself together. No crying." I lift her hand holding the cell and push it at her.

My mother raises her chin, mouth set tight, and eyes narrowed. "This is why I never liked all that nasty fighting and boy stuff." She shakes her head. "It's made you hard. It's made you mean."

"I'm not being mean. I'm trying to protect you."

"It kills you I might find a bit of happiness after Daddy," she says. "I can't believe my own daughter doesn't want to see me happy."

"Happy?" I jab the air with my hands. "Daddy was taking his last breaths, and you were flirting with other men."

"What are you talking about?" Her look of outrage surprises me. "I wasn't flirting! Losing your father devastated me."

"You cried on every available male shoulder, Mr. Murphy, Dad's friends, and your coworker. The night of Dad's funeral, I came home and found you drinking with him."

My mother's face drains of all color. She stands, pushes past me to take off her shoes, and tosses them in the closet, her silence louder than anything.

"You think so little of me." Resting a hand on the dresser, she raises her chin to meet my gaze. "You know nothing of what it was like for me, the pain of losing a husband, my life partner, the man I'd loved for over two decades. How difficult it was for me to continue on without the one person who had my back at every turn. I thought my oldest, nearly grown-up daughter would be the one person who would understand, or at least, who might try to understand. Clearly, that isn't the case."

Before I can think of a response, she's shoving me toward the door.

"Get out of my room. I know what I need to do with the bank and the credit cards. I'll take care of *all* of it." Her tone is brisk, business-like. "You don't need to worry about me anymore. Your sister and I have done fine without you here."

I'm barely in the hallway before the door slams shut behind me, bumping against my butt. I turn and stare at the door feeling bloodied from another round with my mother, heat wavering in the back of my eyes. It's all right if she hates me. She's finally angry, and that's good. She will do something now. Stop being soft. Stop being a victim.

There's a tingling in my limbs, an itch to run. I don't belong here, not anymore, not since my father died. I don't know where I'll go, but I'm not wanted here.

With a heavy sigh, I start toward my bedroom when Kara's shout makes me do an about-face.

"Jay, come quick! You need to see this."

I sprint downstairs to the foyer and ground to a halt as Kara heaves the front door closed; her darkened expression leaves me cold.

"She did a video interview." My sister thrusts her phone before my eyes.

Zoe Bocek's face fills the screen. Bright flashes of light and the green screen behind her suggest a photo shoot. A female narrator's voice explains that Zoe's celebrity has grown. She's such a big deal that she's going to be featured on the cover of the MMA online zine.

"Right out of her days growing up in historic Quebec, family members say that the young French-Canadian girl exhibited a natural talent for fighting. Some may not know that the Bocek family has competitive fighting in their blood. Zoe's grandfather was an undisputed WBC belt holder," the narrator says. Black and white images of Zoe's grandfather in the ring segue into motion clips of a younger Zoe in training—kicking and punching—with the same determined sneer. "Despite a shoulder injury, she's risen to the top of her game, winning all of her show competitions on *The Sin City Fight Club*. Now that the season's drawing to an end, it's just the beginning for Bocek. She's hired an agent and promoter."

Kara and I stand next to each other, watching as the scene changes to an interview room. Zoe and the narrator sit in matching upholstered chairs facing each other. Zoe is wearing black Lycra shorts and a pink exercise bra, with ripped stomach muscles on display.

The host doesn't waste time, plowing forward into the subject of her relationship with Troy.

"We met on the show. I noticed him the first day of casting." Her smile for the camera is coy and her French accent thick. "The first thing I noticed about him, besides his pretty blue eyes, is the way he treats the female fighters. He's straight-up with us. Not all the guys are. Most of them think they're more important, but Troy is different. He has respect for female fighters."

To Troy's credit, that's a fair assessment.

"Were you immediately attracted to each other?"

"I think so—at least I was," Zoe says. "We worked out together. Grew close. He has this adorable little smile."

"Did you know about his girlfriend, Jayden Jones, back home?" the host asks.

An answer I am particularly curious to hear.

"Yes." She shrugs. "But I pulled out all the stops once I found out they weren't exclusive."

"Earlier episodes of Sin City suggest Troy and Jayden were still very much a couple when you met. What made you think he was available?"

My stomach tightens. I'm not sure I'm ready to hear this, but it feels important to know.

"With the way the filming works, those production guys push us together. They like it when things happen. It makes the show more interesting and exciting when you throw all our different personalities together," she says. "From day one, Troy and me, we connected. We spend a lot of time together, during the fights, and hanging out afterward. Let's face it, that boy is *hot*. He doesn't even have to try. He naturally draws girls in, like bees to honey. Buzz, buzz." She flutters her hands like giant bee wings and chuckles.

Kara and I both make gagging noises.

This time, the host leans in. "Were you just one of many bees drawn to his, um, honey?"

"Mmm huh." Zoe laughs, but quickly rearranges her expression. "This experience changed us all. We're like ... celebrities. Going out is like, oh-my-god crazy. Intense. People want to hang out with us and buy us dinner and drinks. All the guys get propositioned. You know, 'cause a lot of women are wolves."

The host howls playfully, drawing a laugh from Zoe.

"But Troy's done with those other women." Zoe sits forward, her face hardened. "Once he and I hooked up, I told him I don't share. There'd be no more messing around with other women."

In my peripheral, Kara gawks at me. "Is she saying there were others?"

My heart is thumping in my chest, my throat uncomfortably dry. I turn and walk straight out the front door. The rain pounds the streets, sending up a hiss of mist as it cools the summer-hot pavement. Seething, I cross the street, not slowing down until I am at Troy's house, hammering at the door with my fist.

When Troy opens the door, I shove him aside to get into the house. My hair is stuck to my face, and rain drips off me, forming a puddle at my feet.

"How many more were there, Troy?" I stare unblinkingly at him.

My question seems to disorient him, and his face is a landscape of shifting expressions.

"Come and sit down." He tries to steer me further into the house.

I jerk away and hold him in place with my glare. He lowers his eyes. "Oh my God, you can't even look at me."

"C'mon, we only saw each other a couple of times each semester. You must've known. You didn't sleep with anyone else while we were apart?"

"No, I didn't know," I hiss. "And I sure as hell didn't cheat on you. Not once!"

"Keep it down, will ya?" He squeezes his temples with his middle finger and thumb. "My dad is in the other room."

"I don't care. You're a liar *and* a cheater."

"They didn't mean anything." He lifts a hand toward me, but I smack it away.

"Don't touch me." I aim my finger at him like a weapon. "Don't talk to me. Don't look at me. Don't *anything* me, ever again. You are dead to me! You hear me? Dead. To. Me!"

I charge through the door and back into the rain, running blindly across the street but cut away from the walkway up to my house. I refuse to go into the house where my spineless, weak mother hates me, and my little sister knows my boyfriend cheated on me multiple times.

I move swiftly, each step faster and faster, until I am running full stride. My sneakers smack the wet pavement, my clothes absorbing the rain, until the fibers, saturated, cling to my skin.

My best friend and yet, all those years we were together, I'd never been enough for him. I've never been enough. Never enough.

The words echo in my head. The tightly wound coil in my chest springs loose, anger racing up and down my limbs as I tear through the streets. I am drenched in rage, ugly with bitterness.

"I hate you!" I yell into the thick, sodden grayness.

Though my lungs feel like they're going to burst, I run and run. I run until an uneven tread of sidewalk catches the front of my sneaker and I sprawl forward, ungracefully. The skin of my palms grate against the coarse cement and split open. I catch myself and sit up, sucking in great gulps of air.

"I hate you." The utterance breaks my lips with a weakening force. On my knees, I lean my head back and let the rain mix with my tears as my shoulders shake with broken sobs.

Headlights pierce the storm-darkened dullness. The chug of a car engine slows with the cry of its brakes as my father's Impala stops beside me. The heavy doors squeal as my mother and Kara catapult from the car.

"Jayden! Oh my God, honey." My mother's hands are touching me, brushing my sopping hair from my eyes.

I can't stop crying. Kara is crying, too.

"I'm sorry, Jayden. It's not right what he did to you," my sister whispers.

"Come on. Let's get you home." Mom slides her arm around me.

I'm too drained to resist and let them guide me into the passenger seat. In the car, my teeth chatter.

"It's going to be all right. You'll see." From the back seat, Kara drapes a sweater across my shoulders. She holds onto my arm as if I might tip over without her support.

Back at the house, my sister rushes to get me a new, extra-soft blanket that she had ordered online while Mom fusses over me, overseeing my change of clothes, cleaning the abrasions on my palms, and tucking me in once I crawl into bed.

"How about a cup of tea?" she asks, her hand on my bedroom doorknob.

"No," I say from under the burrow of the fluffy comforter. She lingers at the door. She wants to do more, say something. Her coddling attention after our blowout earlier is uncomfortable. I just want her to go. When she finally shuts the door, I pull the blanket over my head.

Anxiousness rises within me. I don't want to be here, but I've got nowhere to go. I grab my phone from the nightstand. There are two missed calls and several messages from Kara from earlier.

I begin reading them when there's a knock at my door. I peek out from behind the edge of the blanket. My sister opens the door but hangs halfway in, halfway out of my room.

"When you left the house, I was really worried. I didn't know what to do," she says. "I told Mom what happened. I hope that's okay,"

"It's okay." I push back the blanket and sit up, speaking gently. She's like a timid bunny I don't want to frighten away.

"I was going to call Cooper." She shrugs. "But I don't think he's impartial when it comes to you."

"Yeah, it's infuriatingly overly complicated with us." I roll my eyes, and my sister smiles.

"I thought, if something like this happened to me, I'd want to talk to my girlfriend. I suppose that butthead across the street was the closest thing you ever had to a girlfriend." She toes the edge of the door. "I know of some sisters that are tight, like best friends. Maybe you and I can be more like that, you know, so we can talk and confide in each other?"

My sister, my girlfriend.

Guy friends don't do the deep, emotional talking. They just do stuff. They drink too much. Drive too fast. Hit things and break shit. Wrestle each other. That's the kind of interaction I've grown comfortable with. The talking? Not so much.

"I'd like that. I'd like that a lot." I pat the bed, inviting her to join me. Kara shuts the door and climbs in next to me.

"So, what happened?" She scoots closer to me and pulls the blanket over the two of us.

"There were others. I confronted him about it."

Her brows pop up. "And?"

"He didn't even try to deny it." I sigh and sink back into my pillow. "I have literally never seen someone look so guilty. To think I went to him earlier for advice. He was going to help me, but I'd rather cut off my arm than take anything from him."

Our family still very much needs the money, though.

"He's your past. Move on. As Nanny used to say, you've got bigger fish to fry." Kara gently shakes my arm. "Everything will be all right."

"I wish it were that simple," I say. It's time Kara knows the full extent of Mom's financial crisis, and I tell her.

"I wasn't paying attention. But you—" My sister smacks her hands on the bed. "You knew Alejandro was no good. You were skeptical of Mommy's online relationship all along."

"I wish to God I hadn't been right." Mistrusting my mother's love life isn't something to gloat about. "This has turned Mom inside out."

"What's going to happen? What are we going to do?" Kara's worries hit me.

Lean into it.

I hear the words in my head as if Coach is right there, telling me what I need to do, what I need to hear. A surge of calm washes over me.

"Everything will be fine. They offered me *a lot* of money to fight Zoe Bocek. I'm going to take the fight."

"I hope you wipe the floor with her, Jayden." Kara wraps her arms around me and snuggles into my side.

I smile at my little sister, glad she still has some faith in me. The truth is, I'm so far behind Zoe in training, I'll be racing the clock just to prove myself a decent opponent. But training for the fight is the least of my worries.

SIXTEEN

Cooper is behind the counter at Gloves making notes on a clipboard. The metallic clink of weight plates and the rip of harnessed grunts rise above the fast-tempo music streaming from overhead speakers. I wait until he looks up.

When he notices me, I rush to say, "I'll do it."

"Yeah?" He tilts his head. "What changed your mind?"

I struggle to pinpoint exactly how to answer. I'm both humiliated and angered by the discovery of Troy's pervasive cheating, but so much transpired yesterday, that my decision to fight is more than just a reaction to the breadth of his betrayal. From the earlier conversation between Cooper and me to the fallout with my mother over Alejandro, from Zoe's revealing interview to confronting Troy. From my rain-soaked meltdown to Mom's unexpected concern, to the newfound friendship with my sister and her faith in me. I will not go down without a fight.

"Like your father used to say, when the fight gets tough, you get tougher. I've got a lot of work ahead of me, but I want this fight. Really want it. Even if it's only to prove I'm not afraid of doing it. Or Zoe."

"All right." He taps his pen on the clipboard. If he's seen Zoe's interview, he's not letting on. "I'll call the promoter and formally accept the fight. Then, I'll write up a training plan, and we'll meet tomorrow morning to go over the details. If we're in agreement, we'll get started. There's no time to waste."

"No, none." I nod.

"Well, since you quit yesterday, I have nothing for you." He looks around. "Go stretch and warm up, then talk to Marcus. He can set you up with a workout today. Oh, and your mom. Everything okay?"

It takes a moment for me to remember he'd witnessed my mother's tearful arrival home yesterday. He'd be understanding of the truth, but this is not the time nor the place to show vulnerability. Now, more than ever, I need to exemplify strength.

"Dating drama. She'll be fine," I reply.

I arrive the next morning ready to get to work, but Marcus ushers me into the gym office where Cooper and Van are waiting. Marcus motions for me to take the seat next to Van and his tatted, muscled, authoritative bulk.

"Good morning, Jayden. I asked Marcus and Van to join us," Cooper starts. "They've agreed to be part of your team, Team Bruiser Jones."

I trill in my seat.

"Bruiser Jones Team, assemble!" Marcus says in an announcer-like voice, and my face cracks into a wide grin.

Van simply nods, either unaware or indifferent to Marcus's Ron Burgundy-*Anchorman* reference. His dour expression pivots my attention back to business.

"I thought about what you do best." Cooper shifts forward, leaning slightly over the desk. "We both know that's wrestling and grappling, but it's been over a year since you've wrestled competitively. We need to rehearse those drills, make sure every motion is tight, and figure out when and how we can best implement them. In the meantime, we also need to make sure you can defend yourself. You must be able to block kicks and take punches. Lots of them."

A phantom ache pulses in my jaw. I'll be Zoe's punching bag—at least until I get her to the mat.

"Van and I created a training plan. As your coaches, we lay down the rules. You'll train every day, two times a day, starting at 6 a.m. After the second week, we'll up training to three times a day." He taps the clipboard in front of him. His serious tone wipes away any consideration of sarcastic replies. "What we expect of you: to learn new techniques. Develop a style. Study other fighters and figure out how your strengths match the way you like to fight. To consistently learn and grow, evolve."

He looks at me for confirmation. I break out in a cool sweat thinking of what the next two months will look like as my mother's financial situation disintegrates, visits to the bank and lawyer offices. I may need time off.

"What if I need time off for... stuff?" I ask, eyes on the edge of the desk.

Van makes a gruff, throaty noise.

"From this minute on, there's nothing more important in your life than training." Van pokes the top of the desk with a thick, callused finger. "You show up every day, girlie. Consistency is crucial. Lateness won't be tolerated. You arrive on time. Listen. Don't ask questions."

Heat roils up my neck.

"I can't ask questions?"

"Not stupid ones."

The sharpness of his tone stirs my inner rebel.

"As for your diet, we expect you to eat healthy, eat clean." Cooper consults his clipboard. "Van, what do you think about bringing a nutritionist on board? I can get a few recommendations."

"Negative. Before girlie leaves today, I'll go over her diet plan," Van responds like I'm not sitting next to him. "She'll keep a notebook of everything she puts in her mouth and show it to me every day."

Van's dark eyes pin me in my seat, daring me to voice the protest ready to swan dive off my tongue. We have a stare-off. Making weight is part of wrestling. I've sucked weight my entire career and never, ever needed help.

I inhale and shake it off. "Okay."

"Good. I think we've covered everything. We can make adjustments and fine-tune as we go." Cooper slides a typewritten list and a pen across the desk to me. "Last, the contract. I listed the breakdown of hours and estimate of expenses payable when the fight production company funds come in."

Lots and lots of figures, and neat lines with explanations of the services to be rendered. No one is doing this for free. We all stand to make a pretty penny. The guys' three signatures are already at the bottom. There's one blank line waiting for mine.

"You good with all of this, Jayden?" Cooper asks.

The room falls silent as the guys wait for me to give the nod to get started. I grip the cool plastic arms of the chair and eye the contract before me. The law student in me wants time to review the agreement thoroughly. There's a lot at stake here. For my mother. For our house. For my reputation. But I'm already so far behind, and the one thing I'm certain of is that I trust Cooper. I trust he's chosen the best team he could assemble to get me prepared for this fight. I need the knowledge and support these men can provide. The older trainer appears eager to challenge me, to break me, but I've faced challenges before—tougher ones. I'm not afraid.

I dip my chin and pick up the pen. "One hundred percent. Let's do this."

"Good morning, Cat," Cooper calls out to me as I walk through the door of Gloves fifteen minutes before 6 a.m., bike helmet in hand, a light sheen of sweat dampening my hairline. Mom needed a car, so I gave her the Impala keys. I will bike back and forth to the gym every day, twice a day, regardless of the weather.

Cat—the nickname his father dubbed me. It's what my high school wrestling teammates called me. It feels familiar, like getting battle-ready.

"Marcus and I will work with you most mornings." Cooper walks me to a mat in the back corner of the gym, holding a clipboard and stopwatch. "Van will handle the brunt of the afternoon trainings. Let's start with wrestling drills, work on executing the techniques slowly, with little strength at first, so you get them clean. We'll do them over and over again until you can do them in your sleep."

After I warm up, Marcus wraps my hands with a roll of thin cotton fabric and helps me put on new, slimmer-fitting MMA-sanctioned fight gloves.

"Zoe's most dangerous moves are her kicks. The most important part of your training is learning how to avoid getting kicked and get her to the mat. Those two things will up the odds of you taking this fight."

"No problem," I say, curling my hands into fists, feeling the tightness of the wrap underneath the padding of the fingerless gloves. The padded layers protect my knuckles, but they also impede the movement of my fingers. Adjustments will have to be made. These gloves need to feel like part of my hands, part of me.

The schedule has me working on new techniques and drills Monday mornings. In the afternoon when I return, I check in with Van for boxing lessons, rotating my time on the mitt, pad, and bag.

"No bodybuilding," Van warns me when I go for the heavier weights. "We want you to strength train, not to build body mass. We need you in fighting form, lean, flexible, loose."

Fight promoters send a photographer to Gloves to take pictures of me in my second week of training. The fight is being heavily promoted, and they want to keep the fight on people's minds. I suit up and hear the camera clicks as I climb into the ring.

"Hey!" Across from me, wearing headgear and gloves, the other woman is grinning through her mouth guard. I recognize her immediately as the woman I sparred with the very first day I walked into Gloves.

"Dani, you're not sparring with me, are you?"

"Gloves had a sparring partner vacancy," she says. "You're looking at the newest training member of Team Bruiser Jones."

I smile. "Welcome, and thank you."

"Don't thank me yet." She laughs. "I'm going to unleash some seriously badass kicks on you."

"Good. Don't hold back. I need to learn how to defend myself." I lightly jab her shoulder with a gloved hand. "Glad to have you onboard."

Dani, though a lighter weight than me, is a trained fighter. Her moves are quick, fluid. It's apparent by the way she holds her gloves at the ready, bouncing from foot to foot, that she knows boxing. She already has a relationship with Van. Her soft-spoken obedience to his orders meets with his approval.

On Tuesday mornings, I condition and strength train with Cooper. In the afternoon, Van takes over, and I spar with Dani and learn how to crowd her to keep from giving her room and the opportunity to kick me. Wednesdays are jiu-jitsu and wrestling, and in the evening, boxing.

On Thursdays I spar again, followed by strength training in the afternoon. Fridays, I spend an hour doing drills and end with a run.

Saturdays, I spar again and get a massage afterward.

On Sundays, I do roadwork in the morning, either running or riding my bike. In the evening, I get time to rest and recover.

The drills are grueling, the same ones Coach made us do in high school on the mats of the wrestling gym: pushups, lunges, squats, broad jumps, tumbling, and the dreaded burpee. I curse out Cooper as I grunt through the workouts, but my body is changing, and quickly. Along with being more limber, I am leaner, with much more muscle mass. Having my workouts intensify to a professional level, for the first time in my life, I see the beginning emergence of eight-pack abs.

I leash my doubts about Van when I get to the gym for my afternoon sessions with him. Van works with me on boxing techniques. He's no Coach McCaffrey. He doesn't mince words, and is miserly with his "attaboys," but under his coarse tutelage, I am learning. I practice my footwork, jabs, crosses, hooks, and uppercuts in the bathroom mirror after my showers, as I go up and down the stairs to my bedroom, while I stand in the kitchen making dinner.

Cooper returns by the time I finish up my late-day boxing lessons with Van, and he helps me cool down and stretch.

We have stretching sessions a few times a day, every day. The routine has almost become a well-rehearsed dance. When we finish one move, I automatically prepare for the next. Having Cooper's direct attention by far makes it one of my favorite parts of the day.

"How's the ankle doing?" His regard shoots to my left leg.

"All good." I put my weight on that leg and rotate my knee to show him. He nods, and I lie on the mat and prepare to let him manipulate my body. "Where do you go in the afternoons?"

"Got a gig coaching a summer wrestling camp." He kneels between my legs and raises my right leg over his shoulder. "Two dozen ten- to fourteen-year-olds. Lots of energy, but also lots of fun."

It's easy to imagine him with a group of energetic kids. Just like his dad. It makes me smile.

I pull my attention back to him as, hand on my left thigh, he leans into me, pushing my upraised leg toward me, commanding me to inhale and exhale. With my knees pulled into my chest, he pushes the soles of my feet, guiding my knees to the sides of my body for a lower back stretch. He squats and kneels on my butt. My leg muscles immediately protest under the deeper stretch.

"Inhale, Cat." He works, eyes lowered as he presses his weight into me, coaxing my hips to stretch. "Now exhale."

I let my gaze wander over his face, moving down to his shoulders, his chest, his hips. Hovering over me, his hands on my thighs. My body, already flooded with endorphins, is triggered.

Jurisprudence. Jurisprudence.

My leg vibrates under his hand. Though he's not looking at my face, he must feel it. He probably thinks it's my fatigued muscles and not him who's generating the response. This is athletic training. Not intimacy.

"Good pelvic movement," he says, bringing my attention back to his face. Our eyes meet for a split second, and he immediately releases me from the stretch and hands me a dense black foam roller. "Finish up another five minutes on this."

Before he can stand, I roll up, catch his ankle, and drive my head and shoulders into his stomach, knocking him onto his back. We grapple for a few seconds until he laughs and gives in.

I hold him perpendicular in the pin, both of us slightly breathless. He looks up at me hovering over him and inhales slowly.

"Jayden, you need to stop looking at me like that."

"Like what?"

"Like you're undressing me with your eyes."

My face flushes and I drop my chin. "I'm not."

"No?"

"No," I say more forcefully, pulling back.

Before I can move away, he scoops his arms around me and dump-trucks me, bridging his body, and twisting me onto my back, to pin me.

"I'm trying to be professional here." His breath barely spikes as he holds me, locked in place.

"Stop bringing it up then," I say between gritted teeth, keeping tension on our lock. "'Cause I'm starting to think you want it and you're too proud to admit it."

He releases me, sits back on his heels, and shakes his head. "You are incorrigible."

I sit up and drape a hand over my bent knee. "Am I wrong?"

Standing, he offers me a hand up. "We don't have a lot of time. We need to focus all our energy on one goal—to get you fight-ready."

I take his hand and rise to my feet. He's right. Still, I'm disappointed he won't admit to wanting me.

My first practice fight is two weeks into my training with Natalie, another fighter Van works with, known for her boxing skills. She stands several inches taller and is nearly ten pounds heavier than me. Van says my bulkier, more muscular frame helps balance the difference.

"Leave your ego at the door," Cooper reminds me as I eye my opponent. "You can tap out. It's not the end of the world."

Back during high school wrestling, endurance was my strong suit, and since starting at the gym, I've worked steadily to rebuild that stamina. I easily go the distance, but when Natalie throws a 1-2 punch—one to my stomach, the second to the side of my head—I drop. Marcus checks on me. Embarrassed, I push him away and try to stand, but Van stops the fight.

A week later, another fight. I get dropped again. Outside the ring, Cooper confers with Van. I know by the serious set of their expressions, that whatever they're saying about me is not good.

I climb out of the ring, winded and bruised, and collapse on the mat for my post-workout stretches. It's Van who comes over to run me through the stretches.

"I'm not very good at this." I look away, embarrassed by my obvious shortfalls, embarrassed that I'm admitting this to him of all people.

"We need to work on your defensive fighting skills." His tone is stringent. "I want you here an hour earlier every morning and afternoon. Got it?"

I nod. Something has shifted. Van has not been involved with my cooldown stretches before now. As Van works my legs, I glance over at Cooper. We catch eyes for a moment, and then he walks away.

"Inhale," Van orders.

I take a deep breath and focus on Van's instructions.

All week long, it's Van, interspersed with Marcus—but only them—morning, noon, and night, working with me. It feels like a test, and I don't ask them where Cooper is. I pay attention. I learn.

On Friday, I'm finishing up my second training of the day when Cooper finally makes an appearance. My heart lifts at the sight of him, but his weeklong avoidance eviscerates the pleasure of seeing him. I ignore him and focus on finishing up the final fifteen minutes of my workout, throwing punches at the heavy, black body bag that hangs from a girder in the industrial-like ceiling of the gym. My body shines with perspiration. My workout clothes are saturated with hard-earned sweat.

"How's it going?" He moves behind the bag and steadies it with his body.

A swirl of emotions twists through my body, but I steel myself against it.

"Fine."

He stands silent for a few minutes, bracing the bag as I throw punches. "Spill it, Cat."

I stop, gloved fists raised. "Why is Van the only one coaching me now? Where have you been?"

"You questioning your training?"

"No." I grunt and throw a left cross. Since signing the contract, I haven't questioned one part of my training.

"Boxing is your weakest area. Van is a former WBA boxing champ," he says. "I wanted you to focus entirely on your defense, with no distraction."

My face warms and I slam the bag with a gloved fist. Cooper's right. *Again*. His presence affects me. Even now, it takes enormous mental energy to focus on my workout instead of him. When did I become this easily distracted?

"What else is on your mind?" He's staring at me.

I keep my eyes on the bag, but my punches lose force.

"You know, the only way I even stand a chance at going the distance with Zoe is if I can wrestle her."

"Don't underestimate yourself," he says.

A buzzer goes off, and Van yells, "Time!"

My workout is finished. I lower my gloves and inhale deeply.

"Yeah, I'm strong, but I'm not fooling myself about this, Cooper. She's going make me look like a small-time chowderhead if I can't figure out how to get her to the mat."

He extends his hand for mine. "You got plans Saturday evening?"

I surrender my gloved hand to him. He pulls the Velcro straps loose. His touch, though perfunctory, makes my pulse climb.

"I'm not permitted to do anything outside my training." Trying to control his effect on me, I don't look at him.

"After your last workout, we'll do dinner, and talk over a plan for the fight." He pulls off my second glove but doesn't release my hand. "No one is going to make Jayden 'Courageous Cat' Jones look like a small-time chowderhead. Not on my watch."

SEVENTEEN

A special, courier-paid demand letter comes from the bank that holds our house mortgage. Mom is going on four months behind payments. We cancel all unnecessary services, including the lawn service—I will mow the lawn—and scramble to borrow and gather money to catch up. Mom agrees to let me return some of her online purchases, but many of the return windows have closed. We sit for hours crunching the numbers, figuring out what needs to get paid, and the smallest amounts we can pay, to stretch the money the furthest.

"If I pay the mortgage, I'll be one less month behind, but there's nothing left for July's bills. If I don't pay the monthlies, they'll accrue late fees. This is a lesson in futility," Mom says with a sigh. "I cut up my credit cards, eliminated all spending. My paycheck goes straight to the bank. Yet, it's not enough. Every month, we sink a little further. We're doing everything we can, but we won't be able to hold out for much longer."

I look at the notes I've written on the yellow legal pad in front of me. She's right. The numbers don't add up.

"What do you want to do?" I lay my pen down, noting how exhausted she looks.

I wish I could do more. Wish I had a large, untapped bank account. Or a rich aunt. Something more immediate than the anticipation of the fight purse to come.

She fingers the corner of a billing statement. "I need a loan and probably legal advice."

In full agreement, I'm already considering options as to where to get that advice. One year of law school hasn't provided me with enough knowledge.

"Alejandro said he loved me. We talked about a future together. He was going to take me traveling around the world... I can't believe how foolish I've been." Mom covers her mouth, stifling a sob.

This is the house my parents built, our home, the last place my father lived. I slide my hand across the table, letting my fingers graze the back of her hand.

"You're not going through this alone." It's all I have to offer.

A notice from Brooklyn Law shows up in my email inbox, reminding me to register for fall classes. My mission statement consists of a few vague notes. In the likely event I don't get the scholarship renewed, I'll need Mom to co-sign a school loan, only without the house as collateral, nothing is assured. The fight purse will solve a lot of problems. Maybe I should put law school off for a year.

At nine in the morning, I steer my bike up the driveway and pop off, warm and limber, straight off the morning's sparring workout. Van had nodded more than grunted. My boxing dynamics are improving incrementally. Not enough to make a huge difference in the ring with Zoe, but for the moment, I acknowledge my growth.

Out of the corner of my eye, I see Troy crossing the street. I didn't know he was home. I yank open the garage door and brace for the inevitable interaction.

"Came home for a brief visit with the old man. I'm heading back to Las Vegas today." His eyes flicker upward, but he cannot hold my gaze. "Figured I'd stop by to see how you guys are doing."

"All things considered, pretty terrible." I hang my helmet on the handlebars and push my bike into the garage.

But it's like he doesn't hear me.

"Jay, I need to tell you something."

"That's a sentence that never seems to end well." I tramp to the pair of rocking chairs on the front porch and toss my backpack on one before dropping into the other. Arms crossed, I wait.

With nowhere to sit, he stays on his feet. "You were my best friend. Growing up here with your family was everything to me. I loved your dad. When he died, I didn't know what to do." His voice breaks and rattles me along with it. "I felt useless. When you came to me the night after the funeral, I saw it as my chance to do something."

"What was that, Troy? Sleep with me, *pretend* to be my boyfriend?"

"It's what you wanted, what you asked of me."

I lift my chin. "You saying our relationship was a three-plus year pity-fuck?"

"No, I ... I was with you because I loved you. Still love you, but the thing is ... I was never *in love* with you."

It's unfathomable that he could surprise me again. And yet he has, and it's the worst of all. I struggle to stay upright in my seat and not fold down and crumble at his feet.

"I screwed up, but no matter what," he continues, "I'll always look out for you. That's why I think—"

I see his lips move, but I've barely registered anything past his *never-in-love* admission. By the way he pauses and looks me square in the eye, I know he's about to drop another hefty bomb. I grip the chair's armrests.

"You need to call off the fight. Please. There's no way you can win. You'll just get hurt—*really badly.*"

He's completely bailed on me. My knuckles whiten as my grip on the arms of the chair tightens.

"You should leave now, Troy."

"Jay, listen to me." He holds up one hand as he pulls a white envelope from his back pocket. "I want you to have this."

I stare, unmoved.

"It's a certified bank check. Immediate cash. Enough to help your mother. This way, you can enjoy the summer and go back to law school. You've always been so smart. That should be your future."

"I don't want your money. I don't want anything from you."

"Jay, c'mon. You're my friend. I want to help you."

"I don't want your help. Go away!" I spring from the chair, fists curled.

He backs up a few feet, shoving the envelope in his pocket, turns, and saunters down the walkway and across the street. I hold my breath until he disappears inside his house. I squeeze my eyes closed, forcing tears away. I won't let them fall.

Troy Murphy doesn't believe in me. I'll prove him wrong.

EIGHTEEN

An hour later, as I'm pulling the lawn mower out of the garage, a sleek black limo pulls away from the curb in front of the Murphys' house. Mr. Murphy, at the door, waves as it pulls away.

As Troy said, he's off to Vegas, again.

I think about questions I want to ask him, like, how many other girls were there in college, a steady stream or just one here and there? Maybe I don't really want the answer.

After I finish cutting the lawn, I eat, wait an hour, and go for a five-mile run. Then, I bike back to the gym. During a sparring round, I twist my left ankle—the bad one.

"Marcus, get an ice pack." Van palpates the ankle with his large hands, frowns, and leans back on his heels. "You're done for the day."

We all know I can't afford to lose even a moment of training.

"I'm fine. I want to keep going."

"That's not a suggestion, girlie." Van lowers his chin, a challenge in his eyes.

"It's my damn training. If I say I'm fine, *I'm fine*." I'm adamant, but when I stand, a red-hot wave of pain shoots from the ankle right up the length of my leg, and I nearly buckle under it.

"Whatever, princess, but *I'm* not training you anymore today." Van walks off.

"I'll give you a princess," I mutter under my breath. I wrap my ankle, and limping, I collect my gear and head out of the gym to bike home. It throbs the entire ride, making the last mile a real effort. My energy wanes with the punishing early August heat and humidity, and my cheeks are wet with tears as I hobble the bicycle to the garage door. I drop the bike and lower myself to the ground to glare at the offending joint. Troy is right. I'm out of my league with Zoe. Van and Cooper have me scrutinizing her fights. Video after video, I watch her demolish her opponents with blood-splattering, bone-crunching kicks. That bitch is strong.

"You're not only going to lose this fight, but you're also going to look like a joke. A broken, bloody joke," I say to myself.

I hold back the sob that rattles in my throat, but I'm too lethargic to keep it at bay. Pushing my flimsy will aside, my emotions stampede over me, and tears flow unchecked. I drag my sorry self into the house, grateful no one is home to witness my meltdown.

I cry it out in the shower. Afterward, wrapped in a towel, I collapse on the bed and fall asleep wishing the world away.

The ringing of my cell on the floor next to my bed awakens me. The light in the room has dimmed with the approaching evening. Dazed, I feel around the floor until my hand connects with the phone. Cooper's name flashes across the screen.

"Yeah." My greeting is terse.

"Just calling to tell you I'll pick you up at six."

"Not up to going out."

"Van said you sprained your ankle. Is it bothering you that much?" He sounds concerned.

A slight wiggle of the offending joint tells me it's stiff.

"It's fine, but I'd rather stay home." I stare up at the ceiling of my bedroom, hollowed out. There's so much I want to say, to confide my fears to him. Cooper is a good listener, but if I tell him what Troy said, he'll be mad that I let Troy's words affect me. I don't need a second opinion on that. I'm already angry enough at myself.

"You need a break from the routine. I'm not taking no for an answer. I'll pick you up at six," he says.

"Whatever." Apparently, I am the boss of nothing, not even myself.

In the hallway, Mom's bedroom door shuts. I throw on a hoodie and limp into the hall to knock on her door. I need someone to talk to.

"Come in," she calls.

I open the door and find her sitting on the bed, her back to me.

"I met with a lawyer this afternoon." She twists to look at me. "She said it was best to avoid foreclosure by doing a short sale on the house. Jayden, we're going to lose our home."

My mother collapses onto the mattress, disintegrating before my eyes. I ignore the twinge in my ankle and rush to her.

"Mom, it's okay." I lay down beside her and stroke her back soothingly. "It looks bad now, but it's going to be okay."

I want to make this okay for her, but all I can offer her is vague, baseless hope that she'll survive through this tidal wave wrecking her life. Mom's debt is massive, and even with the promise of my fight purse, it may be too late to remedy the brunt of the damage.

With Mom resting, I head back to my room consumed with the need to further investigate the short sale option. There must be something we can do to slow down the process.

I want to go out even less now, but Cooper will be here regardless. I put on shorts and a sleeveless T-shirt, skip makeup, and twist my hair in a simple braid. I tackle the staircase with care, testing my ankle, but not putting my full weight on it. Kara is in her regular spot on the couch, cell phone in hand, but her attention is riveted to the television and her favorite entertainment news.

"Jay, I don't know if you want to hear this." She looks over her shoulder at me. "But they just said they're going to have an update on Troy."

I approach the front room tentatively. Troy's last mention on TV dropped a bomb on the ruins of our tattered relationship. I can't stomach any more surprises. Careful to keep most of my weight on my right leg, I stand behind the couch to watch. After the hosts wrap up a story about some celeb's new baby, they flash to a photo of Troy after his final *Sin City Fight Club* win, arms raised in victory.

"We caught up with *Sin City Fight Club's* Country Murphy at Harry Reid International Airport. The hot TV series's star fighter told us he's returning to Vegas to train for his first professional match in December. Teammate-turned-girlfriend, Zoe Bocek, met him at the airport. Bocek, coincidentally, is training for her first post-*Sin City Fight Club* fight as well. Her match is against Country's former girlfriend, Jayden Jones. That's a fight nobody wants to miss!"

The camera follows Zoe as she spots Troy coming down the airport escalator. She shrieks. His face lights up. There's a close-up of the two of them embracing and kissing. Troy is smiling, a genuine smile, one I haven't seen in a long time. He and Zoe hold hands, grinning at each other like they have a secret between them.

My heart rips at the sight. Troy and I never held hands. We got each other's jokes and laughed together, something we shared from growing up so close, but we never behaved the way he and Zoe do. You could say maybe it's a performance, a play for the cameras, but I've known Troy long enough, seen his interest flair and diminish through throngs of girls in high school, to distinguish the difference between a passing flirtation from true interest.

The clarity in which I see it startles me—Troy is really into Zoe.

A range of emotions tumble over me. I'm not sure what to think or how to feel. A knock at the door drags my attention from the TV screen. It's six o'clock on the dot. Cooper has arrived.

"I'm going out," I tell my sister and mentally try to reset myself for the night out.

As much as I try to conceal my injury, the pain stymies my gait.

"That ankle is worse than you're owning up to." Cooper puts the truck in reverse, and my skin goosebumps in response to the fingers that brush my arm as he twists to back out of the driveway. "I have a set of crutches at the house. We'll head over to get them and an ice pack before we go out."

"I don't need them," I say.

"Well, I'm getting them, and as your coach, I expect you to use them." He drives the few minutes to his house, parks, and switches the ignition off. "Come inside. Say hello to my mom."

"Right now, I'm barely tolerating you, Cooper. I don't want to see or talk to anyone else."

He shrugs and leaves me alone in the truck. Several minutes later, the house door opens and shuts. Scrolling through my phone, I don't look up.

"Hi, Jayden."

I nearly jump out of my skin. Mrs. McCaffrey is standing outside my side of the truck, peeking through the window at me. I raise my hand to my heart.

"Didn't mean to frighten you," she says. "I just made a pitcher of peach sangria. Come in, and I'll pour you a glass."

Cooper is playing dirty, sending his mother. He knows I'd never refuse her.

"Great. Sure." I get out and notice she's holding a pair of aluminum crutches.

"Cooper said you need these." She helps me angle one under each arm. "He guessed at the height adjustment, but they look good. How do they feel?"

Keeping my knee bent above the injured ankle, I anchor my weight on the crutch handles and take a few steps. "It's good. Thank you."

Cooper is sitting at the kitchen table and has the gall to smile when I make my three-legged entrance. I return his smile with a frosty glare.

"How about that glass of sangria?" Mrs. McCaffrey asks, oblivious to the rancor between her son and me.

"I'll get an ice pack." Cooper pops up from his chair.

"*I'll* get the ice pack. Toby needs a walk. Take him out," Mrs. Mc-Caffrey orders without breaking stride of preparing our drinks.

He looks at me and hesitates but stands and calls the family's beagle. "I'll make it quick."

"Take him down the block. He needs the exercise," his mother adds.

"Sure thing," he says, meeting my gaze.

I chew my lip. I'm not sure what's going on, but from Cooper's expression, neither does he. Once the door snaps shut behind Cooper and the family's dog, Mrs. McCaffrey walks to the back door with a glass of sangria in each hand and a towel-covered ice pack tucked under her arm.

"How about we take our drinks outside? It's such a pleasant night."

I follow her awkwardly with the crutches out into the yard.

"Let's get some grounding in."

Trailing her, I step-shuffle, step-shuffle to the far end of the yard. "I'm sorry, did you say grounding?"

"Yes. Grounding." She bypasses a set of wicker chairs, stops under the shade of a massive maple tree, and slips her shoes off. "Humans are bio-electrical beings. We carry positive charges, which, over time, build up in our bodies. Earth has a negative charge. Grounding, or even hugging a tree, discharges that excess negative energy and helps us fight off free radicals."

Crossing her feet, she folds into a sitting position on the grass, motioning for me to do the same. I don't have a clue what she's talking about, but I set the crutches aside, lower myself to the ground, and kick off my sneakers. The grass is cool and feels good against my bare feet and legs. She hands me a glass of sangria, and we sip our drinks for a few minutes in silence. The sangria is delicious, and I tell her so.

"Thanks. The trick is to mix the fruit and sugar together and let it sit at room temperature for twenty minutes." She passes the ice pack to me. "Other than your twisted ankle, how's the training going?"

I set my drink aside to straighten my leg and prop the ice pack on my ankle. Troy's words echo in my head.

"Not great. After this injury today, I can't help but think how ridiculous this is—me training for a professional fight. I had no business taking this fight."

I wait for her to interject, to say some typical offset to my gripes, but she sits quietly, waiting for me to go on.

"I was, still am, a really good wrestler, but I'm only so-so in MMA." I picture Van's cross expression from earlier. "Cooper and the team have been pouring their time and energy into working with me. I'll be a huge disappointment."

"From what I hear, Cooper and your team believe in you, Jayden. Unfortunately, their confidence in you means nothing if you don't believe in yourself." She lightly touches my knee. "Only you can decide if you want to finish this out, but whatever you decide, understand a weak acceptance is as good as a soft refusal."

If only to fight or not to fight was the only decision I had to make. I cannot tell this woman my family might lose our house because my mother fell for an internet Lothario who swindled her into giving him money and put her over her head in debt. As wonderful and kind as Liz Mc-Caffrey is, it's too embarrassing. I've already weighed the poor woman down with my current dysfunctional state of mind.

"You're right. I need to figure this out. I'm stressing Cooper out," I add with a somber laugh.

"You needn't worry about Cooper. I'll admit, after his car accident, followed by his father's decline, I was worried about him. He was not himself. Depressed, I suppose. We all were. But since you've come home, he's snapped out of it." She smiles at me. "My son is in love with you."

I gape at her, eyes wide. *"He told you that?"*

"He didn't, but he doesn't have to. I can see he does." She leans back on her hands. "Does that surprise you?"

"He never said anything, and well—" I swallow self-consciously and then tip my head. "When he wants to be, your son is a monument of restraint and reserve."

"That's Coop, a bit of a perfectionist. I'm afraid he gets that from me," she says. "He won't openly invest unless he's sure a situation is going to turn out the way he wants it to."

I lean back and look at her. "I hope you don't mind me saying, but this is the weirdest conversation I've ever had with someone's mother."

Mrs. McCaffrey laughs. It's such a free and easy laugh, it's instantly clear she takes no offense. The woman is like a unicorn, unusual and mystical. The bang of the door closing draws our attention to the back of the house. Toby waddles over, tail wagging a mile a minute, but is more interested in our empty glasses than us.

Several moments behind him, Cooper arrives. "Toby watered every bush and water hydrant from here to Middle Road. Can I take Jayden out now?

Or maybe you need me to paint the garage or change the oil in your car first?"

"Nope. She's all yours. If she'll have you." Mrs. McCaffrey stands and extends a hand to me, her lips twisted in a hint of a smile.

I accept her help getting to my feet.

"Jayden, don't worry too much about what everyone else thinks. If you listen to your heart and stay true to what feels right, I have a strong hunch it will all work out." She hands me the crutches and collects our glasses. "Have fun, kids. There's a great book and a bubble bath with my name on it."

She heads back toward the house, leaving Cooper and me standing there looking at each other. A warmth spreads through my limbs as I smile at him.

"What are you smiling at?" he asks, unusually ill-humored.

"I enjoyed hanging out with your mother."

"You didn't just tolerate her?"

"Sorry. That was out of line. This week's been brutal. Mom's been upset. Troy stopped by for a 'visit.' I sprained my ankle, and Van called me a *princess*." I shift my weight and grimace. "All nicely rounded out by seeing Troy and Zoe on TV in full-force PDA, kissing and hugging for the cameras, just before you picked me up."

"I'm sorry. You should have said something. I wouldn't have been so pushy."

He lays a hand on my arm. It's the first time he's touched me in a week, underscoring how much I've missed him.

"No, it's better to be out instead of staying home and stewing about the situation—and this ankle."

"Here. Sit down. You should rest that leg as much as possible." He pulls a cushioned wicker chair closer and holds it while I sit down. Then, he sets up a second chair across from me and gently lifts my injured limb to rest on the seat cushion.

I settle into my chair, warmed by his attention. He spends an enormous amount of time with me, helping me achieve my goals. But is that love?

"Sorry dinner got sidetracked. My mother is a force of nature." He absently tugs on an earlobe. "Do you want to go to a restaurant or maybe order in and chill out here? I'm game for whatever you decide."

The detour of our dinner plans by his mother seems to stress him out, but I don't regret the interruption. The impromptu conversation with Mrs. McCaffrey has given me food for thought. I'm very hungry, though still disinterested in dealing with Saturday night restaurant crowds.

"The backyard suits me fine. Is that okay?"

"Perfectly okay." He nods. "I'll go pick something up. What do you want to have? Asian, spicy Mexican, hamburgers…"

"Spicy Mexican," I interrupt him and grin. "And a salt-rimmed margarita, please."

"Ok, spicy Mexican it is, but no alcohol, Cat. You're in training. We'll write the sangria off as a special treat." He takes his phone from his back pocket and dials the restaurant. "Trust me to order?"

"Yes. My only requirement is food and lots of it."

"On it." He grins at me and places our order. After he hangs up, he puts the ice pack on my ankle and sets up a small table and another chair next to mine. "I'll go pick it up and be right back. Need anything?"

"Just food," I say and with that, he moves swiftly across the yard and disappears into the house.

As comfortable as the chair is, I slip out of it and lie on my back, arms spread wide — grounding as Mrs. McCaffrey put it.

A breeze ruffles the plume of leaves overhead, and a solitary leaf floats down to the grass near me. In a few weeks, as the air grows steadily cooler, many more will trace the same path. Fall is waiting in the wings.

For most of my life, late summer has been a time of preparation for the start of the next year of school, getting back to a schedule. Of new possibilities. But with my mother's troubles and the fight looming, it's hard to stir up the motivation to set myself up for the fall.

A weak acceptance is as good as a soft refusal.

Mrs. McCaffrey's perceptiveness sits heavy on my chest. While I've gone at my training with all I've got, I've wavered back and forth with this fight from day one. Troy talked me out of it. Cooper talked me into it. I am halfway in, stalled and fizzling with indecision—with everything in my life, including my family.

On Monday, they'll expect me back at the gym, training for this fight. Of course, I need to go. Or do I? I agreed to do it, and there's the not-so-small matter of needing the money to save our home, but with me getting clobbered in practice fights and blowing out my ankle, I'm not convinced I'll make it to the fight in one piece.

Overhead, the mellowing evening sun dots through the thick canopy of summery leaves. I inhale deeply and imagine the earth drawing the negativity from my body, neutralizing it.

I stay put, reclined on the grass, hands stretched out over my head, until Cooper returns, a large carry-bag of food in each hand, and a folded blanket tucked under one arm.

"Grounding?" he smiles.

I push up on my elbows. "It was your mother's idea. I kind of like it."

"I suppose you might also like her suggestion of this blanket so we can eat picnic style." He sets both bags down and tosses me the blanket.

"Did you order everything on the menu?" I sit up and unfold the blanket.

"You said lots of food. If nothing else, I am a good listener."

"You are. I *really* like that about you," I say. "And I'm starving."

His curved lips send a current of raw energy pulsing through my body. I busy myself spreading the blanket on the ground, sighing when he unpacks the food. This is how it is with us, ignoring the sparks between us, pretending they don't exist.

We sit across from each other, passing the food back and forth, eating directly from the containers. There's so much food, both of us eat heartily.

I pluck at the hem of my T-shirt. "I'm having serious doubts about this fight."

"I know you're bummed about your ankle," he says, working his way through the last bites of arroz con pollo. "It's only a minor setback. Van will have you do seated workouts until it's healed."

"It's not like I can call it off."

"That's always an option." He lowers the food container. "You'll forfeit the entry-level payout plus the chance at the win bonus, but they'll likely replace you so Bocek can still have the fight."

"I wouldn't be penalized financially?"

"You'd still have to pay Van and Marcus for their time."

"But not you?" I ask.

"I'm not in it for the money." He sits back and shrugs. "Do whatever you want. Go ahead, throw in the towel if you want."

There's a challenge in his tone. I shoot him an annoyed look.

"I don't, it's just... Troy came by to see me before he left for Vegas." I thump the ground with a fist. "He said that while he loves me, he was never *in love* with me."

Cooper lowers his chin. "What bothers you most about his saying that?"

I roll my eyes. "Isn't it obvious?"

"Humor me."

"That I've wasted my time." I turn away, unable to look at him. "And that I was stupid, gullible, naïve."

"If my opinion matters, I don't think you're any of those things." He puts a hand on my shoulder. "You won't look weak *or* make a fool of yourself. I promise you that."

"You always give me more credit than I deserve." I raise my eyes to his. "Why?"

"Isn't it obvious?" He turns the question on me but without the accompanying eye roll. "Since the first time I saw a beautiful but fiercely determined girl best one of my guy teammates on a wrestling mat, I've been a fan. Like my father, I want to see you succeed."

His compliments are like a warm caress.

"Picking up where your father left off?"

"I think you're worth the effort, but emotionally speaking, there's a bit more at stake for me." He laces his fingers through mine and holds my gaze. "Maybe I'm too close to be objective."

My longing is mirrored in his eyes, but when he leans in to kiss me, I put a hand on his chest to stop him.

"Don't." Under my palm, his heart beats in a powerful rhythm. "I'm tired of playing this game of hot and cold with you."

I mentally compel him to challenge me, to try to kiss me again. Instead, he pulls back.

"You're right. I shouldn't have done that. Sorry."

I exhale loudly. "Not sorrier than me. We're attracted to each other. Why can't we just let it happen, and see where it takes us?"

"After what happened with Troy? Nope. Not going to risk doing something either of us will regret."

"I only regret Troy didn't break up with me *before* he cheated."

"That's it? That's the *only* regret you have?" His anger momentarily renders me speechless. "You ever consider why he cheated on you?"

I recover my voice. "Are you insinuating he has a *justifiable* excuse for sleeping around on me?"

"Of course not, but most behaviors usually have underlying motives," he says. "I think Troy had one."

I cross my arms. "Well, please, don't hold back. I can hardly wait to hear your studied psychological viewpoint."

"The two of you together was a mistake. And Troy knew it from day one."

"Wow, just wow." I shake my head. "Troy was my best friend. He was there for me when I needed him."

"He gave you what you believed, at that moment, you needed."

"Are you implying I needed a fuck?" My cheeks flame.

"You—"

"I'm really not in the mood for this. I'm trying to open up to you about how Troy's cheating affects me. To tell you how it feels to hear he never really loved me. It hurts me. A lot. I thought you'd respond with compassion." I swing upright onto my knees. "I'm ready to go home."

I begin shoving the food containers back into the sacks, the burn of frustration heating my face. Wordlessly, he joins in. Once the mess is cleaned up, I stand and pick up the crutches. Though I don't want to use the stupid things, I'm much faster with them. I quickly step-shuffle to his truck and get in. We drive in grim silence, an invisible wedge drawn between us.

He pulls up in my driveway and kills the headlights. Before I can open the door, he catches my arm.

"Listen, Troy was one of my best friends, but I've always known him to put his needs first. Honestly, it never bothered me—until it came to you.

That morning," he starts. I know he's talking about the morning after my father's funeral when he came to Troy's house unannounced and found us in bed together. "I asked him straight out why, after all this time, would he put your friendship on the line. Jayden, he didn't have an answer. We nearly came to blows over it."

Despite pleading with him at the time, Troy wouldn't tell me what Cooper had said. All these years, he'd kept that to himself.

"Maybe being with Troy helped you with your grief for a while, but I knew it wouldn't last," he says. "It couldn't."

He plunges a knife into my chest, where my heart is already bleeding. My limbs go cold. Troy didn't really love me, not the my-heart-beats-only-for-you kind of love. A truth obvious to Troy and Cooper and even Kara. Yet I had been blind to it.

"Why not say this back then, when it would have made a difference?"

"You know I tried. Neither of you would listen."

"Because you were angry. And now I see you were jealous, too." I tighten my hold on the door handle. Sweat trickles down my back.

"I was angry. Yeah, and jealous, too, because I liked you... a lot. And Troy knew it. I would've come to terms with your relationship if I had thought Troy was in it for real, that he was *really* in love with you."

His words, this entire conversation, cut me deep. With so much on my mind, I can't deal with more. Why can't Cooper see that? If I stay a moment more, I'll explode.

"Thanks for a memorable night," I say as I catapult from the truck, leaving the crutches behind.

Nineteen

Mom jumps up from her position on the couch when I slam the door and without the crutches, I'm forced to hop-shuffle into the house.

"What happened? Did you hurt your leg?"

She'd been so caught up in her own situation she'd failed to notice me limping into and out of her room earlier.

"Twisted it during training. It's fine." I sit next to her on the couch, my pulse still racing.

"I'm sorry about falling apart on you again," she says, her voice humbled. "I'm a total disaster lately."

I don't know what to say. I can't imagine the strain she's been under.

"Who'd ever think I'd be foolishly naïve about love at my age?"

"You and me both." I blow the hair out of my eyes. "I've been blindly naïve about Troy. He doesn't love me. He never did."

"No, no, no," she says. "Troy absolutely loves you."

"Only as a friend. His words, not mine."

"Something must have happened."

I shake my head. "We had a long-distance relationship. It was easy to fool myself about him. It's clear, even though it wasn't perfect, that I got way more mileage out of our relationship than he did."

Mom brushes the hair out of my eyes. "What a fine mess we are."

"A mother-daughter dating-disaster duo."

"At least your disaster isn't costing us the house," she replies with a grunt.

My eyes travel the room, unable to believe we could lose it, lose our family home, the place that holds the strongest memories of Dad.

"Mom, what if I asked for an advance on the fight purse?"

That'll mean I have to fight, no matter what.

"Oh honey, you've been working so hard to get ready for this fight. I can't ask that of you. I'd rather you use the money for law school, for living expenses, and whatever the scholarship doesn't cover, without loans."

"I lost my scholarship."

Mom's mouth moves like she wants to say something. She blinks several times before she finally speaks. "I don't understand. You're an outstanding student."

"With Troy fighting in Vegas, I was distracted," I admit. "I loved wrestling but it ended, and for me to continue in some type of competitive fighting, mixed martial arts is the best way. I was prepared to follow Troy into that world. His cheating pulled the rug out from under me. Everything is upside down. I planned to go back to school, but what if practicing law isn't what I'm meant to do?"

Mom scooches closer.

"Since you could speak, whenever you were asked what you wanted to do when you grew up, you said you wanted to go to law school, just like your dad. It was adorable, but I figured as you got older, you'd change your mind. Not your father, though. He was convinced you'd do it. Said he'd been the same way—that he'd known at a young age practicing law was in his future."

That one hits me in the gut, and seeming to understand, she sandwiches my hands between both of hers. We haven't touched this freely since before Dad passed.

"Jayden, you don't have to follow anyone's vision for your future, not even your father's." Her voice is soft but confident. "Your future is yours to make of it whatever you wish. And whatever they pay you to fight, that money is yours. I'd rather you use it for school, but that's up to you. I won't let you alter your life because of the mess I made."

"But Mom—"

"No, Jayden." She shakes her head firmly. "I won't, and that's final."

We sit for a moment in silence. This unbending side of her is annoying.

"Let me deal with the house. I'll figure it out. You focus on your training." She pats my hand and rises to her feet.

Long after my mother goes to bed, I lie on the couch in the dark, swollen ankle propped on a pillow, and stare into the shadows. Fragments of light dance across the ceiling whenever a car passes down the street.

Telling my mother about law school temporarily quiets my anxiety, but I still won't sleep with so much to think about. Car keys in hand, I open the front door and find my sister pulling away from another girl. I've interrupted a goodnight kiss.

The other girl slinks away in the dark to a car waiting at the end of the driveway. I quickly wipe the surprised expression from my face.

"Where are you going?" Kara takes out a tube of lip balm and applies a fresh coat.

If she's annoyed that I interrupted her private moment, she doesn't show it. I jiggle the keys in my hand, unsure I want to share. Her expression is open, unperturbed. She is giving me a chance to connect with her.

"To see Dad. Want to come?"

"Sure," she responds with a brief rise of her shoulders.

My foot remains steady on the gas pedal, cruising twenty miles over the speed limit. At the late hour, traffic is thin.

"That girl—" Hands clasped on her lap, I sense my sister's discomfort, having to justify herself.

"No need to explain. Do what makes you happy," I say. "It's your life."

"Thanks." Kara grins unabashedly, and a swell of pride rises within me.

I applaud my sister for not permitting other people's narrow attitudes to dictate the person she's supposed to be with and fall in love with.

We drive the rest of the way in silence. I haven't been to St. Patrick's in ages, but I know the way by heart. Park hours are posted on a sign at the entrance—open until 6 p.m.—but there's no gate.

I snap off the radio and turn my face to the open window. The darkness within the park seems unnaturally inert. Deep pockets of shadow lend a downright eeriness that slithers down my back, but I came to visit my father, and I'm not leaving until I do. I steer the car down the center lane, crawling along until I get to the section where my father lies in eternal rest. I park and turn off the lights. Dad's plot is only a row away. I limp through the damp grass past a line of plots, wishing I hadn't been too stubborn to take the crutches.

"And we're visiting Dad right now because... why?" Kara asks peeking around.

"I just needed to," I say.

"We should keep an eye out for security guards—or lost souls." Kara clutches my arm as if to help me, but she's leaning into me, hindering more than helping, but I don't mind. It's like she trusts me to protect her. And I will, at any cost.

In front of his headstone, the two of us lower to our knees. There's a bouquet of wilted flowers, the petals scattered on the ground. On the attached weather-curled note card, someone drew a heart and wrote: "I miss you."

It's Mom's handwriting.

"Daddy—" I kneel, head low, wanting to say something, but the words get strangled in my throat.

When I was younger, no matter what was going on, Dad made everything right. Mom often called us two peas in a pod. He once told me he didn't like it when people told him he couldn't do something. It made him want to prove them wrong. I inherited that characteristic from him.

I'd been fifteen and nervous when I faced off with the school board to get permission to wrestle. Dad's support bolstered my belief that I could get the board to amend their outdated rules. I stood at the podium that day, before a room of adults, mostly men, reading off my painstakingly prepared speech, Dad on one side, Coach on the other. Behind me, Cooper, Troy, and the wrestling team sat, along with a handful of parents and classmates. I told the board girls should have the same opportunity as boys and backed it up with facts.

I left the room that day to the sound of applause, my future crystal clear. When did it get so cloudy? A silly question since I know exactly when.

Troy went to Vegas.

"I'm at a crossroads, and I don't know what to do, Dad," I whisper. "Should I fight regardless of the likelihood I'll get my ass handed to me, or do I just forget it, and go back to law school?" I rip a handful of grass from the ground. "I wish you were here to help me figure it out. Could you maybe give me a sign? Something to help me decide?"

I hold my breath and wait, but there's no miracle response from heaven, though, just the long hush of nightfall.

"Hi, Daddy. I miss you." Kara sits, knees tucked to her chest, and rocks herself, the side of her face wet with tears. Her greeting chokes me up and reminds me that I am not the only one who lost my father. Mom and Kara lost him, too. And, to a lesser degree, so did Troy. Dad's death affected us all. Running away has solved nothing in my life. It has only closed doors behind me and is possibly the impetus that sent my life off the rails, beginning with Cooper.

Faint chatter catches our ears, and Kara and I turn with a start. Off in the distance, the voices of a group of shadowy people carry through the park.

My sister's eyes grow wide with fear. "Let's get out of here."

I look around for something to mark my visit. Under my palm, I feel a stone and dig it out of the ground. I dust it off on my shorts and give it to Kara to place on the marble ledge that runs the perimeter of the headstone.

"I love you, Daddy. I hope wherever you are, you are happy and safe," I murmur, running my fingers across the polished face of the stone, tracing the engraved letters of my father's name.

After a moment of silence, we stand and make our way back to the car.

"You can't drop out of the fight," Kara says. "You *love* fighting. Dad used to drag me to all of your meets. They bored me to tears, but even then, I could see how much you loved fighting."

"But this isn't the same. And I hate the gossipy, public theater around this fight."

"Sure, you're a private person, but you've been training your butt off. People would have to be blind to miss how focused and motivated you've been since you agreed to take the fight."

"Yeah, but I don't have Zoe's experience."

"Cooper thinks you have a chance."

"Cooper's an eternal optimist. My only chance lies in my ability to endure a beating and get her to the mat."

"Then that's what you do, Jayden. You get her to the mat."

I chuckle at my sister's certainty that I can make that happen. Sliding into the driver's seat, my phone, perched in the car's console, beeps with a missed call and a voice message from Cooper.

"You're not taking my call, so I guess that means you're still angry with me." The recording pauses. "I just wanted to say, I don't care what you do regarding the fight—take it or leave it—but remember how much you love wrestling. Think about these past few months, how focused and into the training you've been, and how much you've learned and improved. Competitive fighting calls to you. Don't rule out this fight just because you're scared.

"Anyway, you're on a full day of rest tomorrow. Keep off that ankle. That's an order, Cat. Come Monday morning, I'll be outside your house at 4:45 a.m. If you don't come out, I'll know your decision. And I will support that decision, unequivocally."

Three times tonight I've been reminded of my love of wrestling and competitive fighting and by the three people most important to me.

"You're lucky. You had Dad, Coach, and now Cooper helping you figure out everything," Kara says, staring at my cell. "I'm facing a big hairy undecided future without any help."

"You're not on your own. You have Mom." I flick her shoulder with the back of my hand. "And me."

"Do I?" She eyes me apprehensively.

"Of course," I say.

"Okay." With a shrug, she takes out her phone and begins scrolling through the social media app du jour.

My past absence from everyday life makes her mistrust me, but somehow, I'll prove she can trust that I'll be here whenever she needs me.

I lie in bed and stare at the ceiling, knowing sleep won't come any time soon. Kara is right. I've been mentored and supported by some of the best people I know. Right now, all she has is Mom and me. I acknowledge the comfort of knowing both she and my mother are nearby. Unlike visits home before, the three of us are figuring it out.

We have each other. And that isn't nothing.

Adele pushes my bedroom door open and pitter-patters across the room to the bedside. She meows a warning before she jumps up and curls her furry body into the nook between my arms and stomach, as she does most nights.

I stroke her fur, thinking about Cooper and his voice message. I'm not angry at him. Our conversation in his backyard made me uncomfortable. He'd grasped the truth about my and Troy's relationship right from the start.

Somehow, at nineteen, Cooper had understood that sex, the physical act I sought, would be a temporary fix for my grief, like popping pills for chronic pain instead of investigating the root cause. Grief though, as I've come to understand, isn't meant to be escaped. Three years ago, I couldn't see that, and when Cooper wouldn't provide the distraction I sought, I went elsewhere.

I'd shifted the weight and responsibility of my pain onto Troy, who'd also been grieving. The sex, I now realize, acted as a distraction, an unwitting balm for the emptiness, the wounds of death we both deeply felt. Because he loved me, and because I pushed for it, Troy had shouldered the burden and allowed me to falsely hold onto the belief that together we had everything, the perfect relationship—romance and friendship—when, in fact, romantically, we were a poor fit.

Maybe, just maybe I unconsciously knew he was messing around with other girls and just wouldn't allow myself to consider it. Not that it absolved him. My so-called best friend betrayed and shamed me, and worse, with the public watching.

But this revelation enables me to see why he was ambiguous about my moving to Vegas. He'd seen it as his escape, his chance to move on. Deeply humiliated, I pull the purring Adele to my chest and burrow my face in her soft fur. It's time to move forward, to own the mistakes I've made, and let my heart finally heal.

Careful not to upset Adele, I grab a pen and the yellow pad where I've previously scribbled some thoughts for my soon-due mission statement.

I write. And write. Filling three pages with thoughts for my future—my dreams, goals, what I believe in. Satisfied, I put the pad and pen on the night table, shut the light, and close my eyes.

The morning sun shines in my window and stirs me awake. Barefoot, I make my way to the kitchen to grab a protein bar and ice pack, and then limp out to the backyard. In contrast to Mr. Murphy's colorful, well-loved oasis of a yard, ours is a blank slate. I've been away. Mom has a full plate. Kara is uninterested. The backyard upkeep has simply become another chore on a long list of things to do. Conceding that while the lawn and gardens are austere and patchy, at least it's mowed and neat. I find a sunny spot on the perimeter of the pool and lie in the grass.

Half an hour later, the back door opens.

"Jayden? Are you all right?" Mom's shadow stripes across my legs. She's wearing the men's periwinkle Oxford from her closet. "I worried about you after we talked last night. Maybe I came on too harsh."

"You weren't harsh. You made me think. And I'm fine. Better than fine." I stretch my arms wide and smile at her. "I learned this new technique called grounding."

"You want a towel to lie on?"

"No. It works better when there's nothing between you and the earth." I squint up at her. "Take off your shoes and join me."

With a shrug, Mom slips out of her canvas mules and lies on the ground, shimmying closer until the tops of our heads touch. "What's supposed to happen?"

"It's a natural energy thing. It'll make you feel good."

We lie there inhaling and exhaling.

"Is that Dad's shirt you're wearing?" I ask.

"Yes, I kept a few of his shirts and sweaters. When I'm feeling down, I like wearing something of his."

"Nice," is all I can say, I'm so overcome with emotion.

"I have some *sort of* good news," she says. "I put in for a mortgage forbearance to temporarily suspend monthly payments. Being a single-parent widow, the loan manager said there's a good chance I'll be approved."

"That *is* good news, Mom." And it is, mostly. It won't relieve the debt, but hopefully, it'll give us time to catch up. More so, I'm proud of her for taking a proactive step, on her own.

"I'm happy you came home, Jayden. You may not believe it, but I've missed you. And I certainly don't know how I would've gotten through this mess without you," Mom says. "And I want you to know I'm sorry for how I behaved when your father died. I'm sorry I wasn't more patient and understanding with your feelings. I should have been more attentive to you and your sister. I'm your mother. I should've been setting an example, not—" It isn't until she hiccups a sob that I realize she's crying.

"It's okay, Mom." I twist around and tip my forehead to hers. "You were grieving. Losing Daddy was hard. It didn't help that I acted like a spoiled brat, and I'm sorry for that."

She curls her smooth, warm hand around mine. "I need you to know that regardless of how you and I came together, as much as your sister is, you're every bit my daughter. Every bit. And I love you just as much."

A quiet whimper forces its way up my throat.

"I love you too, Mom." I kiss my mother's forehead and return to my position on the grass.

Inhaling, I will myself to let go of the resentments that have held us apart. Hot, tight pressure releases with the tears that trickle down the sides of my face. This place of acceptance and forgiveness has been a hard spot for my mother and me to arrive at, but we're finally opening the door.

"Hey! What are you guys doing?" Kara's voice calls from the back door.

Without opening my eyes, I wave my arm. "We're grounding. Come out and join us. It's good for you."

"Grounding?" She sounds like Mom.

I feel the vibration of her steps in the grass as she draws near to us.

"I found these outside next to the front door."

I crack open an eye to find she's got those damn crutches.

"That guy." I laugh and pat the ground. "Come on, sis. Take your shoes off and get down here with us. Let the earth discharge your negative energy."

"Hmph. It's an actual thing." She kicks off a pair of bright yellow flip-flops, her attention on her cell as she lets the crutches fall to the grass. "Grounding: a therapeutic technique that involves doing activities that electrically reconnect you to the earth."

"You can also hug a tree," I say.

"Eww, I'm not hugging a tree. That's like hugging bugs." She slips to the ground, lying perpendicular to Mom and me.

As the three of us lie head-to-head-to-head, staring up at a picturesque blue summer sky, I'm aware I can't undo what I've already done. None of us can. It's better to focus on what we can do—how I can be a better daughter, a more reliable big sister. Right now, it's enough to enjoy a few peaceful minutes with two of the most important people in my life.

"God, do you remember how much fun we used to have out here? All the barbeques and pool parties?" I turn to look across the yard, past my sister. "Remember that time Dad threw Mom into the pool?"

Mom laughs. "I had just had my hair done. I was so angry at him!"

"I remember when I missed a camping trip with the Girl Scouts. Dad set up a tent, and we camped out for the weekend," Kara adds.

"Oh yeah. I forgot about that," I say, smiling. It feels good to talk about Dad. Talking about him makes me feel like he's still here. Like he's present and not in the past. We need to talk about him more. This is a good start.

Mom shifts onto her stomach. "A lot of good memories for sure."

"But with no one around, I hardly ever come back here anymore." Kara rolls over too.

"Me neither. With no one using it, the pool is just too much work. Without your father, the whole house is just too much." Mom is quiet for a moment before she asks, "How would you girls feel if I put it up for sale?"

After all the stress of trying to figure out how to keep the house, now she wants to give it up, *willingly*?

"But this was the last place Dad lived. How do you think he would feel about us letting it go?" Kara asks what's on all our minds.

The questions drop us into silence.

Though I can't see Mom's face, I feel her eyes on me. An ache blooms in my heart as I let my eyes trace the stone path up to the back door. It's hard to imagine not calling this house home, to not have access to the place where my life's memories begin—where my father's ended.

I consider the facts. It's only a matter of time before I'll be off, away from here, back to pursuing my career, and likely, setting up a new home, my home. And with Kara starting college next fall, Mom will be here alone. It'd be selfish to insist she struggle to hold onto and maintain this house just so I don't have to let it go, so I can continue to call it home.

"For what it's worth," Mom says, taking my and my sister's hands. "I think all Daddy would care about is that we're together, happy and healthy." She squeezes our fingers. "And doing what we love."

"Yes," I add. "I agree with Mom, one hundred percent."

"What if I don't know what I love?" Kara asks.

"You keep trying new things until something clicks and feels right," I reply.

"That's easy for you to say," my sister replies. "You're the bravest chick I've ever known."

The unexpected compliment makes me twist to look at her. It's the nicest thing she's said to me in years.

"Except your sister isn't feeling so courageous lately," Mom says, stifling the hum.

"Because of Troy?" Kara's attentive gaze stays on me. "He's just a guy, Jay. You know I love Troy—we all do—but all the time you were together, he was a tool. He didn't really treat you well."

I flop back down onto the grass. "How is it that everyone saw this but me?"

"Grief and loneliness create blind spots," Mom answers. "The same way you couldn't see the truth about you and Troy, I couldn't see Alejandro for the scam artist he really is. Your father left a hole we've been trying to fill."

Kara's fingers tickle my arm. "All my girlfriends talk about is how fearless you are, Jay. You're Bruiser Jones. You got all up in the school board's face to be the first girl on an all-boys wrestling team. Your legacy is a huge shadow to live under, but, you know, there are perks to being the sister of that girl. No one gets away with treating me or any of my friends any different because we don't have a schlong between our legs."

"Kara, really," Mom huffs.

"Oh, mother." Kara rolls her eyes and turns her face to me. "Jay, all the girls in my class are rooting for you in the upcoming fight. We want you to kick Zoe Bocek's ass."

A full-blown smile rounds my lips. "Thanks for the vote of confidence."

Kara gives me a thumbs-up and lays back. "Hey, if we move our arms and legs in the grass, will we get healthier, quicker?"

"I don't know. Can't hurt to try," I say.

Kara and I swing our arms and legs, doing grass versions of snow angels.

"Come on, Mom," Kara urges.

"Yeah, come on, Mom!" I reach behind me and pat her head.

Mom finally joins in, and our laughter fills the air as the three of us flail around in the grass like little kids.

TWENTY

I drive the Impala to the town beach after dinner. A woman is walking her dog. The day trippers have left, and it's too early and too light out for teens cruising around in their parents' cars. I leave the crutches on the seat and grab my cell phone. A soft breeze rolls off the bay, nudging small waves onto the fine-textured sand of the little beach.

The past couple of days have given me hope and even a bit of clarity. Maybe the reminders of my strength, the gentle pushes to take the fight from Cooper and Kara, and even Mom, are messages from my father.

"If that was your doing, Dad, message received. Thanks."

I lean against the side of the car, stilling myself, and dial Cooper. What I have to say can't wait until Monday morning.

"Hey," he answers on the first ring.

"Are you busy?" I ask. "I'm at the town beach."

"Be there in a few," he says.

I can't help but smile because Cooper is the OG, genuinely kind. Somebody who can be counted on whenever needed, by anyone, but I get the impression he goes the extra mile for me. Maybe that's what love feels like.

A little more than five minutes go by when his truck rolls into the parking lot, tires crunching over sand scattered from the beach. My heart stops, then speeds up, and the damn thing actually flutters. And when he smiles at me through the open window, I'm about done in.

Jurisprudence. Jurisprudence.

I brace my hands on the hood of my car as my knees wobble with anticipation. I feel like I'm fifteen years old again, beaming at him like a lovesick puppy. Maybe this is what love feels like.

Out of the truck, he shuts the door and stops a few feet from me. His smile is like a comfortable pair of blue jeans. Just the right fit. It takes everything inside me not to reach for him, touch him, but a mea culpa must come first.

"You were right about a few things," I start.

"Oh, yeah?" His grin grows wider. "I already like where this conversation is headed."

"Don't get all big-headed on me now." I chuckle and turn my gaze to the water, so I don't get distracted. "You were right about Troy and me. The two of us were a mistake."

I pause to get the words straight in my head.

"Being with him helped me cope with losing my father. Looking back, we weren't normal. We didn't kiss and hug. I wasn't a very good girlfriend. I didn't hold his hand or get excited when he walked into the room. Most of the years, we were in different states. We didn't do 'couply-like' things. We were just friends who stepped over that line. Toward the end, we barely touched each other. I can't fault him for wanting something more than what we had."

"Don't you do that, Jayden. Don't let him off the hook. He didn't do right by you." Cooper grabs my hand and makes me look at him.

"Yes, his cheating was wrong, but I can't lay the blame for all my troubles at his feet." I hesitate, again. "When you rejected me, I went off the rails—"

"Jayden, you don't know how difficult that was," he interrupts. "I swear, I wanted you, but you'd just lost your dad. You were vulnerable. I didn't want to be your one-night hero. I wish had let me explain instead of running away."

"I wish I'd let you explain, too. But my point is, my father's death turned me upside down. Troy was hurting, too. I created this impossible situation for him. For us. Trying to escape sorrow and pain is not a healthy way to start a relationship. Barely out of high school, you somehow already knew this, and that's why you turned me down."

"The only way past the pain..." he starts.

"...is to go through the pain," I finish.

"Ah, little grasshopper, you have learned well." Hands in prayer, he bows.

"Yeah, it only took me all these years to learn." I let out a little laugh. "Part of that lesson is that it's best to be honest and open with the people closest to you. Which brings me to one last thing—the reason I've been a little preoccupied."

"Okay." He leans against my car, intrigued.

"It's embarrassing." I drop my gaze.

"You can tell me. I promise it won't change how I think of you."

I square my shoulders and raise my chin. The best way to do this is to yank it off like a Band-Aid.

"My mother got involved in an online dating scam. And she lost a lot of money."

Cooper's eyebrows shoot up. "How bad is it?"

"It's sunk us. We're on the brim of foreclosure."

"Well, shit, that sucks. I'm sorry." He pushes off the car, arms raised like he's going to embrace me, but stops. "Can I give you a hug?"

I half-smile and nod. "I'd like that."

He wraps an arm around my waist and the other across my back, my head cradled in the crook of his neck. The strength of his arms and the earthy masculine smell his of skin mollify me, and I literally let myself go and sink into his embrace.

Maybe this is what love feels like.

"So, the fight." He pulls back slightly to look at my face. "You took it for the money?"

"Well, at first I wanted revenge on Troy and Zoe, which you called me on. Then, it was for the money. Over the last few days, it's become about so much more, but mostly, it's about me. I want to prove to myself that I'm capable. That I can go the distance."

"I know how important that is for you. You have more than enough talent for this fight, Jayden," he says. "We're going to practice the moves until you can do them in your sleep. No one is going to be less than impressed by your fighting skill."

"You sure know how to butter a fighter up."

"Sounds like we're doing this then." His blue-jean smile seals the deal.

"Yep. I'm all in," I say. "No turning back, for real this time."

TWENTY-ONE

I roll out of bed at four on Monday, put my workout gear on, and ice my ankle. I am standing at the door when Cooper's truck slides to the curb. He barely pulls to a stop, and I'm out the door. The ankle is better, but I use the crutches anyway. It *must* heal, so I'll go easy on it for a few days more.

With confidence is the only way forward. No more doubt. No allowing negative thoughts to prevail. My strength training included learning how to withstand punches and kicks, but I will likely get hurt during this fight. There is no way around that. I'm young and healthy, and I will recover from anything Zoe can do to me.

"Good morning!" Cooper croons as I scuttle into the seat next to him. He puts the truck in gear and pulls out. "How's the ankle?"

"It's good." I look down at my hands in my lap. "Cooper, I need you to train me. Please say you will. Van is great and all, but it's not the same. I need you."

"This upcoming fight is major. The biggest fight of your life. I think it's best if we don't get sidetracked. My presence seems to distract you."

"I'm more distracted when you're not there."

He scratches the back of his head.

"Okay, but you have to promise to stay focused." He glances my way, expression serious. "Your open invitation not only distracts you, but it also distracts me, too. I'm only human."

I take a moment, smiling as I bask in that admission before I respond. "I promise. I need to wrestle you. If I can best you, I can best Zoe."

"I hear a bet coming on." He breaks into a grin.

"Oh, yes. Let's bet!" I grin back. "What will you give me if I pin you?"

"What do you want?"

"Sex," I say with a laugh.

"Jayden," he chastises. "You *literally* just promised to stay focused."

"I meant it as a joke, but hey, why not? With that kind of incentive, I guarantee I'll stay focused."

"No, absolutely not." He shakes his head.

"Why?" I turn in my seat to look at his profile. "Is the idea of having sex with me that unappealing?"

"It's not that." He briefly glances my way, then back to the road. "To bet you is hardly fair. I'm taller and outweigh you by a good forty pounds."

"Both things I know and accept, and more reasons for you to take the bet," I say. "If I pin you, we have sex."

"So, you get something if you pin me. What do I get if you can't?"

"Depends on what you'd like." I splay my hands in appeal. "Name your conditions, McCaffrey."

He swings the truck into a parking spot at the gym and turns off the ignition. "In the unlikely event that you win, the sex doesn't happen until *after* the fight. And, if I win, you stop asking for sex. Full stop."

"That seems way harsh, but okay." I shrug.

"The fight with Zoe is only three weeks away. The bet expires the Friday of the week before the fight. If you haven't pinned me by then, the win is mine."

"I accept your terms. Let's shake on it." I hold out my hand.

He shakes my hand, pushing his lips into a frown that says, "What the hell have I gotten myself into."

A renewed sense of energy puts a bounce in my step, and I gear up and get right to work. To keep me off the ankle, the day's workout focuses on exercises I can do from a seated position. First, I work my arms with the heavy rope and the rowing machine. Then, it's onto floor exercises and so much ab work, I'm sure I'll puke.

By the end of the week, I ditch the crutches and charge full steam into regular workouts, upping my sparring time. Dani puts me through the paces.

My training ends each day on the mat, grappling with Cooper. I am no pushover, but the first week in, I am nowhere near besting him. The stalemate ratchets up my competitive drive. With one week left, I immerse myself in learning: watching videos of wrestling moves during meals and downtime, and listening to grappling tips and advice while I run my miles. I try new moves on Cooper each day. I play my battle song, Sia's "Unstoppable," on repeat.

I will either win or run out of time. There's no giving up. Two days before our bet is to expire, a week before the fight, I try something completely different. We begin grappling normally. I pretend to keep resorting to the old moves until we are upright, facing off, both of our bodies leaning in. I rush him, and he goes low, aiming for my waist, putting me in the optimal position to leap up and onto his back. In that position, I easily curl my arms around his waist, bringing the full weight of my body down on him. Because he's reaching forward, it throws him off balance. We crash to the ground, and I tie up his leg and ram him with my shoulder until his back hits the mat. I twist his legs at an awkward angle that immobilizes him There's that moment in wrestling when you know you've bested your opponent, but as Coach always said, you never let up until the ref calls it. Cooper's stuck. I have him.

"Pin!" Marcus calls the match for me and fist pumps the air. "This girl is killing it!"

After I untangle myself from Cooper, he sits up slowly, trying to hide a wince, but I catch it.

"That old war injury again?" I offer him a hand up.

"What can I say? You're a bruiser, Cat. You got me." Cooper accepts my hand, laughing as he shakes his head. "What the hell was that?"

"They call it a flying squirrel. Saw a high school kid do it on a video," I say, grinning. "It's all about the element of surprise."

I am three strips into cutting the lawn when the O'Brien's Lawn Service truck and trailer pull up in front of my house. The crew gets out and starts setting up their equipment. I stop the mower and walk over to explain their error.

"This address is on our list," the head guy says.

"We had a billing issue. Call your office."

He tells his crew to hold up and makes a call from the cab of the truck. A few minutes later, he strolls over to me. "According to the office, the bill has been paid through the rest of the season." He nods to the workers, and they start up the noisy equipment.

Someone paid our bill.

Annoyed, I push the lawnmower into the garage and dial Cooper.

"I didn't confide in you for your charity," I say when he answers.

"Hello, Jayden," he says, skating around my ill humor. "It's nice to hear your voice."

I'm not as successful at skating around it. "My family doesn't need charity in the form of lawn maintenance—or in any form."

"Lawn maintenance? I have no idea what you're talking about." Despite my heated charge, on the other end of the line, Cooper remains even-tempered. "I have respected your wish and your family's privacy. Though, if you ask, I'm available for whatever you need."

"So, O'Brien's isn't you?" I ask.

"Whatever you're referring to, it wasn't me."

I dip my head in embarrassment. "I'm sorry."

"No worries. But when you find out who's responsible, maybe don't be so hard on them. Some people like to help others. No need to be a martyr."

I look up and see one of the landscaping crew cross the street to start another job—the Murphys' house.

I've thought about Troy many times since visiting the cemetery. Our relationship is battered and bruised, and yet, we cannot erase the long history between us. And, in his own way, he's trying to make amends.

TWENTY-TWO

Zoe and I assemble our teams for weigh-in and rules meeting the night before the fight. Her face is leaner, but her tatted ropey arms are thicker, and oiled for the weigh-in. We take turns stepping onto the scale, our weights recorded by officials. Height for height, pound for pound, her 133 to my 129, we're well-matched. They urge us to stand together for a few publicity photos. We both step forward, my head spinning with the surreal lead-up to this fight. But as we face each other, posing with fists raised, Zoe's gaze is dark, menacing—hateful. I am reminded that we're here because of her. And Troy. They started this whirlwind, and I'm ready to finish it. I flatten my lips and narrow my gaze, matching the bloodthirsty look in Zoe's eyes. After a few quick flashes, I turn my back on her.

Troy mills around in the periphery, but I haven't made eye contact or acknowledged his presence. Even as I ignore him, I wonder what's going through his head. Does he even care that this fight is not only a pinnacle moment in Zoe's life but also in mine?

Is there a part of him rooting for me?

"You looked fierce up there." Cooper steps up to me and hands me my sneakers. "You're more than ready for this."

"I *am* ready." Sitting to tie my shoelaces, I take a slow, deep breath to ease the tension in my shoulders. No matter what happened with Troy, no matter how deep the wound of his betrayal, I mustn't lose sight of why I'm here. Zoe isn't my enemy. She's my opponent, and I'm here to compete—*to win*.

"Thank you," Cooper says, and I glance at him, questioning him with my eyes. "For trusting me to get you here. It's been an honor."

"I couldn't have done this without you."

"Yeah, you could have," he says.

"Maybe." I stand and face him. "But your confidence in my ability made me rise to the challenge. So, thank *you*."

Our private moment ends when Van descends on us and orders me to hydrate and carb load, giving me the green light to consume as much pasta, potatoes, and rice as I want.

The following night is Fight Night. My corner crew, Cooper, Van, and Marcus, keep me company in one of the backroom staging areas. It's a small, impersonal room with a few chairs, a shower stall, and a treatment table; its black pleather cracked here and there. Marcus packs a bucket with towels, gauze, scissors, tape, and ice packs to tend to injuries during the fight. After Van tapes and wraps my hands, there's nothing but time to kill until I'm called into the arena. Cooper blasts Sia's "Unstoppable" and does mitt work with me, maintaining a stream of positivity, but despite it, there's a nervous energy in the air.

Time was limited, but I've trained hard for as long as possible. All that's left is to go into this fight and give it my best shot. It's all I've got to give. Maybe it's enough. Maybe it isn't. Either way, I can't let indecisive thoughts take up valuable real estate in my head. I've been working on my mental game, journaling, and using affirmations. With my ankle taped up for extra support, I switch from mitt work to jumping rope at a metered pace, keeping my eyes trained on the wall, and steel my thoughts from running away by repeating my affirmations: *I am a trained fighter. I trust myself to know what to do and when to do it.*

A backstage organizer pops into the doorway to say, "You're up," and a wave of awareness swells over me. Everything that's happened over the last few months has led me to this moment, and I am ready to meet it head-on.

Non-championship fights by mostly unknowns like Zoe and me are typically a lesser draw, lower in ranking on the night's fight card, and our match is the first in the lineup. My team heads onto the floor of the arena followed by Zoe and her team. A rush of noise fills the air as we head down the main aisle. The volume increases as the crowd becomes aware of us. We're one of several preliminary fights before the main event. No one expects the audience to pay attention to undercard bouts for up-and-coming fighters like us. However, Troy's celebrity status and the media blitz around my and Zoe's personal fight have gained us a following. Many are on their feet, yelling and clapping as the guys and I claim our side of the octagon, opposite Zoe and her crew. On the floor outside the octagon, I strip off my sweatshirt and kick off my sandals. Jacked up on adrenalin and nerves, I bounce on my bare feet, making wide arm circles to keep my muscles warm and limber.

Black mesh fencing encircles the ring. Cage-like, it's raised a few feet off the ground and bathed in bright stage lights. A fight official lumbers over to do a visual check of my front and back, my hand wraps, and the inside of my mouth. Once he nods his approval, Van smears my face with petroleum jelly.

I search the sea of moving faces beyond the mesh octagon for Mom and Kara. I almost give up until I spot Kara next to Mom, jumping up and down, waving her arms, and shouting. What she's shouting I can't tell, but knowing they are here settles something inside me.

Cooper holds up my mouthguard, and I open my mouth for him to slip it past my lips. I ground my teeth down on the pliable plastic until it settles into place. He follows me as I mount the steps and pass through the gate into the octagon. This is it. My body hums with electricity. The noises of the arena blend together, becoming an insignificant whirr in the background.

"You tire her out," Van yells through the black fence dividing us, his directive clear and simple. "Get her to the ground, and do what you know best."

"Hey," Cooper says, drawing my attention. He holds up a little stuffed bear and wiggles it back and forth. Champ, the tie-dyed toy Coach used to bring to our wrestling matches. I grin through my mouth guard and reach forward to rub the top of Champ's furry head.

"For luck," I say.

"This is your fight, Cat. Three rounds. You set the pace." His tone is serious, eyes unblinking. "You worked hard. You deserve to be here."

I nod and bounce around on the balls of my feet, throwing jabs.

My crew and I are keenly aware of the importance of this fight for Zoe—a career fight—but I push that to the back of my mind and mentally reset.

Competitive fighting isn't about emotions. It's about one's ability to outmaneuver, outwit, and overpower the opponent. Zoe is simply another of the many fighters I've faced before. I will hold my own. I can. I will.

The referee signals us out to the center of the ring. Once again, I notice Zoe's muscled arms and the many tats. The ink seems to tell a story, but I don't have time to look at her long enough to grasp the narrative. I meet her stare, head-on.

"I've been dreaming of this moment." Zoe leans in. "Dreaming of the hurting I'm going to give you."

I keep quiet. Smack talk isn't my thing.

Unlike my ice blue shorts and top, her outfit is foreboding black with bright pink trim. The stern features of her face appear carved of stone. We stare each other down as the burly ref dressed all in black calls for a fair fight. Both sets of gloved hands touch, brief double fist pumps, her black gloves to my white ones.

The ref motions us apart and holds out his arms. He points to me and asks, "Ready?"

I nod. He does the same to Zoe, and she nods.

"Fight!" he bellows and steps out from between us.

The bell clangs and everything outside the ring blurs. Zoe is all I see. My mind clicks into battle mode, and my feet follow, moving into a practiced rhythm, side-to-side, foot-to-foot. She kicks and spins without trying to connect. Showmanship. She loves this. She lives for it. Her jaunty smile and bouncing are meant to intimidate me. I block it out. I throw a few jabs, concentrating on how she responds, cataloging the best time to strike.

She throws some early kicks, ones easy to avoid. I skip around to stay away from her fists. To get at her, I need to close the distance between us, but I also need to limit my time in the strike zone of those dangerous legs. Though I bob and weave exactly as Van taught me, Zoe lands a few punches. She swings her right fist like a mallet. I don't know if it's because I'm jacked up on adrenaline or my conditioning, but I barely feel the hits.

She kicks, misses, spins, and kicks again, just like she did earlier. I expect the second kick and reach out to catch her leg, and I yank her off balance and take her to the floor. Our bodies locked together, we grapple, each trying to outpower the other until Zoe manages to pull herself to her feet and me along with her.

She twists, using the momentum to slam me against the cage. Before I can react, she has me in a headlock and begins hammering me with knee strikes to my stomach, waist, and upper thighs. I buck against the hold uselessly, feeling every single blow. The bell rings, and hand cradling my stomach, I return to my corner and collapse on the stool.

Just like a racecar pulling in for a pit stop, my crew immediately flies into action. Cooper accepts the mouth guard I spit into his hand and squirts water into my mouth as Marcus rotates ice packs from my stomach, to face to shoulders.

"Stay loose, relax, breathe," Van says as he rolls each of my arms between his callused palms. "You're doing great."

"I finally found something you suck at, Van. Lying," I say, but Van pays no attention, stepping aside to let Cooper wipe my face and feed me my mouthguard. The one-minute break between rounds feels like seconds before the bell rings, and I'm back on my feet.

Halfway into the second round, I ram Zoe and knock her to the floor. She goes berserk, kicking and punching me so fast, I fall back against the cage. She pounces on me, ties up my right arm, and elbows me in the forehead. Blood gushes down my face and into my eyes, impeding my vision.

At the bell, I blindly totter to my corner. Cooper gives me water and kneads my arms, Marcus applies ice, and Van attends to the gushing injury. He presses an ice-cold metal Enswell eye iron across the cut to stop the bleeding. It should sting, but my heart is pumping so hard, I barely feel anything.

"How's the ankle holding up?" Cooper asks.

It's twinging, but I give him a quick nod.

"Last round. Go for her legs. Get her to the mat," Van barks and smears a thick clear ointment across the wound. "Don't let her put you against that damn fence."

Order received, I stand and smack my gloves together.

"This is it, Cat. Five minutes. Do what you do best. Take her down." Cooper swats my backside and exits the gate.

Five minutes to endure or five minutes to triumph. Five minutes either way.

This is a place I've been before: on the brink of a match that could go either way. And I know what to do.

Take her down. Get her to the mat. This is *my* round.

Focused on these directives, I shore up my resolve, raise my fists, and move forward. As soon as I'm close enough, I swing. She ducks the punch, but I'm able to hook an arm around her neck and strike her in the stomach. She counterstrikes with a series of hip shots.

I'm busy fighting her off when she seizes my right leg. My balance is superior, though, and I remain upright, hammering her with punches to her face and both sides of her head. I lean into her, letting her take the bulk of my weight, and jack my free leg forward, ramming her with my knee, once, twice, three times.

My knee strikes shake her off balance and, weakened by the barrage of hits, her grip loosens. Having the upper hand galvanizes me, and I suck in a full breath and hurl myself on top of her. Before we even hit the ground, I'm pretzeled around her, my arms around her neck, my legs around her torso. Tightly entwined, we slam to the octagon floor as a bundled mass. I intensify my hold, squeezing the life out of her like a snake. Held down by my full length and weight, my shoulder pinning her right arm, she strikes me feebly with her left. I take a few blows until I catch the arm and force it down, trapping it between my thighs, and then I gun her face with elbow strikes. Red stains smear her cheeks. With a surge of adrenaline, I twist and rotate, forcing her face down into the mat, her arm still caught between my thighs. Her response is immediate. Her whole body tightens. Even as I hold her, hammering the side of her face with short pumps of my fist, both of us dripping with sweat, her attention is fixed on the arm caught between my legs. A successful arm bar will end the fight. She wriggles under me, frantically trying to break free. There's no escape. I've got her, and as I squeeze my thighs tighter, her arm rotates toward an awkward, precarious angle.

Another inch, just one more, and the ref will call it.

The hissing roar of the crowd breaks through, followed by the ref tugging my leg loose from the hold on Zoe's arm.

It takes me a few seconds to realize the bell rang. The fight is over.

I uncoil myself from Zoe. She lies still for a few moments before she rolls over and sits up. I offer her my hand.

For a moment, I think she's not going to take it, but finally, she does, and I pull her to her feet. We say nothing and go to our corners.

"You owned that round," Van says. "You had her."

Marcus ices my shoulders as we wait for the judges to decide on the winner.

"Cat, you were amazing!" Cooper shouts.

I spit my mouth guard out. "A few more damn seconds and she would have tapped out!"

"No doubt, but just the same, you did good, girlie," Van says with a bob of his chin. "You did real, real good."

I don't know if it's the unexpected nod of respect from my cantankerous coach or the release of tension from the end of the fight that causes my eyes to well up.

My vision swims as I meet his gaze. "Thanks, Van."

"Don't be getting all princessy on me now." He hands me a towel to dry my tears, and despite the words, he smiles, briefly easing his usually severe countenance.

The decision comes in and the ref beckons us back to the center of the mat. With Zoe and I on either side of him, he holds one of each of our wrists.

"And the winner by the judge's unanimous majority..." the announcer bellows, "is Zoe Bocek."

The ref drops my hand and raises Zoe's high in the air.

TWENTY-THREE

Reporters, photographers, and my family crowd the anteroom. Flashes pop off from the right and left, causing moments of blindness. I am flanked by Cooper and Van, who thankfully field many of the questions shot at me.

"How do you feel about your performance, Jayden?" they ask.

"I'm satisfied," I say.

"Who will you fight next?"

My mouth pops open, but nothing comes out.

"She just finished fighting." Van edges in front of me. "I know you'd like to see her fight again, but for now, let her rest."

Cooper and Marcus get to work wrapping my hands in ice packs and tie another ice pack around my waist to ease stomach soreness. Mom fusses with my face, first applying a fresh bandage to cut on my forehead, and then pressing a cold pack to the injury while Kara snaps photos.

I turn and find Troy near the door, watching me. Cooper follows my gaze.

"I'll make him leave."

Though I can take care of myself, I like that he worries about me.

"No, it's okay," I say, resting a hand on his chest. "I'd like to talk to him."

"I'll get everyone out of here." His eyes travel my face as he softly thumbs my chin. He leans in and carefully avoids the bruised side of my mouth to kiss my cheek. Then he enlists Van's and my mother's help to corral the media out of the room, leaving me alone with Troy.

My ex keeps his distance, a nervous smile etched on his face.

"I'm too tired to bite," I say, and finally, he comes closer.

"You and Cooper, huh?"

I ignore his question, ditch the ice packs, and begin unwinding the hand wrap on my left hand. "I'm surprised you're here. Figured you'd be with your girlfriend, you know, celebrating the win."

"She's mobbed with press." He extends his hand to help me undo the wrapping, but I step back from him.

"I don't need anyone's help." I lift my chin. "I didn't need to have our lawn maintained for the season, either."

"I know, I know, but I wanted to do it—for you. And for your mom." He scratches the back of his head. "You looked great out there, Jay. Hell, you nearly won. I'm so proud of you."

"You didn't think I could hold my own with Zoe." I toss a coil of wrinkled hand wrapping aside and start on the right hand.

"I was worried, no joke, but I knew it'd make you angry and you'd do everything in your power to prove me wrong."

I open my mouth to respond but snap it shut and just shake my head.

"Chowderhead." My response is natural, like muscle memory of the tongue.

He laughs, and so do I.

It's the lightest moment we've had between us since Vegas. We both become quiet and still as the realization of what we've lost folds over our laughter.

"Jay, I've been so stupid. What I did to you—" His voice cracks. "Despite everything that's happened over the last few months, how I treated you,

you're the best friend I ever had. I freakin' miss you—like *really* miss you." His eyes go glassy. "Do you think there's any way you can ever forgive me?"

"Damn it, don't make me cry." But I already am. "We mutually failed at this thing together. We were a mistake that didn't know how to end."

The door springs open and draws our attention. Zoe stands in the doorway, her face ruddy and swollen, a mosaic of yellow and violet bruises. I take pleasure knowing I messed that pretty face up good, though mine probably looks just as bad. She's wearing a clean outfit and looks freshly showered under an unzipped hoodie. I'm still in a bloodied sports bra and sweat-stained fight shorts.

"So, it's like this." Head tilted, Zoe crosses her arms. Her stance is all challenge.

"Chill out, Bocek. You've won the fight and, apparently, you won this butthead, too." I cock a thumb at Troy. "But we go back a long way. Been through a lot together. If you care about his happiness, you might have to put up with me on occasion."

Troy's face nearly crumbles.

"Thank you." He smothers me in a brawny hug.

"Ow! Troy, that hurts!" I smack him away.

"Everything cool?" Cooper pushes past Zoe.

I can barely see Cooper past Troy's large stature. Troy once again blocking my view of Cooper—but that's done.

"We're good." I move next to Cooper.

Troy fist bumps Cooper's shoulder and, moving toward the door, loops an arm around Zoe's shoulders. "Coop, take care of our girl."

The two of them exit the room. Cooper closes the door and turns back to me.

"We need to get you out of those clothes." He pushes the sweatshirt off my shoulders.

"Time to make good on our bet?" I press into him and smile, making my swollen fat lip zing with pain.

"You just finished a major fight." He steers me toward the shower stall and turns on the water. "You need a shower. Then, food and rest."

I'm disappointed but don't resist him. My body's soreness is slowly stepping forward, revealing itself, inch by inch, fiber by fiber. As the steam billows past the shower enclosure, hot water calls to me temptingly.

"Help me undress," I say before he leaves the shower area. "My arms feel like overcooked spaghetti noodles."

With a subtle resignation, he helps me strip down until I am standing before him, naked. He presses a towel to my chest. I take it but let it drop low. I want him to see me.

"I'm a mess, but I still want you." I tilt my head back and meet his gaze, letting him see the open truth in my eyes.

"Where you see a mess, I see strength." He steps closer, his chest brushing against mine. Despite the wear and tear of the fight on my body, a pulse of vibrant energy, greater than the pain, thrums to life.

"Please," I whisper.

Cooper responds by pushing me into the shower. The hot water winds through my braided hair, heating the top of my head. He doesn't leave, though. Facing him, I reach for the bottom hem of his T-shirt, already wet from the shower spray, and lift it up, exposing his chest.

"Jayden, no." He stills my hands, pulling the material away from me, but not before the light catches a red patch of skin that arcs over his right hip and dips under the waistband of his athletic pants.

"What's this?" I move out from under the water spray and tug the waistband lower to inspect the thick foot-long cord of angry skin.

He covers the area with his hand, shielding it from me. "A scar. From my car accident."

I push his hand away and run my fingertips over the rough welt that dimples otherwise smooth skin.

"A piece of metal lodged in my hip. Had surgery to remove it. It's why I stopped wrestling."

"And why you changed schools?" Hurt, angry tears blend with the spray of the shower. Our eyes meet, and he nods. "Why didn't you tell me?"

"Because I didn't want your sympathy. I figured, when and if you came back, I wanted it to be for me, not because of this."

"Wow, Cooper McCaffrey, you're much better at holding a grudge than I'd expect."

"I'm not proud of it."

I inhale and stare at the scar. "Be honest, how bad is it?"

"I have minor limitations. Not a big deal."

"*Not a big deal?* How can you say that?"

He gives me one of those stupid, careless shrugs.

"And our bet?" I ask, angling my chin up at him. "You knew I would win."

"I fought as hard as I could," he says, a smile softening the admission. "You're a strong woman. And a bet is a bet. You won it fair and square."

There's more I want to say, but I am numbed into silence. My stubbornness and refusal to interact with him over the past few years left me unaware, clueless to the months of pain he endured.

He releases my hands and removes his shirt, exposing his well-built muscled chest. Except for the ugly scar, everything else about him is perfect.

"Jayden, I'm okay, really," he whispers and turns me around under the spray of water. Subdued, I brace myself, palms against the tiled wall. He pulls the hairbands from my braid and gently loosens the weaves. When he's finished, he lathers up shampoo and massages my scalp.

With a bar of soap, he moves onto my neck and shoulders, washing me. This battle-scarred man is bathing me. I am torn up inside. I want to resist, to apologize for not knowing he was hurt, for not being there for him, but I'm silenced by his hands on me. They're like magic as they move from my shoulders to my back, down to my glutes, gentle but firm, exquisitely easing the tension of my sore, tight muscles.

I turn to press my mouth to his neck as his hands roam my curves, inciting little moans of pleasure to roll off my tongue. The water splashes my face, and I close my eyes, concentrating on how every inch of me is alive under his touch.

He cradles my face, touching his forehead to mine, and makes me look him in the eye.

"I'm going to let you finish your shower. Then, you're going to rest. As your coach, I will make sure you get it."

"Cooper—"

"Shhh." He touches a finger to my lips. "Can you trust me, that at this moment, I know what's right for you?"

When I nod, he continues. "The fight traumatized your body. We're going to give your muscles time to regenerate. And when you're feeling better, we'll continue this discussion." He presses the bar of soap into my hand. "Now, finish up."

On his way out of the enclosure, he taps the faucet. The water goes cold.

"Hey!" I yell but when I try to turn it back, he stays my hand.

"Cold is better for your muscles," he says. "Stay in as long as you can tolerate it."

TWENTY-FOUR

I use a portion of the fight purse to dig my mother out from under her financial load. Mom, mind made up, wants out from under the responsibility of home ownership, so we begin the monumental process of clearing out our home.

The first week, though, I lay low, alternating heat and ice packs on every part of my body, back, stomach, arms, and legs. My body downshifts, conceding to the trauma of the punishing battle. The first few mornings I can barely crawl out of bed. I use the time to finish writing my law school mission statement. I write about how this summer showed me a great deal about myself—that I'm determined, and a fighter to the core, but that I'm also able to cooperate and work for a better outcome. Writing this down settles something deep inside me. Anything seems possible.

Cooper comes over before and after work to run me through a series of stretches. I hate the stretches, but I love our time together. My muscles remain tight, but as the days pass by, the pain substantially fades. To my disappointment, Cooper remains pretty much hands-off unless he's helping me stretch. Despite that, I remain optimistic.

Mom and Kara move about the house with a mission. Boxes and large trash bags line the hallway and kitchen. I shuffle around, helping do light-weight stuff, like cleaning out drawers and cabinets. Kara holds a yard sale one weekend. I am given the job of cashier, where I get to sit and accept payment. Embarrassingly, my presence attracts a lot of attention. Many shoppers recognize me. Some have come because of me. Some ask to take photos with me.

Cooper comes over to move the big items into the driveway and stays to further help by selling a few of my mother's infomercial purchases, just shy of the original selling price. He's good with people. He knows how to read them. He's always known how to read me.

The hand-holding couple that walks the neighborhood stops by to browse. Cooper and I wait on them. I admire how kind and in-step they are with each other, and not just in the walking sense.

"Nice couple," Cooper says as they leave, hand in hand of course, with a lightly used peppermill and a stack of novels.

"They are." I turn to him, inspired. "What do you say to a road trip? Just the two of us, to get away for a couple of days? My treat."

"Oh, right. Our bet." His sunglasses prevent me from seeing his eyes.

I flinch. He *still* views sleeping with me as settling our bet.

"Jayden! Look what I found." Kara, cheeks flushed, drops a dusty cardboard box with a thud at my feet.

Inside the box are two piles of hardcover books.

"Daddy's law books." I grab the brown, thickly bound book on top, Black's Law Dictionary, smiling as I open to a random page, the unforgettable scent filling my nostrils.

The first word my eyes land on is Jurisprudence.

I burst out laughing and look up at the sky. "Dad, this could only be *you*."

"What's that?" Kara looks over my shoulder.

"This word I've been using to help me through some... trying moments," I say. "Dad is talking to me."

Kara hugs me from behind. "I think he's always talking to us. We just need to listen."

I tip my head to hers. "I agree."

We box up the leftover items that didn't sell at the end of the day, and as Cooper and I load them into the back of his truck to take to Goodwill, he says, "So, that trip you mentioned. Are you up for it?"

"I should be good by next weekend."

"Then say no more. I'm in. With the weather cooling off, it's a great time to do some hiking," he says with a smile. "Leave the reservations to me."

I am the best little patient all week. I rest, eat well, stretch, and do light workouts, hoping the only muscle soreness I'll experience this weekend is the overworked muscles between my legs.

Packing for our trip, I come across the wristlet purse I used the night of Jess's grad party, the three-count of condoms still inside. I toss them in my toiletry bag. If I have my way, three won't be nearly enough, I think with a laugh.

I pause and retrieve the condoms from my bag. Bringing protection says I expect sex—or at least hope for it. But it'll say all I need to know if Cooper *doesn't*.

My sister is in her disaster of a bedroom, with several boxes and lumpy trash bags surrounding her. It looks like she's cleaning, but it's hard to tell. It doesn't look much better under normal circumstances.

"Hey, I'm returning these." I toss the rubbers at her.

They hit her shoulder and slide down into her cupped hands. "You didn't use them that night?"

"No. Things went sideways." I shrug.

"I don't need them. It's probably not permanent, but I'm not seeing any guys right now." She offers the packets back to me with a knowing smile. "But you'll definitely need them for your weekend away."

"I'd rather he bring his own provisions."

"Leaving it up to the guy? That's so unlike you."

"Cooper knows what I want. When he's ready, it'll happen." Remembering the injury to his hip, I exhale and lean against the doorjamb. I don't want to give him a reason to hide anything from me again. I plan to give him the time and space he needs to trust in me again.

"After Daddy died, I was hurting. And I spread that hurt around. I hurt Cooper." I roll my lip under my teeth. "I hurt Mom. And you, too. Kara, I'm sorry."

"It's okay. I'm just glad you came home, Jay. We missed you." She hugs her knees.

"I really missed you, too." I fold to the floor and hug my sister. "I promise, even when I move out, we'll still see each other regularly."

"Good, 'cause things are better with you around. Better, and more fun." Kara wipes tears from the corner of her eyes as a smile wiggles out. "For what it's worth, I'm sure you won't be disappointed this weekend."

I wish I was as confident as her, but I promise myself, that until it happens, I will assume nothing.

I am both excited and nervous when Cooper arrives Friday morning and puts my weekend duffle bag, borrowed from Kara, in the bed of his truck.

"Where are we going?" I say after I climb into the passenger seat beside him. He's planned our getaway and, despite my asking, has told me nothing.

"The place we're staying at is a cottage—small, cozy, but private," he says as we set out for our hour-and-a-half drive east.

Private. Cozy. It sounds perfect.

After a short silence, he turns to me. "I have some news. Van received several calls inquiring about you."

"Oh?"

"You've been offered a half dozen fights."

"Oh."

"You could conceivably fight for the next few years and make some really decent money." When I fail to respond, he reaches over to pat my knee. "What do you think?"

"The only way I might even entertain the idea is if you stayed on as my trainer."

"Classes at Brooklyn U start in next week. I'm not sure how much time I could commit to." He watches the road. "I'm sure Van would stay on. Despite some rockiness, you two worked well together."

"Yeah, we did, but I couldn't do it without you. I wouldn't want to."

"Your decision shouldn't be based on me or anyone else. This is all about you and what you want."

"Taking another fight would mean putting off school, and possibly not finishing my law degree." The thought creates a pinch of discomfort in my chest. "Remember that day you told me I wouldn't be content going back to law school until I finished with competitive fighting on my terms? You were right. I wouldn't have been."

"This isn't a decision you need to make right now. This is our getaway weekend." He turns down a tree-lined country lane. "What do you want to do after we check in? Go for a hike, a bike ride, or get lunch?"

"I'm open to whatever." I know exactly what I want to do, but I'm adamant if that happens, it's his decision.

The cottage is rustic, stained wood clapboard with windows trimmed in bright sunny yellow and a slate path that leads to a generous covered porch, where several wind chimes hang from the eves and sing softly in the breeze.

It's cozy, all right. One bedroom, a tiny kitchen, and a small den area, but the decor is far from rustic. Crisp white walls and cabinetry with plush gray furniture and fuzzy throw rugs. It's Pottery Barn meets Tiny Homes.

I dump my duffle bag in the bedroom where a well-dressed queen-sized bed dominates the small room. Imagining myself falling asleep and waking up beside Cooper, surrounded by the fleecy soft gray blanket and fluffy pillows, brings a smile to my face.

When I return to the main room, Cooper is sitting on the couch scrolling through his phone, his overnight bag abandoned nearby. On the kitchen counter, he's placed a few bags of foodstuffs we've brought along. I take a six-pack of beer from one bag and pop the top off two bottles. He puts his phone down when I offer him one.

Standing in front of him, I take a sip, not sure where to settle my gaze. I rotate between the couch and his arms, the couch and his legs. After a pull from his own bottle, he puts the beer on the table and kicks off his shoes.

"Guess it's time. Take off your clothes." He begins to unbutton his shirt. "Or maybe you want to have a few more beers, and we can just... stumble into it."

"*Excuse me?*"

"Isn't that how you want it? To ditch our clothes and go at it?"

I raise an eyebrow. "Not a totally unpleasant suggestion. But that's not exactly how I thought this would go down."

"What *do* you expect, Jayden?" He settles back against the couch, shirt open to his navel. "We're here on the premise that I make good on a wager for sex."

"Forget the bet. No more games."

"You sure about that?"

I nod and twist the beer bottle in my hands.

"Being with you these last few months reminded me of how much I like you. I've been thinking, perhaps we could have more, like, make a go of it."

He scrubs a hand over his chin. "You're saying a relationship, not just sex?"

"Of course. What'd you think I meant?"

"I don't know. With you, anything past sex is not a foregone conclusion." The acrimony in his voice startles me. "I suppose I'm a bit of a romantic, but I thought our first time would be more than a passing urge or mindless escape from whatever's currently got you riled up."

Offph. If I was under any misconception that I hurt this guy, he's blown the roof off that delusion. The years-long chasm between us needs closure. I sit next to him and put a hand on his knee.

"Cooper, I promise, what I feel about you isn't a passing urge." I clear my throat. "I grew up wanting, needing, to be seen as tough. I thought admitting to feely, touchy kind of emotions would make me appear soft, weak.

"I was a stubborn, tough girl who made decisions that hurt you and my family. I'm trying to make up for my mistakes. I'll never be perfect by any stretch of the imagination." I peek up at him. "But what I feel for you is so much more than I've ever felt about anyone. It's real and tangible, and if you'll have me, I want to try and build on whatever this is between us."

Pushing my hair aside, he leans in and kisses my cheek. "Thank you. I—"

"You don't have to say anything. I'm not fishing."

"I know you're not, but there's something I want to tell you."

I exhale. "Okay, hit me."

"I thought I was over you, but when you came home, I realized I'd been lying to myself. And still, I resisted because I refuse to be second to Troy. But time hasn't changed anything." He reaches for my hands. "I'm in love with you."

My breath catches, and I beam up at him. His unicorn mom was right. This, *this*, feels a lot like love.

Our eyes meet, and as he leans in to kiss me, his hand slides flat against my stomach, his touch generating a blaze that spreads like wildfire through my body.

Between kisses, he whispers, "How about we go check out the bed?"

"Yes," I say. "Let's."

In the bedroom, we lie together, kissing while we strip away the barrier of clothes. A strong thrum of desire runs through me as I admire the body I am about to be deeply intimate with. He descends over me, his warm, solid weight pinning me to the mattress. Even as our hands explore, pet, and caress, I cannot look anywhere but into his thick-lashed green eyes. When I plead for release, he reaches for a condom, and finally, *finally*, we give in to what we both want.

Propped up on his forearms, his gaze stays glued to my face as the energy of our bodies together makes the air hum. It builds, like a crescendo of feels, until our language is reduced to guttural sounds of pleasure.

Our bodies press together, breaths rushing, hands drawing each other closer still, as we rise and crash, then descend to a blissful plateau.

"That was incredible," Cooper whispers, brushing my lips with his.

"Mm-hmm." I grin. "All the years we wasted when we could have been doing this."

"How about we promise to not waste anymore more time?"

"I fully concur," I say, sliding my hand down his side to touch the puckered skin of his hip with the pads of my fingertips. "While we're making promises—promise you'll never keep me in the dark, like how you were injured in the car accident, and you knew I didn't know about it."

"I promise." He pulls my hand from his scar and kisses my fingertips. "And I'd like a promise from you that you'll stay to talk and work through any situation, however difficult or upsetting, the future brings us, and not to run off."

There's no place to hide from his gaze. I am seen in all my imperfections.

"I'll stay and fight. Fight for us." My fingers brush the soft hair at his nape. "You know, I wasn't positive we were going to have sex this weekend. I didn't even bring condoms."

"You didn't think I would bring some?" He shakes his head and smiles. "I have a whole box. Thirty-six, minus one."

I throw my head back and laugh. "You bought an economy-sized box of rubbers for the weekend? I totally underestimated you."

"Barring some superhuman record, I don't expect to use all of them this weekend." He tightens his arms around me. "Though I do plan to pay my bet generously."

"I like the sound of that." I wrap my legs around his and frame his face in my hands. Staring into his eyes, my breath catches, and I recognize what I'm feeling is more than desire. This emotional vulnerability, this intense connectedness—something I always expected to feel but hadn't before now—is intimacy, the kind that comes when you're fully in sync with another, like when you're in love.

"Cooper," I say his name, my voice tender, unrecognizable to even myself.

"Yes, Jayden?" He smiles, the emotion in his eyes warming every inch of me.

Like a runaway train, I can't stop what flows past my lips. "I love you. I love you so, so much."

TWENTY-FIVE

Two purchased coffees in hand, I make my way up to the floor where the faculty offices are located. There are groupings of chairs along the walls for each office. A steady procession of students up and down the hallway creates more commotion than usual. I imagine they're all here for last-minute changes to their class schedules for the semester that begins this week: additions, drops—or, like me, getting a very late start on registering. Instead of barging into the office, I find a chair and sip one coffee while I scroll the newsfeed on my cell and wait to be called in for my appointment.

I lower my phone to my lap and put my head back. It's no use. I can't concentrate. I left this very spot in May, skeptical I would return. Yet here I am. Back at Brooklyn Law.

The air beyond the scent of my coffee stirs with the movement of sharp minds and conversations of legalese that make my pulse buzz. As I sit there, something loosens inside me, a breaking free, a relief that causes the corner of my lips to curl in a smile.

"Jurisprudence," I whisper just as the office door across from me opens.

"Hello, Jayden." Professor Dumfries stands in the doorway with an expectant look.

"I brought you coffee." I rise and hand her a cup and a small bag of sugar and creamers.

"Thank you." She takes the offering, and I follow her inside the office. "How's your mother and that awful dating situation?"

"I think she learned a valuable lesson about trusting people online. Unfortunately, it was an expensive one, but she's on her feet," I say. When I left last week, Mom had been happily immersed in decorating the new apartment—on a budget we figured out together. "My mother's a fighter. She's going to be okay."

"I'm glad to hear that." Her lips round in a sympathetic smile as she motions for me to sit and returns to her seat behind the desk. "By the way, I like your pin."

I touch my Ruth Bader Ginsburg pin and smile. I'd found it while cleaning my room for the move. "My high school wrestling coach gave it to me when I graduated."

"I was in the last class Ginsburg taught at Columbia. Made quite an impression on me." Dumfries told us this in class last year, but I won't stop her from telling it again. "She could cite history and cases without looking at notes." She rests her forearms on the desk with a nostalgic expression that makes her look younger and more approachable, like a nice grandmother instead of a stern law professor. "She said, '...things that you regard as an impediment turn out to be great, good fortune.'"

Dumfries lets the quote sit with me while she adds every sugar packet in the bag to her coffee.

My father's death, Troy's cheating, the stilted relationships with my mother, Kara, and Cooper— and Zoe—those were my impediments, my hurdles. This summer, I faced them down, one by one.

What doesn't kill you makes you stronger.

The professor gives the joe a quick stir and lifts her cup. "To a great woman."

"To a great woman." I lift my cup, too.

"So, Jayden." She puts the coffee aside and faces me. "This moment begs a larger question. How do we carry on this great woman's work?"

"'Fight for the things that you care about but do it in a way that will lead others to join you,'" I recite Ginsburg. "And to do that, I need to finish my law degree."

"Any thoughts about the area of practice you'd like to focus on?"

"I'm thinking equality and human rights. Ultimately, though, I aim to be a judge."

"An admirable goal." The professor steeples her fingers and sits back in her chair. "I saw your MMA debut."

Warmth floods my cheeks.

"I've followed your progress through the news," Dumfries continues. "I'm not an enthusiast of that sport, but I can see you're remarkably strong and talented at what you do. How do you think it applies to your law goals?"

"Fighting requires a kind of strength that's mental as well as physical. What happens in court, the art of justice, is a fight too. The events of the summer provided me with a lot of clarity. I did the work I needed to do to get back here, where I'm supposed to be."

"Your mission statement says as much. It's well-written. And convincing. I forwarded it to the scholarship board. You should hear back in a few weeks." She gives me a smiling nod before focusing on her computer screen. "Your fall schedule looks to be in order, but the bigger question remains." Her attention returns to me. "Looking forward, will you be content to fight in court and not in the octagon?"

Professor Dumfries prints out the forms and signs off on my schedule. Our meeting ends with her leaving that last question open-ended for me to consider. In the registrar's office, I pay the tuition and get the paperwork stamped, making my fall term enrollment official, but the fact remains that I have two viable routes open to me.

Right now, I'm looking at two more years of law school. Once I successfully complete my studies, I must take, and pass, the bar exam. Then, I'll have to practice law to build experience and my reputation before I can even seek an appointment as a judge. The route to becoming a judge will take years and be mentally laborious, and with less financial compensation as I work my way up the ladder.

Or I can continue to fight competitively. Van and Cooper tell me the additional fight offers keep coming. Apparently, Zoe's and my match had huge audience ratings. Wherever I go lately, someone somewhere recognizes me. On the streets, strangers shout, "Bruiser Jones" and fist bump me.

If I wanted to, I could fight for the next few years and be quite comfortable financially, too.

My options are amazing, and more than anything, I love that I get to choose.

I make the walk from the subway to my new Brooklyn apartment, with a spring in my step. The summer's heat and humidity have given way to crisp fall mornings and evenings. The sidewalk is littered with yellow and orange leaves from the row of trees that line the road.

I climb the steps to the third floor and am met with the mouthwatering scent of sauteed garlic and onions as I draw closer to the apartment door. I insert the key in the deadbolt as Billy Joel's iconic voice floats to me through the closure, and I hum along.

Cooper is moving about in our apartment kitchen, cooking a meal for us. I never tire of coming home to him. To be fair, the living situation is still new, less than a week old, but being that we're both going to school in Brooklyn, moving in together was an easy decision and suits us well. He's neat and pretty good in the kitchen, too, just as his mother said.

But goodness, every time I come home, I want to pinch myself. This is my life.

"Hey there." I step into the narrow, galley kitchen and greet him with a big grin.

He grins back and simultaneously we both lean in to give and receive a kiss. At first, it felt silly to kiss him *every* time I saw him, but it quickly became habitual, and now it's just another element I enjoy about our couplehood. We *always* kiss, whether we're aggravated or busy—no matter what. The brief physical contact reminds me that, regardless of what the day throws at me, this man loves and respects me. I plan to show him every day that the feeling is mutual.

That is love.

"How'd the meeting with your academic advisor go?" He gives me his full attention.

"Dumfries saw the fight." I snag a peeled carrot from the cutting board in front of him. "She questioned my earnestness of returning to classes."

"And are you earnestly returning without doubts?"

"I love competitive fighting, but MMA is not wrestling. The cuts, bruises, and pulpy sore muscles. One fight takes weeks to recover."

"The downside of professional fighting," he says. "It's the price you pay, and some would say, you'd be richly rewarded."

For many, like Troy and Zoe, the money and celebrity status would be enough to convince them, but not me.

And if it were fear that kept me from taking the next fight, I might be less sure of stepping away from it all. But the one thing I am clear on is that I am not afraid.

"It burned me that Troy, as a guy, had choices after college that I didn't. But this summer, the fight—preparing for it, being able to compete professionally—that's what I wanted. The opportunity to go to the next level and not be denied that choice because of my gender."

He moves closer and threads his fingers through mine. "You certainly have the opportunity. And as far as ability, you've always had that. You've cut the path wide open, Courageous Cat. It's literally your call. You can do whatever you want."

Those words are music to my ears. A lightness fills my chest.

"It's enough to know I can make that call. I've retired my gloves. I'm taking the fights to the courts. It's law school for me."

His eyes beam with unspoken pride, and he makes me think of his dad.

"Will you miss wrestling?" he asks.

"Nah," I say with a smile. "Not with a live-in grappling partner!"

I quickly twist his arm behind his back. He tackles me with his head and shoulders, and the two of us tumble to the ground. I'm laughing so hard that he easily captures my arms and pins me. When I go limp under him, his hold softens, and he kisses me.

"I love you," he says.

"I love you, too." I wrap my arms around him and kiss him back.

Cooper is steady and sure. There's no reason to run or fight. I'm ready to stake my claim, plant my flag.

I choose this life.

Acknowledgments

I don't remember when I decided to write about a female competitive fighter, but I recently found an article from 2017 about a female high school wrestler that I saved. My husband, Brian, who loves wrestling and MMA fights—come to think of it, *all* things sports related—was a wrestler in high school. Whenever I needed fighting terminology and wrestling moves, he was my go-to source. He was also an early reader and is my favorite car trip, vacation, and walking partner, and my favorite cook. He's amazing in the kitchen. Yes, I know I'm lucky! Thank you, honey.

Thank you, Bruce Link. Watching you compete in high school wrestling tournaments as a teen was my first exposure to the world of competitive fighting. You were fierce despite your size, but had a kind, gentle heart. Through marriage, you became my little brother, and after thirty-plus years, I could never imagine life without you — though now I must. Yours is a legacy of warmth, of easy smiles, wholehearted embraces, nicknames, silly hats, and the laughter you brought to our lives. Rest in peace, my brother.

My author friends: Kimberly Wenzler and Deborah Garland. These ladies are my corner crew, always there for me whenever I call for help—repeatedly, and sometimes daily! I treasure their insight and feedback on anything from storytelling to cover art and everything in between. I am grateful for the wisdom and strength they freely share with me, and most of all, for their friendship. Kim, thank you for being my accountability partner, my phone-a-friend, pancake breakfast partner, and always providing me with all-around solid advice. Deborah, thank you for sharing your publishing knowledge and savvy marketing strategies with me, for invaluable brainstorming lunches, and for being my go-to writing retreat partner.

Thank you longtime friends Suzanne Kelly and Ann Marie Maud for always cheerfully being my first readers.

Thank you to the lovely Veronica Jorden. Developmental editor and one-woman cheering squad, an amazing person who has now worked with me on all four of my books. Her enthusiasm and gentle guidance have become a never-to-be-missed contribution to my stories.

Thank you to Kelley Riegert of CookieLynn Publishing Services for your editorial insight, and Erin McClary, for your proofreading and astute editorial comments. It was a pleasure working with you both.

Thank you to the ladies of Wine Not Read book group who provided feedback, especially Janice, Elaine, Tracy, and Kimberly.

Reviews, Reviews, reviews

Lions, tigers, and bears — Oh my! There's no need to fear leaving a review. I promise, no one will show up on your doorstep to browbeat you for words, but if you enjoyed this book, please pop on over to your favorite book website and let me know. Even better, recommend it to a friend. Recommendations and reviews are greatly appreciated.

Enjoyed this book? Try another book
by Suzanne McKenna Link

Saving Toby, Save Me Book 1 - Claudia reenters Toby's life through an unexpected job offer, only to find herself drawn to the town's notorious bad boy. As their connection deepens, Claudia must navigate strained relationships and personal challenges to stand by Toby through his darkest hour.

Keeping Claudia, Save Me Book 2 – The girl Toby has long dreamed of is finally within his reach, but one last secret hides in the dark corner of his past. The one that could undermine it all. Falling in love is easy. Staying in love is hard.

Finding Edward, Save Me Book 3 – At the dying request of his grandmother, Edward must go to Italy to find his biological father, a man he didn't know existed. He experiences a new culture, meets a cast of colorful characters, reignites his passion for art, and falls in love. A journey of discovery begins with one step.

About the Author

Suzanne McKenna Link works for a family of newspapers that cover events in and around the area she lives, on the South Shore of Long Island, New York.

An avid interest in psychology and human nature has the native Long Islander digging deep into the reasons for her characters' behaviors. As a result, her characters come to life on the pages. To find out more and to sign up for author updates, visit suzannemckennalink.com.

Ways to connect

Goodreads, FaceBook, and Instagram @SuzMcKLink, TikTok, or Literary Love Blog (suzannemckennalink.blogspot.com).

www.ingramcontent.com/pod-product-compliance
Lightning Source LLC
Chambersburg PA
CBHW070848260626
47170CB00007B/2543